THE FOURTH WALL

THE FOURTH WALL

A novel

SORJ CHALANDON

Translated by Cheney Crow

THE LILLIPUT PRESS
DUBLIN

First published in English 2026 by
THE LILLIPUT PRESS
62–63 Sitric Road,
Arbour Hill,
Dublin 7,
Ireland
www.lilliputpress.ie

First published in French in 2013 under the title *Le Quatriéme Mur*

10 9 8 7 6 5 4 3 2 1

Cet ouvrage a bénéficié du soutien du Programme d'aide à la publication de l'Institut français.

A CIP record for this title is available from The British Library.

Paperback ISBN 978 1 84351 966 9
eBook ISBN 978 1 84351 967 6

Set in 11.5 pt on 16 pt Sabon and Perpetua by Compuscript
Cover design by Luke Bird, lukebird.co.uk

Printed and bound in Czechia by Finidr

For Valentine,
who asks me whether she'll be allowed
to take her snuggly to heaven ...

PROLOGUE

'Here we are. These actors are going to perform the story of Antigone for you. Antigone is the small, thin girl sitting over there, silent. Staring straight ahead. Focused. Intent. Thinking that in a few moments she'll become Antigone, the small, slender, dark-skinned introvert that no one in her family paid much attention to. Until now. Her metamorphosis. Her choice: to stand alone in defiance, against the world, against Creon, her uncle, her king. She knows this could lead to her death. Life is full of invitation and promise. Life appeals to her, but she has chosen. Her name is Antigone and she must enter this new self, fully engaged, to the end.'

Jean Anouilh, *Antigone*, 1942

1

TRIPOLI, NORTHERN LEBANON

Thursday, 27 October 1983

I fell down. Struggled up, made my way into the garage, stumbling through rubble. Flames, smoke, dust – I spat out the plaster burning my throat. I squeezed my eyes shut, clasped my hands over my ears. Collided with a low wall, tripped over wires. The explosion had torn away half the ceiling. Burning cement was falling, hitting the floor with a slapping sound. Behind the carcass of a car, a crater. A pit of war, asphalt opened like petals to reveal its heart of sand. I threw myself into its fractures, staggering, my body limp, my stomach churned to rubble. I was shaking. I'd never shaken so hard. My right leg was desperate to flee, to escape me, a frightened grasshopper in tall grass. I pressed it to the ground with both hands. My crazy leg. It was bleeding. I had felt nothing.

I believed that wounds and the wounded were one, united. That pain howled its message at the moment of impact. But it was blood that announced the bad news. Not the impact, or pain, just my sticky sap. My trousers were torn. And smoking. My leg flashed its pain like an infected tooth. My shirt was stuck to me with sweat. I had grabbed my bag, but my jacket lay in Marwan's car with my papers, my money, everything I had left. I never thought a tank could open fire on a taxi.

'Get out, George!'

We were driving along the coast. The sun was rising behind the hills. Just after the turn, a huge sand-coloured Syrian tank, an ambush. It blocked the road. My Druze swore. He braked sharply. I was sleeping. I startled awake. He panicked, backed up onto the embankment overlooking the sea. The sleeping carapace awoke. Almost nothing, a breath. The metal of the gun turret pivoting.

'Take cover, idiot!'

I plunged my arm towards the back seat, found my bag, grasped for my jacket, my passport, without taking my eyes off death. Then I gave up. The steel mouth pointed directly at us. An uproar in my head.

'He won't fire! He can't fire on a taxi!'

A red diamond and a yellow circle were painted on the turret. Familiar shapes on a schoolboy's board. And three Arabic numerals stencilled in white. Marwan crossed the road bent almost double. He moved towards shelter, a shattered garage. The walls were studded with shards of shells, black with soot. I opened my door, ran towards the gaping ruin.

'When shells fall, open your mouth,' my friend had told me the first time. If you don't release the pressure, your eardrums explode.

As I entered the garage, he ran back out.

'I left the keys on the dashboard!'

The keys? The words were absurd. The turret followed us. Me going in, him going out. It hesitated between his terror and mine.

The shell flew as I stepped into shadow.

I fell the way one dies, onto my stomach, my forehead crushed, my neck pinned to the ground by a blast of fire. Half inside, half outside, my feet on the embankment, my hands on cement. My body was in shock. A powdery light ripped through the concrete. I stood up. Heavy smoke, grey dust. I was suffocating. I had sand in my throat, my lip torn open, my hair smoking. I was blind. Silver sequins pierced my eyelids. The shell had hit, but it hadn't spoken yet. The lightning after the thunderclap, fragments of steel. Smell of gunpowder, hot oil, burnt metal. I threw myself into the hole as it blew. My whole stomach rose up my throat. I vomited. A stream of bile and bits of me. I screamed my fear. Fists clenched, ears bleeding, covered with salty earth and greasy shadow.

The tank moved. It creaked towards the garage. I couldn't see, I heard its power. The turret paused. Right, left, rusty gears. The shell casing had ejected. A clang of hollow metal echoed on the road. Silence.

'It's a Soviet T55, an old granddaddy.'

I startled. A raspy voice, poor English. An older man on his back, in the hole, next to me in the dim light. I hadn't noticed.

'Head down. He'll try again.'

Arab headdress, a keffiyeh, white beard, a cigarette between two fingers, he smoked. Despite the tank, the danger, the end of our world, he lay there smoking, his mouth half-open, a peaceful cloud of smoke brushing his lips.

'Is that comfortable?'

He gestured towards my stomach. I was crushing his rifle, its buttstock against my thigh, its magazine digging into my gut. I had thrown myself onto an assault rifle to escape a tank shell. I lay still. He nodded his head and smiled. Outside, the tank began to move. The scream of mishandled gears.

'He's backing up,' the old man whispered.

The shadow of the tank had given way to dawn gathering over charred grass. Incinerated. It was still backing up. I held my breath until I heard seagulls laughing. I hoisted myself onto one elbow, my mouth wide open. I looked for Marwan, first in the tumult, then in the silence. I waited for my friend to come back, waving his car keys over his head, laughing. Singing that he was crazy to have gone back to the car. Even crazier for following me into this idiotic quest. He would take me in his arms like a brother, bless the heavens for sparing us. I waited a long time. Hoped. Outside, shouts, orders, the buzz of war. A burst of machine-gun fire. I rolled onto my side. My leg bled in brutal spurts. The Palestinian yanked out my belt and shaped it into a tourniquet around my thigh. I lay on my back. Pain, a sledgehammer at work. The old man slid a blanket under my head, lifting me carefully up to the rim of the hole.

Then I saw Marwan. His legs stuck out into the road. He'd fallen onto his back, his clothes ripped away by the explosion, his body bloody and naked.

Up the road, the tank was still coughing. The moan of the wind was back. The breath of the sea. The old Palestinian turned onto his side, on one elbow, his cheek in his hand. He looked at me. I shook my head. No, I wasn't crying. I was out of tears. He said we have to save some for life. That I had the right to fear, to anger, to sadness.

I heaved myself into a seated position. I pushed away his weapon with one foot. He moved closer. He and I, in the hole. Fastened to his breast pocket, the enamel insignia of the Fatah. He took my chin gently in one hand. He turned my face towards the daylight. Then he leaned down. Under his worn moustache, his lips were open. I thought he was going to kiss me. He examined me closely. He was searching for something within me. He grew serious.

'You've seen death, but you haven't killed,' the old man murmured.

I think he was relieved. He lit a cigarette and sat on his heels. Then he went quiet, watching the fragile light outdoors.

And I didn't dare tell him he was wrong.

2

SAMUEL AKOUNIS

For months I didn't know that Sam was Jewish. He was Greek and claimed nothing else. My buddies and I wondered about him. He was foreign, older than we were, different in every way. I remember one day in April 1974, marching towards the palace of the Mutualité in Paris. We filled the street. Sam followed along on the pavement, tense, his face stern, unreadable. To our shouts of 'Palestine will conquer,' he answered, 'Palestine will survive.' I didn't ask myself what that distinction meant to him. I carried a bucket of green paint. Behind us, comrades carried the other colours: white, red and black. Two hours before a Zionist meeting, we planned to paint a Palestinian flag in front of the entrance to the building.

'This is not a day to raise the flag,' Sam protested.

The day before, Thursday, 11 April 1974, three members of the Palestinian Liberation Front had attacked the city of Kiryat Shmona, in Galilee. Their target was a school, but they found it closed for Passover. Instead, they entered an apartment building where they murdered nineteen people, including nine children, before killing themselves.

'Couldn't we postpone our protest?' Sam had asked.

In our group, he was the only one opposed to this war painting. We put his idea to a vote. On his side, he stood alone. Opposing him, all those who thought the slaughter changed nothing about the pain of Palestine.

One of us had even claimed, 'It's the cost of the cause.'

'Nine children?' Was Sam's response.

He stood up, imposing, calm. In the three months he had been a refugee in France, I had never heard his voice harden, seen him make a fist, or even frown. When we fought, he refused to use a weapon, even an iron rod. He said a Molotov cocktail was neither argument nor answer. Sam was tall, his body visibly battered yet muscular, strong as an ancient olive tree. Some people mistook him for a cop. His short grey hair stood out in our long-haired leftist group, his tweed jacket contrasted with our leather, also his way of checking out a place, the scrutiny in his gaze. His way of never taking a step back. Except slowly, defiantly, with a glacial smile that chastened any adversary. We all feared the police, the extreme right, and Zionist ambushes, but he feared none of their blows. After surviving dictatorship, the battle of Athens and prison, he said our battles were a form of light opera. He didn't judge our political commitment. He just made sure that in the morning, we'd all be at roll call. That there would be no dead in our ranks. He called our anger a slogan, our wound a bruise, and said the blood we shed would not fill a handkerchief. He dreaded the facts of struggle, not the belief in it.

One day at an intersection, he kept me from yelling 'CRS = SS' with the others. Simply, with one hand on my arm, his dark eyes probing mine. We were trapped by tear gas. Between two ferocious fits of coughing, he asked me if

I knew of Alois Brunner. I looked at him, confused, alarmed at his calm. Alois Brunner? The Nazi war criminal? Of course I did. The tear gas smelled like sulphur, our rocks gashed the sky as we shouted, police batons beat cadence against their shields. We were on the pavement, Sam and I. He grabbed my iron rod and threw it in the gutter. He pulled his scarf from his face and pushed me ahead of him. I struggled fiercely against him.

'You're an idiot!'

He led me towards the police cordon the way a plain-clothes officer drags his prey towards the police cruiser.

'Show me Brunner, George. Point him out!'

We were facing the line of CRS officers, alone in the middle of the street, as our comrades flooded back all around us. The police were ready to charge. One officer walked the ranks, screaming over the noise.

'Which one is Brunner? Tell me!'

Sam wouldn't let go of me. He pointed at one of the helmeted men.

'That one? That one? Where is the bastard?'

Then he let me go. The police attacked, shouting. Sam opened the door of a building and pushed me inside. I was crying, shaking, breathless. And he was suffocating. Beyond the closed door, the street was fighting. Screams, shouts, moans, chaos of tear gas. I sat on the low post box, my back to the door. Sam was bent over, one hand against the wall, trying to catch a breath. He pulled the scarf down from my face.

'Alois Brunner wasn't there, George. Or any other SS. Not their dogs, not their whips. So don't ever yell nonsense like that again, got it?'

I got it. A little. It wasn't easy for me. I could have answered that a slogan was an image, a sketch of a thought, but I didn't have the courage. Or even the desire to contradict him. I knew he was right.

'Protect your intelligence, please,' Sam said. And then he helped me stand up.

In Athens, he had chanted, 'Bread, education, freedom.' The most beautiful appeal to rise up ever distilled by the anger of men, he said. And it was he, the Greek resistance member, who challenged the idea of the Palestinian flag. He repeated that smearing paint on a street corner the day after a massacre was wrong. He was more tense than usual. He looked from one face to another to try to convince us. He had trouble breathing, mangled his French, mixing his language with ours, his words stripped back to the accent of an exile. I believe that day it was the Jew who spoke, secretly, the man who wanted to survive, not conquer. When the vote came, he raised his hand. Only his, alone. And all our hands next, to show him up. He had lost. I remember all of us, boys and girls, foolishly applauding, excited as children at a circus. Not to commend the death of nine children, but to proclaim our determination.

'None of you has ever been in danger,' Sam responded.

My Greek friend lowered his eyes. He could have left the room, but that wasn't his way. He would never shut the door on a friend. He just spoke his truth, what he felt was right. And even volunteered to go with us.

'So the flag won't be painted backwards,' he said flatly.

* * *

In January 1974, when Samuel Akounis came into my life, we already had two Chileans in our ranks. They belonged to the Revolutionary Left Movement, and had left Santiago a few days after the military coup d'état. After a month in London, they had chosen France for the language and Paris for its Commune. They were in hiding. The Greek had just arrived. From Athens to lecture hall 34B of the Faculté at Jussieu, to testify about the Regime of the Colonels. The hall was packed, I was in the front row, on the steps, my right leg straight out. I had goosebumps. A member of the resistance, there, in front of us.

'My name is Samuel Akounis. And today I bring you greetings from the students of Athens Polytechnic Institute who faced the tanks of the dictatorship.'

'Only the male students?' a voice broke in from the audience.

Silence in the hall. A few women applauded the remark. The Greek smiled. He was amused. He looked at the young girl, standing in her row. Her name was Aurora.

'I thought that was self-evident, mademoiselle. But in your country, it doesn't seem to be the case.'

He spoke magnificent French, like a language learned in secret. He drank the glass of water on the table, watching the silent crowd. The man seated next to him urged him to continue. He wasn't part of our group, or a professor. He had entered the room with the Greek. I knew his face.

'My name is Samuel Akounis. And I bring you greetings from the male and female students of Athens Polytechnic who stood up to the tanks of the dictatorship, a word that deserves to be masculine ...'

Applause, laughter. Aurora raised her hand to announce her surrender. And then Samuel told his story. Without effects, without emotion, a concise and sombre account. On 14 November 1973 the student associations of the Polytechnic vote to go on strike. Hundreds of others converge from every college, calling for the fall of the dictatorship. Overnight, they become thousands, gathered around the building. The next day local residents join them. Young and old, families with children. The Polytechnic is occupied, its gates padlocked by students. They organize food, security, allocation of tasks. Food supplies, sleeping arrangements, authorization of comings and goings. An infirmary is set up, a radio rigged to broadcast across the city. Barricades are built on the avenues. More people arrive: committees of farmers, workers, simple folk tired of the Colonels. The renowned artist Nikos Xylouris, from Crete, sings among the strikers, 'The Enemy Has Entered the City'.

The Greek spoke on. The hall stayed silent. We weren't used to such restraint in word and gesture. He told his story as one might to a friend, in confidence, catching his breath as if he were emerging from under water. I thought of asthma. And thus, of Guevara. He expected neither congratulations nor compassion from us for what came next. This ending that we knew by heart, from having read it so often in newspapers that didn't understand anything about it. The heroism that we had shared with all our anger, the dismal beauty of bare hands against tank cannons. How many of us had imagined ourselves chained to the gates of the college, facing death? I was one of them: I imagined myself on the tank, throwing a grenade into its open turret, then the ovation from a crowd of raised fists. I re-enacted the heroic gesture in my mind. Sometimes I carried a Greek flag, sometimes a red banner. After a few beers, carried away by the violins of Mikis Theodorakis, I sacrificed myself to the howling tread of a tank. Watching the film *Z*, I saved Grigoris Lambrakis, carrying Yves Montand on my back.

I was there, face to face with the Greek, listening violently. I was ashamed of my secret imaginings. On the edge of sleep, I fought history with bare fists. And it was ridiculous. In 1967, to protest the war in Vietnam, I burnt my draft card in Central Park. In 1969, I protected Catholic neighbourhoods in Belfast. In 1971, I married Angela Davis after rescuing her. In 1973, I was saving Greek insurgents. In 1974, I lowered my eyes when I faced one.

I had dreamt myself a hero. I didn't dare look Samuel Akounis in the eye.

He described the climactic night, Saturday, 17 November. After fifty-six hours of occupation, more than twenty tanks move into position around the school. Inside, more than five thousand resist. Ten thousand more fill the surrounding streets. 'Don't be afraid of the tanks!' the rebel radio repeats non-stop. Students attempt to negotiate an honourable exit. They ask for thirty minutes to vacate the buildings, the area. But an M40 tank rams the gate, lit by battlefield projectors. It crushes the iron gate cluttered with students. No one jumps onto the turret. No grenades. No dream. No little French Mao with his table leg. Just chaos and crushing defeat.

'I was on top of the gate when the tank rammed it. We fell onto each other. The police threw canisters of tear gas. Others turned their guns on us. People died all over the city. Thirty, maybe forty. Hundreds of wounded. Many refused to go to the hospital to avoid arrest.'

The Greek drank another glass of water.

'I was wounded when a metal bar of the gate pierced my thigh like an arrow. I limped home, threw some things into a bag and sought refuge with friends in Salonica. I was a known figure of the opposition. The next day the police came for me, too late. I had spent a year getting a tourist passport with a visa valid in Europe. A week later, I was in Italy. And today here, among you who supported us. I know this, and I thank you for it.'

I coughed my embarrassment. The others applauded. In the top row of the lecture hall, a boy pulled a Greek flag from his bag and waved it like a handkerchief of welcome at an arrival dock.

'Samuel Akounis has spoken little of himself, so I will do that,' the man seated next to him announced to the crowd. 'Out of respect for the honour he does us by joining us today.'

The Greek looked uncomfortable, but the man went on. After a few carefully articulated sentences, I remembered. His voice. A cloudy tone, somewhere between breath and whispered secret. He was an actor. No major roles, but I had seen him the previous autumn, costumed by Jacques Marillier in *Le Malade Imaginaire*. But here among us, in a jacket and jeans, his shirt unbuttoned, without stage makeup, I hadn't recognized him.

'The man before you today began his opposition to the regime of Papadopoulos on 22 April 1967, the day after the coup d'état,' the actor began. 'It was a Saturday, and I was in Athens ...'

Unlike the Greek, he orated. Struck poses, grimaced, his text intense, his audience captive. I found this invasive, unnecessary, but the large lecture hall hummed with palpable suspense. I turned back to Akounis, ignoring everything about the speaker except the story he shared.

'Martial law had been declared. Tanks and soldiers had taken up positions throughout the city, surrounding all public buildings. There were no newspapers, no telephone service, no radio except the military's. Banks, museums and restaurants, all shuttered. Stoplights were shut off, their colours blank. No buses, no taxis, only ambulances and jeeps. The city moved in slow motion, on foot. Soldiers were ordered to shoot on sight after sunset. Citizens were warned.'

The Greek filled his water glass and slid it across the table towards the actor.

'That evening I had reserved a seat for the production of *Ubu Roi*, directed in French by Samuel Akounis ...'

I was struck. *Directed*. A director. The Greek came from the theatre world, as I did. My knee hit something. I stood up. I couldn't sit any longer. I leaned against a wall, shoulder to shoulder with my comrades. A director. Of course. Obviously. His manner of organizing his words, his movement, the restrained elegance of it all turned the spotlight on us. My heart raced. A mood, a sequence, a look. Greek, resistance member, artiste. A lot for one man.

'I was convinced the Rebetiko Theatre would be closed as the others were, but I decided to check, just in case. That didn't take bravery; the theatre was across the street, facing my hotel. The outside marquee lights were off, the posters down, but a young man held the door open for those with the temerity to attend. That man was Samuel Akounis. He pulled down the heavy security gate behind me. Inside the theatre, twenty or thirty audience members. Two cast members were missing, Queen Rosemonde and Captain Bordure.'

The actor drained his water glass. The Greek looked away.

'It was a strange production, a mix of actors and unpainted marionettes. But that night the group improvised. What happened onstage reflected the drama in the streets.'

The actor stood, facing the crowd, acting out one role, then another, leaping between poses, playing the main characters, one after the other. Despite this pantomime, there was no laughter in the lecture hall. Faces stayed tense.

PAPA UBU

Shit!

MAMA UBU

Ah! Now isn't that lovely, Georgios, you're a big hoodlum!

PAPA UBU

May I not strike you in the head, Mama Ubu!

MAMA UBU

It's not me, Georgios, it's someone else who should be murdered!

The actor stood, silent, his imaginary dagger raised, before taking a seat.

'Yes, Samuel Akounis had his actors rename 'Papa Ubu' Georgios, the first name of the leader of the military junta.'

The actor turned to the Greek.

'There was an informer in the audience. Or someone who could not bear the offence to Jarry, the playwright. Two days later, our friend here was arrested and interrogated by the Asphalia. His fingernails were torn off, his torso burnt with cigarettes, his feet battered with lead pipes. Then his torturers suffocated him with gas, sprayed aerosolized chlorine in his mouth.'

He stopped talking, considered the effect on his audience the way a lawyer looks at his jury.

It wasn't asthma.

'He was not tried or imprisoned, but immediately deported to the detention camp at Oropos, where he spent a year with hundreds of other dissidents, including Mikis Theodorakis.'

I flushed. Lowered my head.

'After his release, he was placed under surveillance but never wanted to leave the country. It wasn't until the occupation of the Polytechnic, where he had staged a scathing production of Anouilh's *Antigone,* that Samuel Akounis accepted exile.'

The actor stood one last time. That moment must have been one of his greatest roles. He turned to the Greek, bowed, then applauded him. I clapped with him. Before the others, before the entire hall burst into applause, I stood, clapping, breaking the clenched-jawed silence.

That's when I made my way towards him. Aurora was approaching, too, a bag slung over her shoulder. The Greek hadn't moved. He was looking down at his hands when I extended mine.

'My name is George. I am a director.'

'I'm Aurora. I am trying to do theatre.'

He stood, vaguely surprised. Smiled at us. I didn't like this girl who had taken a swipe at him for saying the word 'revolution' should be masculine in gender, yet now fawned over him, her eyes brimming with regret. Her presence intruded on our moment.

'I was also wounded in the leg ...'

The Greek turned back to me.

'Last year, by fascist sympathizers.'

He nodded. I don't know why I said that. Bluntly, after all this man had just told us. Ashamed, I turned my eyes to the floor. My knee cracked. I shifted positions. He was still gripping my hand.

'It's an honour,' murmured Samuel Akounis.

He was thirty-four years old, Aurora was twenty-two and I was twenty-four.

He would become like a brother to me. And she would become my wife.

3

ALOIS BRUNNER

On 23 July 1974, Sam invited me to Boulevard de Sebastopol for a drink. Just me, not our small group. He had come to meet me at the college where I taught. We recognized each other as contrasting creatures. He was all joy, I was all sorrow. His heart was filled with springtime, my mask was autumn.

'I've suffered too much to be unhappy,' he often said. Then he would look at me and smile. 'But you, you can still indulge.'

From that moment on, we joked about our differences. My world filled with darkness, his with light. I responded to his nimble mind with awkward humour. Our conversations relied on this simple system, and we never strayed beyond it. Nothing intimate, nothing personal. Prudence on my part, and respect. Wherever we walked together, I felt myself a one-man cortège, bound to honour a tortured man.

'You're more tortured than I am,' he said one day when I questioned everything, drowning in doubt.

But that evening on our café terrace I felt almost light-hearted. All day the news on the radio had been about Greece. After the coup d'état in Cyprus, the Colonels had relinquished power to the people. The dictatorship was over. Seven years of suffering erased in a single stroke. I had shared the news with my students during break, with the voice of a professor handing back excellent work.

When Sam showed up at Jussieu that July morning, the girls hugged him, full of congratulations. The boys asked him how soon he would leave.

'One day, surely,' the Greek replied.

I had known for a long time that he stopped by our headquarters out of courtesy. When he came to a few meetings, when he raised the red flag, when he joined our demonstrations, it was never by conviction, but to thank us for having supported him. And, at this point, what was left of our group?

Our leaders had dissolved the movement. *The People's Cause* had ceased printing nine months ago. Since then, other members had disappeared into other lives. One comrade had hung himself. Another shot himself in the mouth. Michel, returned to his gangster life, had been killed by the owner of a café. Big Jacques, a worker at Renault, rejoined the assembly line. Those who held on were still militant, but heavy-hearted. The most recent partisans had gone back to being children, deserting the front lines for the banality of the rear. Headquarters looked like a ballroom at dawn, our scattered pamphlets its wilted dancers. We had a hard time silencing our battle songs. I thought of the soldier wounded by the herald of peace, the drabness of days returned to the quiet of social norms. Once our truths had worn out, we were ideological orphans. And I knew that the days ahead would sing without us.

That's why I stayed close to Sam. He was my remaining proof. Not a slogan, a censored book, a motto painted on a city wall, Samuel was the incarnation of our fight. His arrival among us, as late and understated as it was, renewed the force of my conviction. Gave me courage. He was my resistance and our dignity.

'Dignity? The most beautiful word in the French language,' said Sam with a smile.

From our pavement table on a nondescript street, I watched the people pass. Sam ordered a beer. I had a glass of house wine. Anticipation. He'd asked me to join him, he had something to say. We had never met one-on-one. He teased me in public and I struggled to find lame retorts.

'Are you happy?'

I said that to break the silence. He nodded, his lips covered in foam, his eyes shining.

'There are two men who make me happy today.'

I leaned in, pulled my chair closer. I loved personal conversations.

'First, Karamanlis. He'll go back to Greece, for sure. He'll form a government that will abolish royalty and all that outdated nonsense.'

Sam peered at me over his glass.

'Do you realize what this means? Konstantinos, my friend, prime minister?'

I nodded, laughing. No, I hadn't realized. I didn't even know Karamanlis had Greek friends in France.

Sam unzipped a worn Olympic Airlines bag, with its coloured five-ring logo. That tattered bag was one of the only things Sam had from home. He pulled out a folded newspaper and opened it up to show me the front page.

'My second joy is Eddy Merckx!'

I was stunned. I had read nothing but *The People's Cause* for years. Lately, *Libération* had become the only alternative. Sam was holding *L'Équipe*, a daily paper devoted to sports. He spread the paper across the table, pushing aside our drinks and all of Greece.

'You know he's won eight stages! He came in first in the time trials and swept the twenty-second stage!'

No, I didn't know. Once again. The Tour de France had ended two days earlier. The Belgian had won for the fifth time. So what? For me, 21 July was important because the Cypriot National Guard had managed to defend the city of Kyrenia from a Turkish assault. And the South Vietnamese national army, the Fantouches, had launched an offensive against the communists in Tây Ninh.

I was uncomfortable. He was talking loudly, laughing, losing his command of French. He said that life was that, too, a man on a bike choking down kilometres, screaming in pain. He said sports were another form of resistance. To oneself, to difficulties, to bad weather, to the melancholy that suited me so well.

'Are you listening to me, George?'

I startled. A bit disappointed, lost in thought. Drifting. This magic moment between us, the Greek fighter and the internationalist militant, had devolved into the caravan of the Tour, with its tooting horns, advertising banners, waving spectators, the screech of party whistles.

'Were there any Greek riders?'

Sam laughed at my feeble attempt. I think he read my thoughts exactly.

'I don't understand sports, I'm not a nationalist,' I said.

My words were inappropriate, thoughtless. Sam froze, his glass mid-air, his eyes on mine.

'Anti-nationalism? That's the luxury of man who has a nation.' He went silent, his eyes clouded. I'd never seen him like that.

'Talk to me about your parents, George.'

That caught me off guard. I had told him very little, to avoid revealing I was orphaned. My mother died when I was a child. Then my father, overwhelmed and burdened by me, dragging himself to the grave.

Sam let my silence whisper the rest. No one could put back together the schoolboy who picked a flower to say goodbye to his mother.

'And me? Do you know who I am and where I come from?'

It was obvious to me. Samuel Akounis, Greek partisan.

'I was born in Salonica on 4 January 1940, to Yechoua Akounis and Rachel Aelion. I called my older brother Pepo and my sister Reina.'

I watched him speak, almost not understanding. But I did. My body tensed, almost shaking as I realized: Samuel Akounis was Jewish.

'My father's ancestors came from Mallorca, in Spain. My mother's, from Portugal. The centuries erased their memory and their names. I know they worked in wool for the Ottoman Empire. My father was Communist, my mother Zionist. He was a baker. She raised her children. We lived in the Hirsch quarter, near the railway station. When the Italians invaded our country in October 1940, Yechoua Akounis joined the Greek army. He was wounded in the abdomen. He believed we were Greek forever. But he was the only one.'

Sam got up, abandoned his full glass. I was surprised at this. He put money on the table for his beer and my wine. Then he asked me to join him. I pushed back my chair. He wasn't leaving, wasn't walking away from me. He needed to move. As if none of that story could be told sitting down over a drink. He looked straight ahead, at the movement of the waning crowd, sunlight fading into the ground, the trees murmuring with summer.

'My parents had no nation, they had a star.'

I apologized. He smiled.

'You're sorry for what?'

When the Germans arrived, Samuel was sent to his aunt Allegra. She took him to Corfu, to the Italian zone where they went into hiding, shielded by the olive trees of a family of farm workers until the war ended. Yechoua, Rachel, Pepo and Reina left for Birkenau on the convoy of 15 March 1943.

Sam stopped and turned to me. 'Do you know how many Jews from Salonica died in the camps?'

I shook my head.

He walked slowly along the Parisian boulevard. 'Nearly 55,000. It was Brunner who engineered the Shoah of the Sephardi.'

He jabbed his elbow into my arm. 'Alois Brunner. Remember?'

He contemplated my obvious distress. He laughed. He said I had butterflies in my head and too much heart.

* * *

A few days later, we talked theatre for the first time. Sam was invited to the festival at Vaison-la-Romaine for a production of Anhouil's *Antigone* directed by Gérard Dournel. Liliane Sorval would play the daughter of Oedipus, King of Thebes. And her uncle Creon would be played by Jean-Roger Caussimon. Performances at the Maison des Jeunes et de la Culture, posh dress rehearsals, panel discussions. The Greek accepted all requests, refused nothing. He was the emblem of epic (political) theatre.

'I'm going to get back to work soon, but I'm not quite ready. I've been looking around, listening and learning, catching up on time stolen from me.'

It was the second time he'd mentioned *Antigone*. He'd produced it at the Polytechnic in Athens, before the tanks. Now he was setting out to find it again in the south of France.

From deep in his bag he retrieved a copy of *Antigone*, published by La Table Ronde in 1945, with brown and black etchings by Jane Pécheur. He waved it in the air like a clenched fist.

'I went through a lot with "the small, thin girl". And she fought beside me.'

We were near the Palais Royal, at another outdoor café.

'The small, thin girl?'

Sam tensed up. He had a way of shifting his eyebrows, squeezing his eyes almost shut, a look that radiated intense concentration.

'Don't you remember the opening of the prologue? "*Here we are. These actors are going to perform the story of Antigone. Antigone is the small, thin girl sitting over there. Silent.*"'

His theatrical voice was a different voice completely. It whispered the silk of the words.

'When the curtain rises, the actors are on stage, busy not seeing us, protected by the fourth wall.'

'The fourth wall?'

I had heard that expression but never knew what it meant.

'The fourth wall is what keeps the actor from fucking the audience,' Samuel Akounis answered.

An imaginary facade that actors create at the edge of the stage to strengthen the illusion. A wall that protects their character. For some actors, it's a remedy for stage fright. For others, the boundary of the real. An invisible fence that they breach occasionally with a line addressed directly to the audience.

'Remember the first seconds. All the actors are present, none in the wings. Nothing backstage, no bustling entrance, no applauded exit, no slamming doors. Just a circle of light that each speaker enters. And darkness that reclaims the one who's just spoken. The set? A few steps, a draped curtain, an ancient column. It's minimal, sparse, pure beauty.'

That look, again. Still.

'Don't tell me you've forgotten *Antigone*!'

I tried to buy time, my glass pressed against my lips.

'I've read it, like I read Boris Vian. As teenager. I even improvised a conversation between her and Voltaire.'

'Voltaire?'

'*Candide*. Optimism about mankind. I don't remember.'

'And Antigone, pessimism?'

Sam laughed. Not insultingly. He never insulted anyone who'd just spoken.

'Tomorrow I'll go to Maspero's and buy you a copy. I want you to read it again.'

'Anouilh's version?'

Sam shrugged his shoulders. Yes, Anouilh. Of course, Anouilh. Obviously, Anouilh.

'And Sophocles?'

The Greek brushed aside the name. He said Sophocles limited Antigone to her fraternal duty and submission to the gods.

'In Sophocles, her wrath submits to the divine. Anouilh's small, thin girl is like you.'

'Like me?'

'Over the course of twenty-four centuries, she evolved, from a ritual chorus offered to Dionysus, into a modern story, shifted from the religious to the political, and also from the tragic to absolute tragedy ...'

'How is that like me?'

'A heroine of "no" who defends her own freedom? Take a guess!'

I smiled back at Sam. Okay for Anouilh. 'Thank you for offering it to me. I will read it.' I promised with the nonchalance of someone answering a passer-by who's asked what time it is. I had no idea of the importance of the gift Samuel had just given me. Neither of us realized that this café terrace in July would change his life and mine. Just then, he sensed that I wasn't really listening. My feeble promise, my body angled away, towards the waiter, ordering another glass of wine. But he didn't hold it against me.

The next day, Sam gave me the book. We had planned to meet at the local Maoist group's headquarters. During the school holidays, workmen had changed the classroom locks. School security oversaw the work. Two of them entered the room at Jussieu that we had been using illegally for two years.

'Can I help you?' Sam asked.

One of the security guards wore gloves. We called him 'Moustache'. A Corsican, always first to the scene when something went wrong at the university. Twice he had approached me angrily. He knew I was from the Sorbonne, that I had no justification for being at Jussieu. When he learned I intended to teach, he pitied my future students. He wasn't the type to write you up or file a complaint. He fought fair, hit hard, got hit back. Some friends swore he'd done time in prison, the only place he said he'd bumped into a door when he got bloodied. I respected him for that.

Security guards had never entered our headquarters, but that day there were only three of us: me, Sam and Aurora. Moustache stepped towards the threshold.

'I asked you a question,' the Greek repeated.

'Should we ask for their student IDs?' The guard smiled.

The other shrugged.

I moved towards them, my fists raised. 'Get out of here!'

The two guard dogs feigned surprise.

'Three against two, we're in for it!'

Moustache put one hand on his colleague's shoulder.

'Come on, let's get out of here before they take us down ...'

And they went back into the hall, laughing.

Sam and I didn't need words. A few years earlier, hundreds of us had taken over that campus. From basement to balconies, it was ours. When police breached the doors, the buildings became a city that we defended street by street. A seminar table yielded four iron rods. Chair backs struck their shields. We had stashed Molotov cocktails in every niche to cover our retreat. But that summer sealed our collapse. No violence, no defiant slogans screamed. One by one, we abandoned our fortress. And now they were changing the locks.

As we left what had been our headquarters, I looked back into the room with its burnt-out fluorescents. In 1972 I had written 'Never Give Up!' in red letters to the left of the window. Aurora locked the door with her key. With a hard kick I broke off the part of the key protruding from the lock. And picked it up to keep.

'There are other venues besides this one,' Sam said as we left the building.

He had given me *Antigone*. I accepted it as a goodbye letter. I was sad and worried about us. My friend smiled. He'd been breathing with difficulty since our run-in with the guards.

'Don't get all worked up. No drama here. We'll see each other again.'

I laughed. He knew my fears but respected them. He would never put me in danger. I knew danger. I had an animal awareness of it, a caveman's instinct. I sensed it in the street, in a gesture, in an undue word. I read it in silences, looks, needless laughter. I felt it in promises and in threats. I suspected it in friends and enemies. But not in Sam.

4

NATALIA STEPANOVA

NATALIA STEPANOVA
Your father was a two-bit hustler. A louse!

LOMOV
And your aunt was a back-room cancan girl!

I stood up. Something in Aurora's character wasn't working. Her stance, her movement, her gestures, her tone of voice, nothing was working. Her belly? Maybe. Our child growing inside her. How can a woman six months pregnant embody a girl newly betrothed? She couldn't find her character, couldn't become Natalia. She felt it. We both knew. I walked around her.

'Lomov is out of control. And you? How do you react? You need to strike back!'

Aurora leaned against the wall, one hand on her belly.

'"Injustice disgusts me!" Natalia spits out that line. So when you insult Lomov by calling his aunt "a back-room cancan girl", I want to see your body hurl with disgust. Vomit those words, Aurora! They're a slap in the face. I haven't seen that. You haven't struck. He has to feel the blow!'

Aurora sat on the floor. Lit a cigarette. I hated when she did that. She'd promised to quit.

'I want you beside yourself, incensed! Got it?'

She did.

'It's Natalia's pride that you're defending. *Oxen Meadows* is her land, the pride of her family, her blood, her race, as Chekhov says! Lomov wants to seize that for himself! Fight for it! We die for our land, Aurora. Natalia is willing to kill for hers.'

I wanted to direct rage. The real thing.

My wife nodded. She understood. She understood instantly.

In the autumn of 1975, she realized how carefully I watched her. All it took was a look, a hand on her shoulder, my palm turning her hip as she moved onstage. She had done theatre in middle school and secondary school, then in parish halls and university politics. When the political scene burnt out she'd gone back to theatre. I did theatre in middle school and secondary school, in parish halls and university politics. When the political scene burnt me out, I went back to theatre. We'd watched each other in lecture halls at Jussieu, been chained together in street demonstrations, run away from brutal police crackdowns. Sam had made friends with her. He said that the stage was a better fit for her than a megaphone. That any playwright's lines were more worthy of her than our slogans. He talked theatre with her. He wanted to get her out of the streets. He protected her like a child.

The day I decided to stage *The Marriage Proposal*, she insisted. She had pale skin the colour of chalk, blue eyes, high cheekbones, wide-set eyes. A Breton from Finistère, she embodied my image of Natalia Stepanova. We performed in the meeting halls of young workers in the Red Belt movement. Five free performances. Theatre had become the vehicle of my resistance. My weapon, my protest. To all who accused me of walking away from the fight, I quoted Beaumarchais, 'Theatre? A giant that mortally wounds all it strikes.' My voice filled with emotion in places other than the streets. I added laughter, a thrill long exiled from our sombre halls. First, in the school where I taught. Then in hospitals. Retirement homes. Immigrant centres. I was tired of militant theatre, of performing on a street corner for ten grave-faced friends. I was sick of the present, the reactionary scene. Burning the American flag, the red flag waving in the wind. I wanted something more complex, more intelligent, somewhere in the grey zone, more subtle. So I went back to words that predated our slogans, our tracts. Performing Gatti, Jarry, or Brecht is not a betrayal, Sam affirmed when I had moments of doubt.

He opened a theatre. A real one, with walls and a roof. He said the troupe was the fabric of his theatre. To create a family for the duration of a play wasn't enough for him any more. He wanted to act with certainty, as he had facing tanks in his old country. A community of friends, committed forever. Like his peacetime heroes Roger Planchon and Patrice Chéreau, his was a theatre of language, of image. A pocket-size dream in the north of Paris that he baptized 'Little Diomedes' in homage to Diomedes Komninos, a sixteen-year-old shot in the head on 16 November 1973 as he walked towards the Athens Polytechnic. Sam asked me to join him as an actor, but I said no. I wanted to direct. He wanted to direct me. He asked Aurora, too, but she chose me. He was our best man.

'May the devil take me! Marriage is a bothersome affair,' Sam said with a smile on our wedding day, quoting Gogol.

He refused to wed. He feared seeing his children die. His girlfriends were always Greek. I never knew whether they fell in love with Sam, or Akounis. Former militant, current director, or just the handsome man with the right words?

In the autumn of 1979, we wanted to restage *A Marriage Proposal* for workers on strike, for the anger of the text and its humour. Making the proletariat smile was a battle like any other. The metal workers at the Alsthom factory at Saint-Ouen had occupied the site. They weren't trying to change the world or set the fields on fire. A thousand women and men were fighting for a thirteenth month of pay and a fifth week of paid vacation. Performing Chekhov for these workers, we would be entertaining militants.

On 14 November 1979, the day of our performance, the CRS forced their way into the occupied factory. At 6 am, behind the police clubs and shields, executives opened the gates to non-striking workers.

Friends had warned us early that morning. A union member told us that women were crying. A man yelled that he couldn't survive. At three in the afternoon, Sam, Aurora and I arrived. To perform Chekhov. Sam advanced, menacing, with the brass candelabra. I had nothing but rage in my fists. I wanted to hear what the pigs had to say about it. An officer asked us to move back behind the barrier. No violence. Not another word. The workers had left, the lock that hung on the iron gate pried open by a yellow vest as a precaution.

I fell to the pavement. Backwards, suddenly, as if struck by a stray bullet. My back, my head, my hands hit the ground. I lay there, open-mouthed, my eyes a blank stare, my body shaking, then still. Sam understood. He looked straight at the police, then the strike-breakers. He took a close look at the broken lock. He stared into the crowd of yellow and blue, gone silent and fearful. He looked to the sky, to the vanquished factory. He wore the mask of tragedy. His eyes, his mouth, the deep lines on his face, the worn plaster of his brow, all turned down. He leaned over me, his arms raised to the gods.

TCHOUBOUKOV

Oh! ... What's happened here? What do you want?

NATALIA STEPANOVNA

(Moaning, hands on her belly) He is dead!

TCHOUBOUKOV

Who is dead? (*He looks at me.*) He is really dead! Lord, Lord! Water! A doctor! *(Sam takes an empty glass from his bag, holds it to my mouth.)*

TCHOUBOUKOV

Drink ... No, he's not drinking ... Oh, he is dead. I am the unhappiest of men!

We froze in place. A long minute. Me, lifeless. Sam, motionless. Aurora, mute.

When we stood, the silence grew. First me, a dead man come to life. Then Sam, who had leaned over my last breath. And last, Aurora, her head in her hands, her mouth open, her eyes lifted toward November.

We left the pavement the way one leaves a stage. But expecting nothing.

'He scared me, that fool!' one cop exclaimed.

We accepted that as an ovation.

5

LOUISE

My childhood ended on 9 January 1980, at six in the morning. I don't remember wanting that. Our daughter was named Louise. After Aurora's grandmother, a sardine-cannery worker from Douarnenez who had broken her life against its chains, her hands full of fish. The choice of first name was for her. We had explained it that way to our parents, who were thrilled. But our friends knew it was also to honour Louise Michel, the teacher who chose black over red, mourning the illusions of our soldiers. Louise, the inspiration for my thesis, *Louise Michel and Human Rights*.

Both Louises were fighters. Aurora saw in them a shared rage, and pride. My wife had seduced me with her smile and the story of her grandmother. A 'Penn Sardin' whose wooden clogs clacked down streets, marching with demonstrators right up to police cordons. A scarf on her head, she chanted the cannery workers' fury. At the top of her lungs. Fists on her hips, the way fish-workers stand. She sang leaving home in the morning, she sang filling cans and walking home at the end of the day to make fish soup. In 1924 the workers went on strike for one franc an hour, not the eighty centimes the boss paid. One of the women

– they were all women – was illegally elected to the city council, though women had no right to vote.

Since the beginning of the year, Aurora and I had been counting the weeks, then the days. We wanted Louise on that Wednesday, 9 January, the day Louise Michel, militant revolutionary leader, Communard, closed her eyes for the last time.

'I'll make it happen,' Aurora promised.

And she did, offering us another Louise to share the name.

I did not witness the birth. I was in the hall of the clinic, then in the street, the metro, back in the street, at the door of the delivery room, out on the frozen pavement, circling the final hours I remained unattached.

* * *

Aurora and I were married surrounded by friends. Marriage. I didn't take it seriously, but my wife did. She proposed. She wore a gypsy dress to cover her ballooning belly and I wore a fisherman's sweater, three buttons on the shoulder that closed the round neck. One wedding party before ours was decked out in white. Celebratory, fancy. The next one, too. The bride waited, a short veil over her eyes, and her fiancé eyed us almost fearfully. Aurora's dress was new, purchased specially for this occasion. My sweater was also new. It was high-quality wool, ivory-coloured, almost white. I had left my leather jacket behind, along with my combat boots. We had both ironed our jeans to give them a party crease. Our outfits weren't conventional, but they were acceptable. We had dressed up to honour the ceremony. But the mayor humiliated us. A right-wing official, with his scarf and his scorn.

'A republic has respect for its institutions.'

That's how he greeted us. Aurora and I, with our sketchy friends. He said that marriage was a specific act on a specific day that required a specific attitude and appropriate attire.

'A republic has respect for its differences,' answered Sam, my witness, my best man, without raising his voice.

The mayor was stunned. He united us with the enthusiasm of someone performing an unpleasant task. Before the ceremony I had been upset with the idiots who had pinned Lenin on their lapels. Afterwards I was proud. I was upset about my wedding sweater. And about the wedding dress, a mix of spring colours, expensive, paid for by a group of friends. We had done our best, but our best wasn't enough for the mayor. When the mayor spoke, Aurora cried. Our child must have been crying too. The mayor saw, maybe even understood, but the harm was done. So we chanted our Red anger, fists raised, on the steps of City Hall. I never wore the sweater again. Aurora tore up the dress as soon as we got home. Once more, we had seen what we were up against.

* * *

I became a father that winter, my belly full of fear. A history student doing theatre for tomorrow, suddenly a man holding tomorrow in his arms. Louise was ravishing, I thought. Human babies look alike when they reach the light. I sat on the stool by the bed where her mother rested.

I had let my women rest. My women. I had run out like someone escaping. I drank. I went into a station café, the first one on my path. A departure bar, zinc counters, worn faces, drinks that get refilled at a nod.

'I'm a father.'

I told everyone, no one. The man next to me, talking into his drink. The owner, who found me as interesting as a blank wall. I bought one man a glass of wine, another a beer. Then I moved on, out to the station platform, the empty tracks: no arrivals, no trains. Just parallel rails running towards a goodbye. I didn't want to go home. Not yet. The apartment, the living room transformed into a nursery, the little bed prepared, the white dresser, the mobile of stuffed animals ready to assuage an infant's fears. I didn't want that silence.

I jumped down onto the gravel beside the tracks and walked. Darkness shielded me. I climbed into an old railway carriage, abandoned among forgotten trains. I took a seat in a compartment, next to the window, like a traveller on his way. Under the baggage nets, a photo of Clermont-Ferrand, with its black stone cathedral. The lighting was soft, the orange of the bridge lights, the white of the train signals, gilded by evening. I pressed my forehead to the window. Railway workers were making their rounds in the distance. I could see lanterns that swung from their hands. I feared nothing. Especially not men who worked the railway. What was I doing there, gentlemen? I thought hard. I closed the book on my childhood. I gave myself one night to catch my breath. A home? Of course I have one. Keys? Yes, here they are. The flat one is for the front door, the small one for the letterbox. The third one? The broken one? It's the key to paradise. It opened a secret room at the university. A roof that was ours, a refuge, a haven. It was our matrix. You don't understand? Doesn't matter. We were fighting for you. For you, who work the railways. For the workers at the rake factory, the workers on strike at Alsthom, the battered women, scorned youths, disrespected immigrants, miners deep underground, sailors on their sea. It was for you, gentlemen, comrades, friends. For you, who always knew. So please, let me sleep. Let me have this final night, this still journey in this empty railway carriage. Let me gather my thoughts. Let me become a father before I have to fully enter fatherhood. Please.

I slept until the frozen morning. It was 5 am and Louise was one day old. I waited at the gate for the hospital to open. I felt light-hearted. I was at peace. I was a father. The only example I had of a father was the absence of mine. It took me a night to accept that. I was a father, I ran limping into the empty hall to get back to my women.

* * *

I was born on Tuesday, 16 May 1950. I arrived, disrupting the lives of two young people. My father didn't want children, my mother wasn't sure either way. Her belly hid me from him for months. He was Protestant, she was Catholic. The Virgin was watching, so she kept me. And he kept us. But nothing beyond that. I was her business, on a par with errands, grocery shopping, cleaning house, dust under the beds. I think my parents loved each other before I came along.

He was Parisian, born and bred, raised on rue de la Roquette in a working-class family. His father was a blacksmith, his mother a corset-maker. One December day, my uncle told me, they stood in line, with the homeless, at the Charity Office. My mother was from Mayenne, born on a farm near Commer. The year both her parents died of meningitis she was fifteen. Her aunt in Montreuil took her in. For the first few years my mother worked alongside her aunt as a laundress, learning a trade, before her aunt re-enrolled her in school. My father and mother met later, during the war. They spent those years looking elsewhere, fighting for coal and bread. Then our flags came back out of the closets. He was a history professor. She became a schoolteacher. In August of 1949, she took her husband to Mayenne. She wanted to see the trees, the sky, the farm where she grew up. Her parents' land. That's where they made me unintentionally, one night in the tall grass.

I have few childhood memories, and fewer photos. I found them one evening, just before I left my father's house. Four snapshots on old lacy-edged paper that was once the rage, the images barely larger than a postage stamp. In the first one, I look like a girl. A white blouse tucked into puffy shorts and a lace pinafore. I was holding the hand of a woman cut out of the frame.

'Your mother's hand,' my father said, without conviction, as if he didn't recall.

Another showed a baby carriage in the sunshine of Savoy. I was tucked inside, invisible to the viewer. The third told the tale of an adolescent hiding his face with one hand. Just a glimpse, a crew cut, a blurred wince. The final photo was the most painful, from 1955, at my mother's burial. I had just turned five. I don't know who turned a camera on that lost child, clicked the shutter that day to freeze time. The photographer must have crouched down by the road. Only dark trousers are visible, and sombre dresses of mourning, the cemetery gates. Off to one side, away from the others, a kneeling shadow, delicately dressed, picking a flower to wish his mother goodbye. I stole that photo from my father. I found it in an old biscuit tin that held so few of them. I took it when I left. I've carried it with me ever since.

I moved from childhood into an unruly adolescence at a boarding school where I counted the noisy days. I learned to fight. To stop listening, stop hearing. To follow my instinct the way a wolf follows a scent. In class, I was an average student in middle school, still average at secondary school. Mathematics frightened me. I never understood that language. I had nightmares about being called on to solve a problem at the board, in front of the class. But I loved history, and theatre most of all. Directing myself. Acting, dressed as someone else, with different gestures and movements, another voice, other words to speak. Since preschool, I had been acting. I directed little plays. I created roles before I could read. In middle school I formed The Company of Dunces, a handful of students I led in rehearsals for the festivities at the end of the school year. In secondary school, I created The Four Boards Company and Pocket Theatre, each with its own trends and talent pool. I earned my baccalaureate in 1968. No written tests, just a long oral exam where I was asked how I was doing. I talked about Rimbaud, Ronsard, and love. For the history section, we discussed the present.

'Order has given way to freedom,' I claimed. I had read that slogan on a wall on my way there. The professor smiled. He was wearing an armband. Students swore he'd been beaten by the police. I knew nothing about it. He nodded as I spoke, like a bobble-head dog in the rear window of a car headed for the beach. He wasn't being gracious. He agreed, and it was intoxicating.

I passed my baccalaureate exam in May, enrolled at the Sorbonne in October, when the battle was over. I wanted to study theatre, but my father insisted on history. He offered me his tiny job, his role in the world, which was all he had to offer, and I accepted. Bachelor's, then master's degrees. I failed my teacher's exam twice, stayed enrolled at the university, working part time as a monitor in the dining hall, then on the playground of a secondary school, hoping one day to assume my father's role at the front of a classroom. Theatre?

'Theatre is for the weekend, like gardening,' my father declared.

So it was. We had History in common, but no common history. No flesh memories. I have none of my mother, no trace of her lips, no sense of her hand, no facial expressions. From my father, I had nothing to hold onto because there was nothing. I don't remember his hands, his fingers reassuring me when thunderstorms raged. Not even his anger, his joy, his shouts. His voice. I don't remember my father's laugh. Even now, when I think of him, I feel the silence. Some children are loved, hated, beaten, forced to work, or smothered in tenderness. I was intact, untouched. I smiled often, acting out the paternal embrace in the theatre, the kiss on the forehead of a child ready for sleep. Sometimes I brought maternal tenderness, open arms, offered breast, eyes shining with promise.

I came into the world because a woman loved a man. She left without time to love me. I was an extra mouth, then an extra heart.

I was twenty when my father died. And I stood there, looking at him. People entered the room. Some kissed him, some touched his hand. I stood over the coffin, my head bowed, the wooden moulding crushing my painful thighs. I dominated his body. I could just reach out my hand. My skin on his. Even marbled and loose. I could unite us with one touch. But I couldn't. He lay with his hands folded. I stood with my arms crossed. Like I was punished in my corner, not daring to breathe. Two studies of death.

I stood there all night. I refused a chair, a glass of water, a biscuit, brutalities buzzing with life. In the morning, they had to push me gently aside to close the casket. His hands were what I saw last, on satin, stippled with black death. I still could have. Slid my fingers under the top, blindly grabbed at his sleeve to hold onto him. But I didn't move. I leaned against the wooden stand. I was orphaned. Moved ahead, to the front line. Of our two lives, mine remained. I told myself it was mine to defend. Against any who would do harm, any who would do good. A life to defend. This phrase was my slogan when I fought. To be more than just an envelope, a dead skin people drag behind them like a shroud. My friends chanted communism, I had my own rites. To fight was to keep standing. Not on my knees, not lying down, never. When blows knocked me down, I saw my father's corpse. His folded hands made me ashamed. As a child, as an adult, I resisted. I went from ink-stained fingers to knuckles ripped bare.

* * *

I took Louise in my arms. I held her a long time, my hand at the nape of her neck. She was a beating heart. She smelled of life. I was unshaven. I didn't risk putting my cheek to her skin. I spoke to her quietly, just for myself.

'I love you, I love you, I love you.'

Murmured three times. The missing words, from one child to another. I put my lips on her forehead. I had never sensed such beauty and such violence. I was no longer alone. I would have to protect two lives. Defend them with all my strength. A mother, her daughter. I feared for them both.

'What did you say, George?'

I raised my head. Aurora was sitting up in bed, propped against a pillow. She was watching me. So I repeated.

'I would kill for her.'

'Don't say things like that, you frighten me.'

I leaned over my child.

A guard, a soldier, a sentinel.

'I will kill for you, little woman.'

6

JOSEPH BOCZOV

I frighten myself. I know something flows inside me besides tears and blood. I carry fury. At boarding school, I flipped my bed over with both hands to release the rage. I hit a teacher who had told another student he wasn't finished. It was true. He hadn't finished. Near-sighted, practically blind, he moved his finger slowly along each line as he read. His named was Bashir, but the teacher called him 'bushman'. When Bashir stumbled over an answer he didn't know, he clicked his tongue, and the teacher imitated the language of the African bush, told him to go back to his cave, climb back up a tree. He told him to come to class barefoot if he couldn't get used to shoes.

From September to November 1962, Ambroise Vançay, instructor at Thomas-Edison middle school, mistreated the Algerian Bashir Tayebi, repatriated to France with the baggage of his 'Harki' father, a soldier who had fought with the French against the uprising. And I let it go on for too long. Hour after hour, to the great amusement of those who knew themselves to be truly French. One Friday, before the last class ended, Bashir dropped his glasses. Thick as a submarine porthole, they skidded across the floor, then passed from shoe to shoe, from one end of the room to the other. I looked up at Vançay. He was watching the game. He saw everything. One eye on the clock, the other on the glasses. Bashir stood up, held out his hands. He didn't cry, he didn't shout. This boy had learned not to beg. In a quiet voice, he asked for light. His glasses.

Vançay sat on the edge of his desk. He took off his own glasses, examined their greasy lenses in the fading daylight. He blew on them twice, then wiped them carefully. When the bell rang, he announced, 'See you Monday' without even looking at the class. The others ran out, tramping across the floor in their wooden-soled shoes. I picked up Bashir's glasses, handed them to him. Not a thank you, nothing. He ran out of the room, filled with shame. Only the teacher and I remained in the classroom. I approached his desk without a word. I struck him in the face with my bookbag. Violently, instinctively, driven by desire to inflict pain. The leather scraped his cheek. He lost his balance. His glasses fell. I stomped on them. I crushed them. I can still feel the sound of the glass breaking. And see his astonished face. He crouched down to pick up the debris. And I left. Without waiting. That Sunday I looked up at the sky, believing my life would end.

On Monday, 26 November 1962, I took my seat in the second row, on the left side of the room. Vançay had taken out his mathematics notebook. He wrote the date on the board. He had different glasses, round and black, serious. Bashir Tayebi had come back with only his fog.

Nothing happened. Not a word, ever again. The teacher ignored us. Bashir, me. I was relieved and disappointed.

I had been imagining a public confrontation. I folded my open penknife. I was twelve.

* * *

'Violence is a weakness,' Sam had told me.

He had opened his door for me in December of 1975, after an ambush we had set up for a group of right-wing extremists. A few days earlier, friends of ours had recognized someone leaving a New Right forum in the 15th arrondissement. They set him straight in no uncertain terms, and took whatever he had with him. The militant was brave but foolish. He had written the time and date of their next meeting in his notebook. All the details. He must have been too proud to tell the leaders he'd been beaten up. The night of their meeting, about a hundred of us gathered in neighbouring streets in groups of five. There were about forty of them, maybe more. They were having dinner at a crêperie. Aurora and a friend from Censier had reserved a table inside. They had dressed up, done their hair. One of the men raised his drink in her direction and smiled. When the men asked for their bill, the women came out to alert us. The men had been drinking heavily. They had trouble splitting up when they reached the pavement. Two of them were singing Sardou, arms around each other, glasses raised to the dark windows above.

'Don't ever call me "France" again,

France let me down …'

I went in with the first wave. Since I couldn't run fast, I hit whatever came close. I was screaming. We were all screaming. A pack of dogs. We surged out from both sides of the street, iron rods raised and ready. All of us wore gloves and helmets, scarves covering our faces. Their side melted into a single cluster. Them against us. We were the vengeance of the masses. I remember my strength. My anger. And my brutal joy. My knee was hit, and my teeth. It hurt. I didn't care. I moved sideways. My gait was disturbing. A barbaric dance that looked intentional. Every ten steps, I stretched my leg out in front of me, whipping the air like a demon. I struck the first one in the back. He had slipped on the pavement. He was drunk, had fallen down, stumbled back up. He was making his way back towards the restaurant when I struck with all my hate. The blow pushed him forwards. His forehead struck the window hard. He turned around, crazed. I hit him three times. Nose, chin, mouth, gripping my bloody rod with both hands. Then I crushed his lips, broke his teeth. I was screaming. Inhuman. I masked his screams with mine. The table leg was in his mouth. I pulled it violently towards his ear. And the broken-off steel took off his cheek.

'Kneecaps! Break his kneecaps!' A comrade shouted.

When they came after us, they crushed our knees. It had been the enemy's specialty; now it was ours. To keep them from running, from walking, from lining up in demonstrations. To force them onto crutches, into wheelchairs, into a lifetime of pain. To wound them deep in the flesh, as I had been. I hopped from one to another. None escaped us. We fought three against one. Methodically. The men on the ground were crouched in foetal positions. They tried to protect their necks, their foreheads, leaving the rest to us. Lines stuck in my head, pulsed through me, absurd. 'My heart is beating terribly fast ... *The Oxen Meadows* ... both my eyes are blurring.' A line of Lomov's, to Natalia Stepanova. That morning I had been rehearsing the scene with Aurora. Tomorrow we were going to perform Chekhov at an Immigrant Council Hall in Corbeil. 'My heart is beating terribly fast.' Several of the partiers were on the ground. 'Both my eyes are blurring.' One lost a shoe as he ran off.

I was a militant. I was a theatre director, a monitor in a Parisian middle school, a lingering history student at the university. I was fighting the enemy. I was entertaining the enemy of my enemy. I was educating children to turn them into friends.

'Shit! They're unarmed. They have no weapons on them!' someone from our group yelled.

'And me? I was armed at Luxembourg?' I answered.

* * *

Two years earlier, on the morning of 26 March 1973, we had tried to take back the university buildings at Assas from the 'Black Rats'. That's what they called themselves. 'Anthracite' was their mascot. A comic strip character from the 1950s, a dark rat with one torn ear, an elongated nose and mouth with bad teeth. They put him on their posters, their pamphlets. He was their signature. In children's stories printed in the magazine *TinTin*, Anthracite was the leader of the bad guys. He dreamt of money, strength and power. The leader of the good guys was 'Chlorophylle'. I could never tell if Chlorophylle was a boy or a girl. A dormouse, a small rodent with dark rings around the eyes that gave it a wounded look, like it had been hit. Anthracite was tall, sly and unscrupulous. Chlorophylle was small, intelligent, and full of compassion. In the book, the dormouse wins every time. In the street, things weren't so clear. And I hated the thought that our adversaries had a sense of humour.

That day, Anthracite beat Chlorophylle. The rat let us pass through the rue d'Assas, into the law school. It was too easy. We were helmeted, armed, ready for the final assault. Inside the sewer, we were ready to evict the rat for good. That's when he emerged from all directions, in black hordes. From hallways, streets, classrooms. He was ready. He knew. It was a trap. We couldn't hold them off. Most of us were cornered inside. The police arrived. My friends had never been so glad to raise their hands in a sea of police batons. I tried to escape. Four of us, all from the Sorbonne. We ran for the door. The enemy swarmed the streets. I turned left. Threw down my iron rod. Emptied my improvised tear-gas bomb before I let it go, but the wind was against me. I couldn't breathe. I think I was the only one it hit. I ran around the rats the way a runner evades defensive players on his way to the goal. There were five running after me. I thought they would quit. Only two of them did. I dashed into the Luxembourg Gardens like a refugee rushing into a church. I don't know why I thought they wouldn't bring the fight past the gates. That they would attack a person on a November street, but not under a blooming spring arbour.

They caught me just beyond the sandpit. I used the last of my strength to get past the children. Mothers were screaming as I fell. I had my helmet on, tried to protect my knees. I rolled into a ball. I was wearing a groin guard, elbow pads, cardboard between my jacket and my two sweaters. I thought about Chlorophylle. A ridiculous image. When I fell and my chin struck the ground, I imagined the dormouse frowning, hands on its hips, acting the bad guy. I was surrounded. Being kicked, hit with an axe handle. One of them brandished a baseball bat. He bashed in my helmet. I didn't cry out. Nothing. I yell when I give, not when I receive. I willed myself silent as the horde worked me over. Without a word. No insults. Nothing, just lumberjacks taking down the next tree. I was exploding. I didn't know what suffering was, real pain, life-threatening. I met it there. They didn't miss a bone. They weren't just hitting me, they were demolishing me. Putting me out of commission. My head, my neck, my arms, my legs, my whole body was cracking. I pulled my helmet down over my forehead. And the rat hit right on target. My right knee, unprotected. A deathly pain, a searing blade shot through my body and exploded in my skull. I wouldn't walk again. Ever. I bit through my tongue. My temples were throbbing. The blows stopped. I still felt them. My fearful heart took over when the rats left, smashing my skull, swelling my lips, blasting my body with insane contractions. I was bleeding. I was going to die. They said I raised my fist against the policeman who bent down to check my pulse.

Open fracture of the right knee. Fragments of bone. Wired together. Seven months in a brace. A cane, then crutches, physical therapy, pain ever since. When I go up stairs, when I go down, when I bend that knee. My knee stopped working in the spring of 1973. Also three broken ribs, broken nose, broken collarbone and humerus, stitches in my forehead, my neck, sixteen broken teeth, chronic issues with my right eye. But my anger intact.

To those who said the members of the New Order were barbarians, I replied that we were at war. They attacked, we fought back. For one eye, two eyes, for one tooth, a mouthful. Their weapons were no more unforgiving than ours, our tactics were equally monstrous. We were brothers in violence. So, no. Don't criticize their viciousness. Especially not that.

Racism, antisemitism, scorn for anyone 'other'. Their ideas were the real threat to us, what we needed to overcome. Like their hatred of the present, their disgust with equality, their aversion to difference. That was pure savagery. But their method of defending their ideas was no different from ours. When I fell onto the grass at Luxembourg, I was thinking of that. I had lost. It was my turn. I was angry with myself for not having beaten them. They were going to celebrate my pain, and that's how it was. I took up violence to defend humanity. They violated humanity with the same weapons I used. It was too late to turn back. I accepted that no one understood. I understood those who rejected brutality on both sides, red and brown, equally, ours and theirs. But I could not accept when someone who gives a beating criticizes the beating he gets in response.

* * *

I returned from the crêperie with evidence of the attack. A torn jacket with a shiny iron cross pinned on the lapel. I handed it to Sam. He wouldn't take it.

'What's this for?' he asked.

'Fear has switched sides,' I answered.

'Violence is a weakness,' Sam replied.

I just shrugged my shoulders. I asked what he would have done, at the Polytechnic, if he'd had a weapon, huh? And if he could have defended Diomedes Komninos, wouldn't he have done it? Would he have let him get shot and do nothing?

Sam was reading a book when he let me in. His calm drove me crazy. He often turned off the lights and read by candlelight. He listened non-stop to a brief passage from Duruflé's *Requiem. Pie Jesu*, the motet repeating as the organ and the orchestra retreat, leaving only the voice. Since May, Sam had explained, the composer had been cloistered at home, after a serious automobile accident. My friend said the musician would not write again, ever. That this liturgical work was Duruflé's legacy to Akounis. *Pie Jesu* moved him deeply. He wanted a mezzo-soprano in his room. He dreamt of that purity for Antigone's farewell.

ANTIGONE

I no longer know why I'm dying.

And the singer's breath, time suspended, her first notes, the cello in the distance, light as the wind.

'Answer me, Sam. Please. If you could have saved Diomedes ...'

He looked at me. Stood with difficulty, his breath making a whistling sound. He brought me a mirror. Reached into his back pocket. Pulled out a black kippah, with gold stitching, polished by joy and grief. His father's. Who had gone to his death bareheaded. He put it on. He moved close to me, put his hand on my shoulder, holding the mirror in front of us. Samuel Akounis and I. Two friends in a photo.

'Tell me what you see, George.'

I didn't move away, but I didn't like the game. He was at the theatre. He was talking the way we recite lines, as an enemy of the unnecessary word. I wondered how he had been able to remain among us in our fight over the last two years. Without really criticizing, without letting anything show, no anger, no insults. So who was he? A Greek director who had produced *Ubu Roi* during the dictatorship and had been mistreated for that. And what else? Nothing else? No. Nothing. He had turned the other cheek. He had talked about theatre. He had left the path open for the Colonels. He had climbed onto a gate, fallen, been injured in the leg. A domestic accident. And then he had fled. He had sought refuge in France. He had been lauded by the democrats. He had been invited all over. To denounce dictatorship, he had talked about theatre. He had been lifted up in triumph by different flags: red, black, Vietnamese, Chinese, Chilean, Palestinian, Basque. He had raised his arms. He had smiled. He had talked about theatre. Instead of gathering an army to save a sixteen-year-old boy, he had used his name to build a company.

He had used our fights as a response. He had created a scenario with our struggle. He had kept his distance, never took the stage. He had stayed in the wings, watching what we were. I had never loved a man so much. In my life, ever. I was upset with myself for not having understood his silences.

'Tell me, George. What do you see? Who do you see, George?'

His kippah bothered me. It made him different, other, distant from me.

'I am going to tell you what I see, George.'

He moved away, handing me the mirror.

'I see a man who refuses injustice and indifference. A good guy.'

He studied my reflection.

'I see a middle-school monitor who got lucky enough not to get killed a year ago at Luxembourg. And not sent to jail either. Who kept his job because his friends mobilized to make that happen, and an official who owed him nothing had understood.'

Sam adjusted his kippah.

'But he was lucky, the good guy. He knows it. He's on borrowed time everywhere. At his tiniest misstep, Justice will pursue him. And it loves easy prey.'

He moved away, leaving me alone in the frame.

'Aurora loves you. The theatre, too.'

He put down the mirror.

'What we're going through is hard, but it isn't war. You're not in the Resistance, and Giscard is not Pétain.'

He poured himself a glass of ouzo.

'This may surprise you, but I don't believe your little friends from Assas are Nazis or Fascists. Those words are meaningless here.'

'So, maybe they're democrats?'

'Dangerous racists. That's what they are, but they're not Alois Brunner.'

I remembered.

He went to his bookcase. Inside a book, he kept an old photo, streaked with yellow. A serious man. Or a severe one. There was something of Sam in the way he looked. In the angular face, the fiery eyes, the taut mouth. His cheeks were hollow, his soul on fire. The man wore a coat and a heavy scarf. He stood in profile, his hair combed back, against a grey wall.

'Let me introduce Joseph Boczov,' Samuel Akounis said, smiling.

I remembered. Of course. One of the faces on the Red Poster that accompanied our fight. A companion of Manouchian, executed alongside him on 21 February 1944 at Mont Valérian. 'Hungarian Jew. Train derailer. Twenty attacks,' the Nazis had printed under his photo. He had left his native village at twenty-three. Not to flee, but to join the Republicans in Spain. Defeated with them, he was interned in a camp in France, deported to Germany, escaped. Made his way to Paris, where he joined the FTP. And threw his first grenade at the train station in Belleville.

'Look, George. Look closely at this face. Boczov is facing a firing squad. The photographer is an enemy. Their bullets will kill him. Look at his eyes. Look at the line of his mouth.'

I looked. Joseph, Samuel, and one kippah for the two of them.

'He's about to die, he's already dead. He has no hope, no future, no morning awaits him. He will leave a vanquished world, with a cohort of millions of victims and slaves. He doesn't know. He will never know what tomorrow will be. He doesn't know if his fight has been in vain. If his death will have any meaning. Look at him, George. He is going to die. He can't do anything more. But he still dreams of ripping a solider apart. Look how calm he is. How handsome. He promises them nothing but death.'

He put the photo back in the book. A German cookbook. Sam was never where you expected him to be. Then he stood in front of the mirror.

'You know what I see in the mirror? Not a resistant, not a hero, not a legend. But a Jew from Salonica. Greek by exile, French by choice and theatre director because, when I'm out of ideas, I invent a character. That's all, and that's fine.'

'And us, Sam? Aurora, me, our friends, what are we to you?'

'You are what ended my wandering.'

He took off his kippah. Put it on my head with a weak smile.

'Boczov won your war, George. He's the one who won it.'

7

AURORA

'If Sam hadn't come to France we would never have met,' Aurora said one sleepy Sunday afternoon.

Maybe not. I'm not positive, though. I'd noticed her and her friends, more focused on the status of women in the fight than on the fight itself. When Aurora stood up that day in the hall, when the Greek spoke for the first time, I knew who she was. I knew she would say something about our speaker's use of a masculine noun.

'All words should be allowed a feminine form,' she called out in a meeting in 1973, as we were writing a pamphlet supporting the Polisario Front.

'All words?' I repeated, using a feminine form for 'word', laughing.

She called me macho, congenital idiot. Every time she ran into me, she called me *id-Mao,* for idiot Mao. That suited me. It was light-hearted. I wanted to make her smile and she kept me waiting.

One day someone I knew vaguely made a sexist remark, and I asked him to explain to the group why, to acknowledge his sexism. I took the lead in that battle because I found him disgusting. And because I liked Aurora. I intervened in favour of equality. I cited Mao, his report on the investigation of gender equity among peasants in Hunan in

March 1927. 'Women are not only subject to the power of political, clan, and religious authorities, they are also subject to the authority of men. These four feudal-patriarchal systems restrict the freedoms of all people.'

'Thank you, Mao. How do you integrate that in your life?' Aurora asked.

'I do my best,' I answered.

She was standing up, facing me. All our comrades were seated.

'You've got work to do on that.'

'Help me improve!'

She spoke, I replied. Retorts putting me down gave way to gentler barbs designed to persuade, as the intensity of our back-and-forth sounded progressively more like two glasses tapping in a toast.

'You were so arrogant!' she claimed, much, much later.

'And you, so proud!'

As our arguments lost their edge, a few sly smiles emerged in the group.

'We'll let you two sort this out,' one of our leaders suggested.

Aurora blushed. Sat down. I did the same. Each of us a mirror of the other. It was the following day that Sam came to our lecture hall at Jussieu.

Aurora was not a Maoist. She hadn't read Marx either. She didn't like anything with a structure. She was a feminist, anti-authoritarian, passionately devoted to her freedom and she had found in our movement the means to protect herself. There were about thirty girls with us, unlike the Leninist militants. One day they were marching with their female friends to demand abortion rights, arms raised, forefinger and thumb joined as a symbol of the female sex. The next day they would raise clenched fists in support of the dignity of immigrants piled on top of each other, crammed into housing on the outskirts of our cities. The whistle of the Women's Liberation Movement in the morning. The violence of Maoists in the afternoon.

* * *

When Louise was born, Aurora decided to leave politics behind. To carry on the fight for dignity, but in other ways. The Autonomists frightened her; direct action was not her style. She wasn't oiling guns, she was offering her breast to a child. I knew that. From the beginning, I had sensed that Aurora would stop at the edge of the precipice. She was a French teacher; I was an eternal student of history. A monitor twenty-eight hours a week to earn a living, I'd reached the age limit set for university students by the Ministry of Education. My ongoing status as a student drew smiles. So there I was, a monitor in a mediocre middle school.

At night, we had fits of coughing at the house. Louise was born early. She was born small. She was born fragile.

'I swear, nothing will happen to you,' I had whispered to her when she was born.

'That sounds deathly boring,' Aurora had replied with a smile.

I knew what I meant. No one will diminish you. No one will harm you, ever. Neither one of you.

'Nothing will happen to you, either,' Aurora added.

No. Not to me either.

* * *

On 10 May 1981 I also decided to pause the fight, proclaim a truce. Louise was fourteen months old. We headed towards the Bastille to celebrate as a family. Aurora carried a flag from Brittany, the *Gwenn ha Du* of her childhood. I had pinned a Lenin patch to the stroller. We suddenly found ourselves not just a small group, but a huge crowd. I missed Sam. We hadn't managed to get close to the Place de la Bastille. We'd been swept away. An African woman slipped a good-luck bracelet onto Louise's little wrist. An old Arab emerged from a grey side street to join the celebration. I had seen him earlier, partly hidden by railings. He had raised the collar of his shirt and donned a tie to honour the day. It was raining. He walked straight ahead, his head high. The Arab didn't know it. Aurora didn't realize it. But that stranger guided us through the evening. When he moved forwards, I followed. He paused, I paused. He turned, I turned, we changed direction. I followed his happiness in secret. He walked with a cane. He laughed when we did, raised his hand to acknowledge us, respecting this foreign victory. He straightened his tie. Pulled down the sleeves of his jacket to cover his too-white shirt. He was tiny. He was alone. He was beautiful. He had a grey moustache. And glasses too big for his face.

At one point he stopped, ceding his space in the crowd to the joy of the French. He looked at his watch and walked away.

'Shall we go?' Aurora asked.

Yes. It was time to go home. We walked back down the rue Saint-Antoine. At the corner of the rue Jacques-Coeur, the old man reappeared, leaning on his cane. I don't know what came over me. I put my hand on his shoulder. He flinched. Turned around.

What could I say?

'I'm sorry, I mistook you for a friend of mine.'

He smiled, looked down at Louise, who was crying. Said she was beautiful. Our child was hungry. We left.

8

JEAN ANOUILH

Sam didn't want me to come to the hospital. He was waiting to be freed from his tubes. So I waited, three months, for him to call. In January of 1982, when he realized that his IVs and monitors would be there until the end, he let me visit.

I hate hospitals. The smell, the cleanliness, the eyes already veiled in mourning. I learned about Sam's illness in the press. Ten performances of Brecht's *The Resistible Rise of Arturo Ui* had been cancelled after the dress rehearsal. Just a few lines in the paper, instructions for ticket reimbursement. He hadn't told me.

* * *

Since 1979, Samuel Akounis had split his life between Beirut and Paris. He had returned to France the first time for our wedding, to be my witness at our civil ceremony. And had managed a second trip to hold Louise at the baptismal font. Sam was like me. Not quite a believer but reasonably Cartesian. Somewhere between those questions, Aurora had made a dent. It was for her, because of her, and thanks to her, that we entered a church to get married, a year after our daughter was born.

Our best friends were there. Some of our friends wore jackets, as I did. An old one from Jussieu with a patterned tie. This time Aurora wore a white dress. No one made fun of us. She was happy, and I was, too, with Louise in the front row, on a friend's knees. The priest spoke little and his words rang true. He didn't care where we came from, but he wanted to be sure where we were going. And equally certain that we would go there together, she and I.

Aurora promised. And I promised. The day of that ceremony, the son of God was more elegant than the elected official of the Republic who had united us. The priest married us with a joy that heightened mine. On the stairs, our friends threw rice dyed red. A rain of remembrance, to excuse the rest.

Sam hadn't been able to get out of Lebanon that day. But he still promised to be Louise's godfather.

'Really, now?'

I think he was joking. But two months later, Aurora held him to his word.

'What haven't you made me do?' he muttered, holding the candle in his hands.

He had his kippah in his pocket. He put it on as he left the church, with Louise in his arms, for the photo. My Greek had lost weight. A lot of weight. He turned away to cough. He was hoarse, claimed fatigue, a bronchitis he couldn't shake. He was producing two shows in parallel. Brecht in Paris and Anouilh's *Antigone* in Beirut. One day he appeared in the newspaper *Libération*.

'A Greek to show off for the Lebanese.'

The headline was unusual, but the article was positive. In a bio on the last page, the newspaper sketched Samuel Akounis. The child hidden from the Nazis, the Greek resistant, the Jew turned Zionist, still pro-Palestinian. The theatre director beloved by Parisians, but not committed to them.

'I do Boulevard theatre,' he replied to fans of tragedy.

Drama was a gift he wrapped in farce.

The article explained that he knew what doors to knock on to keep his theatre afloat. No one lived on ticket sales. So he passed the hat unabashedly. Cultural centres, charitable associations, government ministries. 'He could have stopped there,' *Libération* continued, 'but Lebanon grabbed him by the throat.' Antigone also had him under her spell. But the journalist couldn't have known that.

Sam had always wanted to stage Anouilh's dark play in a war zone. To offer each role to a different camp. To make peace between parties in conflict. His first thought was of Greece, now at peace. To mix former oppressed and oppressors in the cast for a single performance, in the theatre of Dionysus, at the Acropolis. He imagined the audience under a summer moon, seated on grass and ancient stones. 'Why *Antigone*?' the journalist had inquired. 'Because it's about pride and one's land,' Samuel Akounis had answered. He had found his Antigone, a Greek actress who had known prison. And also 'the Nurse', mother of a lost militant. But his comrades detested the idea.

'You're mixing victims with executioners,' one communist accused.

He did everything he could to convince a retired police officer. Don't you have children involved in theatre? Relatives? Friends, perhaps? He ran ads in the paper to no avail. The only response was death threats. That was January 1976. Sam gave up. And he eked out a living, renting his 'Little Diomedes' to a group of political satirists.

He came to see me one evening, upset, breathing with difficulty. Some Lebanese Christians had attacked a Palestinian settlement in the Karantina section of Beirut. Thirty thousand people crammed into makeshift shelters covered with sheet metal. After the area was bombed, the militia had sorted them into groups, ignoring their white flags. Women and children to the left, men of fighting age to the right. Hundreds of dead. Then the area was dynamited so intensely that no one was left breathing and nothing could grow back. Two days later, Palestinians, Lebanese and foreign militias entered Damour, a Christian suburb south of Beirut. Women, children, men. The living murdered, the dead profaned in their tombs. The torture of a town for the martyrdom of a neighbourhood.

I remember Sam's face. He was crushed, feverish and in pain all at once. I felt it. I knew. He had found the setting for Antigone. The fervour lasted for months. He sought out his actors. He contacted the French embassy, the consulate, the cultural centre, the French Association of Artistic Action, charitable groups and clubs on each side of the conflict. Muslims first. A group of young Sunnis in Hamra.

Then a group of Shiites from a theatre in Ta'zieh, whose only repertoire was the story of the death of the prophet Hussein. Sam also discovered a Palestinian company, in Shatila, that continually performed a poem by Mahmoud Darwish. With time and patience, he unearthed two Druze performance companies in the mountains. Then Christian actors, in Achrafieh and Deir el-Qamar.

He told them all only that he was Greek, a director, and that he wanted to produce *Antigone* in Lebanon. Each community thought it was the only one solicited. Sam could not explain his project to me in a letter. He waited to tell me in person. Acting on advice from the Greek embassy, he had also told the French Ministry of Culture, and religious authorities. And informed the Lebanese government.

Every letter he sent was the same, with the same enclosures: a copy of the rights to perform the play, the performance agreements and a recommendation signed by several theatre directors. With, most importantly, a few words of encouragement signed by Jean Anouilh.

For days, Sam waited. Then weeks. After four months, the Christians answered. Then the Shiites, three brothers. The Druzes' reply came in July 1976. And the Sunnis' in November.

They all agreed to meet the Greek.

They wanted to know what this man expected of them.

* * *

Sam was alone in the room. His voice was weak. He apologized. Yes, he should have told me that he was ill. He'd had issues with his lungs since his arrival in France. He had trouble breathing, headaches, and pain in his joints.

'I never smoked in my life.'

Then he had thought back to the torture he'd been subjected to, the tear gas down his throat. One day, after exhausting himself climbing a flight of stairs, he spat up blood.

'I don't like what I see here,' the radiologist had told him.

Also, that Sam was late looking into it.

He had lost his appetite. Lost weight. In Beirut, he had been cared for by the doctor at the Greek embassy. In Paris, an oncologist took over. Too late to operate. He tried chemotherapy. Useless. After the lungs, it reached the liver.

'I feel like throwing up.'

He said that. And that his head throbbed, that his mouth tasted like cardboard and his tongue was one big canker sore.

I was mad at him. Mad at myself, too. The end of the movement had scattered us. Life had conspired to add distance. Sam had given me his address in Beirut, and his phone number, but I hadn't called. He existed. For me, that was enough. I thought our friendship grew with the distance between us, but I was wrong. I had lost three years of him.

I stood up. The window faced Paris's beltway, the périphérique, visible in the distance. Winter had seized the city. Paris shivered under sheets of frost. Samuel smiled. He watched his visitors the way a director casts a role.

There was the mortified type, who wouldn't meet his gaze for fear of falling ill. In the eyes of the mortified, Sam recognized his decay. The mortified character stroked the edge of his sheet, not his hand. He didn't stay long. It was too hot. He'd be back soon. The following week, definitely, of course. Maybe.

There was the anxious type. 'How did you know you had that?'

Because he also had headaches, sore arms, cough and shortness of breath. Sam had to reassure the anxious ones. See a doctor? Yes, good idea. Especially if the anxious one smoked, though Sam had never touched a cigarette. A doctor you'd recommend? Do you have a pen I could use?

There was also the knowing one. Who had been through it, and took up the whole room. He compared. His sister had been there, recovered, or not. She had suffered at the end.

'You don't have a morphine drip? That's crazy. Everyone has those now!'

He took in the size of the room, checked out the bed, watched over the nurse who came to change an IV bag. He didn't reassure or empathise, he inserted himself into the medical protocol.

And there was the tourist. Who paid no attention to the bed. Who had a brush with a cancer patient. Barely inside the room, he went straight to the window and admired the view.

'Ah, not bad. You're doing pretty well for yourself.'

The tourist did what he could. He smiled. Winked. Screamed with fear in his head. He had visualized himself in that bed when he entered the room and the image had haunted him all night.

'And me? What kind of visitor am I?'

'You? The friend who shows up late. And therefore angry.'

Sam smiled. He was missing some teeth on one side. His skin was yellow, his eyes rimmed with deep, dark rings and streaked with blood, like he'd been hit. The backs of his hands were blotched with brown. His nails were dark, almost black. My Sam. I didn't recognize him when I entered the room. I held back tears. He was withered by time lost.

'None of this is your fault, you know?'

I knew, of course. He opened his hand. I placed mine in it. I had never held my friend other than with my gaze.

'What can I do for you?'

'A lot. You can do a lot.'

I drew closer. He smelled acrid, of ether and eucalyptus. He was unshaven. I put the back of my hand to his cheek.

'Do you know why I never grew a beard or long hair?'

I shook my head. No. I didn't know. As a teen, I had started growing a moustache as soon as my father told me Frank Zappa looked like a monkey. I loved his music. So I tried to look like him.

'In Salonica, the Nazis cut the beards off the old Jews,' Sam wheezed.

'They did it in the street, to humiliate them. They made the sons sweep the pavements with their hats and cut their fathers' beards.'

My friend measured his breath. He didn't say his words, he exhaled them.

'In July 1942, my father was arrested by the Germans in Salonica. He was taken to Liberty Square, with tens of thousands of others. They were clustered together in the sun, forced to do idiotic exercises. Up, down, up, hands up, head up. My father had a full beard and payot, side locks. An SS cut them, then shaved half his face, cut his skin with the dagger. Most of the men were sent to public works. But he had blood on his shirt. So he was sent back to us, for eight months of reprieve.

'When the Greek Colonels banned beards and long hair, I decided to make sure they could never degrade me like that. So I kept my hair short, cut close, stayed clean-shaven and wore a suit. All things that puzzled your friends when we met.'

Sam closed his eyes. He was exhausted. He wanted to tell me about Beirut, about *Antigone.* I had to come back, soon. He said life was slipping through his eyelids. Tomorrow?

The next day, I took my place again at the head of his bed. Sam was sleeping. I waited. Aurora cried when I told her he was sick. She would come later in the week, with two old friends from Jussieu. Sam called them the 'Pétroleuses'. Affectionately. On the bedside table was his copy of

Antigone, the 1945 edition he had shown me years before. And his father's kippah. His breathing was bad. Whispering voices rose from his chest, moans caught on rasping breath. I thought of hell. A Bosch painting. Insect men up to their necks in flames. I slowed my breathing to match his. When his breath didn't come, I held mine. I watched his heart beat on the monitor. Then I closed my eyes. I counted the beats. I fell asleep. Two nurses came to bathe him. He was still asleep. I touched his fingers and left.

I came back two days later. Sam was awake, propped up on two pillows. He was waiting for me.

'*Antigone* is going to happen in Beirut.'

I nodded. I knew. Sam had found his actors, even a few understudies. They hadn't rehearsed yet, but they had all met, once, in a building owned by the Greek embassy.

Antigone was Palestinian and Sunni. Haemon, her fiancé, a Druze from Shouf. Creon, King of Thebes and Haemon's father, was a Maronite from Gemmayze. The three Shiites had refused their roles at first, since 'guards' seemed unimportant. They accepted after one was renamed as Creon's page, another 'the messenger'. It was up to the director to work that out. An old Shiite woman had been selected as Queen Eurydice, Creon's wife. 'The Nurse' was a Chaldean, and Ismene, Antigone's sister, an Armenian Catholic.

Casting had taken two years. All the young cast members had done some theatre except Eurydice, whose only role was to knit for the poor of Thebes. Sam had initially introduced himself as Greek. He would play 'The Chorus,' an essential voice in ancient theatre. Later, he admitted he was Jewish. So, three Shiite replacements had to be found. And another Catholic, who also refused to participate after this revelation.

'You are going to stage *Antigone*, George.'

I moved closer.

'Sorry?'

'No, I'm the one who's sorry. I no longer have the time or the strength.'

He closed his eyes. He was like a frail, very old man.

'The hard part is done. Your characters are ready. They are expecting you.'

My characters?

This time, I was the one who couldn't catch my breath. He could barely whisper. His voice had a metallic sound. He explained that each actor had learnt their lines, and a few rehearsals would suffice. There would be a single performance, in October. A neutral performance space, neither East nor West Beirut. On the demarcation line. An old school, a depot, anything. He wanted a space that spoke of war, worked over by bullets and mortars. Four walls, or just three. A roof didn't matter. He had seen a decaying cinema that he liked. He envisioned the communities coming into this shadow theatre from both sides of the line. He imagined them with folding chairs, cushions, water bottles, pistachios. All factions, gathered together. Two hours on an autumn night. With fighters, their weapons lowered the length of an act.

'You see?' Sam asked.

No. But he saw it. He described the stage in rubble, the three doors painted on a pocked wall. The faces of the audience. The circle of white light. His actors. He was on stage.

'Here we are. These actors are going to perform the story of Antigone for you. Antigone is the small, thin girl seated over there, silent ...'

He struggled to raise his arm, pointing to a corner of the room.

'See them, George?'

He had opened his eyes. Returned from the dead.

'You see them now?'

'Yes,' I said.

I saw Samuel Akounis fighting for his life. Arms pierced with tubes, skin covered in brown bruises. He closed his eyelids once more, letting a tear slide towards his temple. I hesitated. I wanted to erase this furrow of chagrin, but I didn't do it. Terrified by his request, by the grey sheets, by his unhappy heart snaking across the green screen. Samuel Akounis was fighting for Antigone's life. He fought lying down, mustering all his strength, every bit of courage he had left.

'Take my notebook, on the bedside table. Read it, finish it, fill it up. It will be your road map. Take the plastic bag, too, and everything in it. Next time, I'll give you a record and a gift for the Palestinian actress.'

I looked at the black notebook, its purple stripe, the elastic that held it closed. It lay on his father's kippah. Sam was watching me. He seemed disappointed by my silence.

'Say yes, George.'

'Yes.'

I didn't have regrets right away. Not in the room. Or in the hospital corridor. Or on the street, breathing in the full life of winter. Or on the stairs, climbing slowly towards my daughter's voice. It was when I faced Aurora that I had doubts.

'You promised what?'

Louise was two years old. She clung to my weak leg. She was so like her mother. A miniature Aurora. The high cheekbones, the hair. And a little of me in her anxious eyes.

'Answer me, George. You promised to go there?'

I put my daughter in her little wicker chair. It had been her mother's when she was a child. And her own mother's before that. And her mother's mother, the sardine worker from Douranenez. Our apartment was haunted by evidence of her path.

'Did you even think about us?'

Honestly? No. I had reached the door of our apartment before my family entered my thoughts. At the hospital, only Samuel existed. His strength, his will. He and *Antigone*, his final fight. It was January 1982. I told myself three trips would be enough. Making contact with the actors, a few rehearsals, a dress rehearsal, then the performance in October, the way Sam wanted it. Two to three weeks each time, stretched out over nine months. I was no longer enrolled as a student. I could sort it out, using my monitor job's leave days, rearranging my duties, juggling the days and weeks.

Aurora picked up Louise. It was time to eat. I followed her into the kitchen.

'I'll do it.'

She took the bib from my hands, and the colourful plate. She didn't want this quiet ceremony as her battlefield. So I left the room.

'You two really calculated this one, didn't you?' My wife's voice, from the other end of the apartment.

'What do you mean?'

'Those photos you took for Sam?'

I went back into the kitchen.

'What photos?'

Aurora was warming a small pan.

'Stop, please! The photos, they were for this?'

I didn't know what to say.

Before Louise's baptism, Aurora had asked me for five ID-size photos. A surprise for Sam. For my birthday, he wanted to make a collage with his face, mine, and the faces of our friends. He said this to my wife. I went to the photo booth at the Gare de l'Est, made funny faces for every flash, even crossing my eyes. Aurora had laughed. Sam said they were perfect. And then time passed. Sam never mentioned the gift again.

Louise had her worried look. Aurora waved me out of the room.

'And you realize you've never left France?'

This time she was right. Two childhood trips to the Black Forest, a souvenir from Switzerland, a photo of Turin. As long as Franco was alive, I said no to Spain. And Greece, too, because of the Colonels. Franco was dead, the Colonels deposed. I'd run out of excuses, but now there was no time. Or interest. Travel had never been a pleasure.

Packing a bag, closing up the house, leaving, abandoning my routine, left me cold. I knew France. Intimately. I knew its orchards, its mountains, its coasts, its regional borders and its frontiers. That wasn't enough for Aurora, but it suited me.

'And there's a war over there. Remember?'

I heard the sound of the spoon scraping against the glass jar, Louise's babbling. Yes, war. I remembered. It was precisely because Sam wanted to impose its opposite that he had chosen Lebanon. Aurora knew all that. She also knew I'd made up my mind. She wasted few words on it, aware she couldn't change my mind.

Aurora put Louise to bed. She was afraid, for herself, for our child. She was speaking. This time it wasn't to recite a few lines of theatre in a community centre, but to take a stand against full-scale war. It was sublime. Unthinkable, impossible, grotesque. To go to a country full of death wearing a clown nose, assemble ten factions involved without knowing who's who. Recruit a soldier from each camp to act out peace. Get this army onto a stage. Direct it as one leads a ballet. Ask Creon, a Christian actor, to condemn Antigone, a Palestinian actor, to death. Ask a Shiite to play a Maronite's page. None of that made sense. I told her she was right. Her objections, valid. War was insanity? Sam said peace must be, too. So we had to undertake the inconceivable. Staging *Antigone* in a war zone would shock the fighters. It would be so beautiful that guns would be lowered.

'For an hour,' Aurora snickered.

She was sitting. I squatted between her knees.

'An hour of peace? And you want us to miss out on that?'

She was smiling again. She wanted guarantees. To know who would be waiting for me in Beirut, who would protect me from that city, and who would get me out. She wanted a return date for each trip. She wanted the names of the actors, all of them. She wanted to know that everything would be ready before I got there. That nothing would be left to chance, nothing. She wanted me to cancel if there was even the slightest doubt, the least sign of alarm, any possibility of danger.

'Swear to me.'

'I swear.'

'No, not like that. Look me in the eye. Swear on your daughter.'

'I swear on my daughter.'

Still crouched at her knees, I took Aurora's hands in mine. She studied me for a long time, troubled. She squeezed my hands so hard they hurt. Louise called out in her sleep.

'She's going to miss you,' my wife remarked.

Then she stood up and went to see her child.

9

MAURICE DURUFLÉ

I read *Antigone*. I hadn't done that. In 1974, when Sam had given me Jean Anouilh's play, the book sat on my bedside table. Then it got swallowed by magazines and time. Later, I opened it, read a few pages. My heart wasn't in Thebes. The garlic, leather and red wine on the breath of Creon's guards didn't draw me in. I put the book on a shelf and forgot about it. Eight years ago.

I read *Antigone*. Disturbed, intensely moved, writing down lines to say out loud.

* * *

Thus, *Antigone*. The story of the small, thin girl, daughter of Oedipus and Jocasta, rulers of Thebes. After their mother's suicide and their father's exile, the two sons fight to the death for the throne. To death, truly. Neither will survive. Creon, brother of the deceased queen, becomes king. Of his two nephews, Eteocles and Polynices, he had preferred Eteocles. He ordered that Eteocles be buried with royal honours and refused to bury Polynices. He went beyond refusing; he issued a royal edict that condemned to death anyone who attempted to honour the body, now abandoned to the sun and the scavengers. He wanted to leave the 'renegade, disloyal thug' unmourned, unsepulchred. Polynices had wanted Oedipus killed, and Creon knew that.

One morning, one of the guards tasked with watching over the body noticed that dirt had been disturbed all around it. And scattered over the body, as ritual required, giving him a shroud of dust. Creon was enraged. One of his subjects had offended him. A traitor had given funereal honours to the pariah. In a ditch nearby, the guard discovered a child's shovel, small and rusted. At noon, Antigone was caught. She had returned to finish the ceremony, alone, dirt under her nails, her knees skinned. Ismene did not go with her. Her sister, so much prettier than she, had done everything she could to dissuade her.

Creon was distressed by the terrible news. Antigone was his beloved niece, engaged to Haemon, his own son. So he tells her he will forget what she did, keep it secret. Everything can be fixed with a slap and a diet of dry bread, but Antigone refuses. 'You are the pride of Oedipus,' Creon scolds. She replies that she does not believe in happiness. She can't compromise with life. She wants death, and expects it.

Mortified, Creon turns her over to the guards, who bury her alive. But as they are sealing the tomb, the king finds out that Haemon, his son, chose to be buried with her. They quickly scatter the mound of loose stones. Too late. Antigone had hung herself with the strings of her belt that now lay wrapped around her neck like a child's necklace. Haemon is holding her in his arms. He is crying. Seeing his father's grey hair in the twilight, he stands, sword in hand. Creon backs away. His son casts him a look full of scorn. And thrusts the blade into his own belly.

Creon lost everything. Only Eurydice, his queen, remained, forever knitting for the poor of Thebes. But when he goes to her, his heart shattered, he finds her corpse. After she had finished her last row of stitches, she put down her needles. Lay down on her dead son's bed. Surrounded by his stuffed animals, she slit her throat. She was smiling when Creon came in.

CREON

She, too. They're all sleeping. That's good. It's been a hard day.

(A long pause. He speaks mutedly.) It must be nice to sleep.

I closed the book. I was ready for the small, thin girl. Ready to greet within myself that victim chosen by fate. Ready, too, to undertake this fraternal duty. All I knew of her was that she refused to live. All I knew of myself was my desire to live.

* * *

I remembered Sophocles. I bought his *Antigone.* And Brecht's. And Friederich Holderlin's translation, which had inspired Anouilh. In Sam's notebook I wrote, '*Antigone, here and now.*' Born in Greece, reimagined in the hands of the Reich, or performed during the occupation of Paris, Antigone was timeless. For our time.

'*No costumes. Every actor in street clothes,*' Samuel Akounis had written. '*It should look like a rehearsal. Surprise the audience with the disconnect between the text and the clothing. For Anouilh's premiere at L'Atelier, Antigone wore a black evening gown with a gold cross around her neck. Creon wore a tuxedo, waistcoat, a white bow tie and patent-leather shoes. The guards wore trench coats and fedoras. (Gestapo?) The desired effect is not Thebes, but occupied Paris, in winter. The play must speak to the present.'*

On page after page, Sam gave directions for the play. His comments were not new. The first one had been written a year ago. He knew he would have to turn over the direction to someone else. His writing was clear, slanting, precise. He had written in French. He had been writing for me. I was certain of that.

'Don't mistake Sophocles' brutal Creon for Anouilh's, who is full of bitterness. For Sophocles, Creon is the tragic character. For Anouilh, Antigone holds the tragic role …'

The name Duruflé appeared frequently. *Pie Jesu*, his requiem. In one margin, the name of the singer Pilar Lorengar, with a question mark.

'There will be a cello and a mezzo-soprano. Imperative! I want to hear her sing "Pie Jesu Domine, dona eis requiem. Dona eis requiem sempiternam," at the exact moment the guards take Antigone away.'

'Holy Jesus and Master, give them rest. Give them eternal rest.' He had rewritten the text in French. A sketch to show the actors' body positions on the stage. I was holding Samuel Akounis' Will. He had given it to me on his hospital bed, with the letter from Anouilh and his father's kippah. I had refused. He had insisted. He wanted 'The Chorus' to wear it on stage. So the velvet skullcap responds

to the veil of one, the beret of another, and the keffiyeh that Antigone would throw over her shoulders.

'You will be "The Chorus", George. Wearing the kippah.'

He smiled weakly.

'You will be the Jew.'

* * *

Along with his notebook, his directions, his drawings, Sam had included letters of interest from each actor, with their names and addresses. All of them had written to him in French. Some wrote just a few words. Others spoke of their lives, their neighbourhood, their passion for the stage. One had even sent a resumé. I sensed Beirut for the first time. In the creased paper, the youthful handwriting. All that was real. Antigone and Creon had attached a photo to their letters.

Imane was young, slender, with a blue veil pulled tight over red hair. Barely twenty years old. I found her violently beautiful. Too much so, perhaps, for the 'small, thin girl'. White skin, silky hair. *'You'll have to impoverish this face,'* Sam had written on the back of the photo. In red, he had also written: *'Formal approval from Yassine, her brother, a Fatah fighter.'*

Charbel looked about thirty years old. He had to add another thirty. *'Make-up, grey hair. Handsome hardness.'* The young man's face was like granite, with a disquieting look. I couldn't tell if he had posed for the role, or if it was really him. I put the photos side by side. Antigone, Creon. Imane, Charbel, my foundation. Seven phantoms yet to be discovered.

I called Imane one Sunday in January. An Arab voice, a child. Then a man, another man, and finally Antigone.

'Samuel?'

'Hello, Imane, my name is George.'

I was talking, Antigone was listening. I could hear her breathing hard. The connection, the telephone, the emotion. I told her everything. She knew about the cancer, the hospital. She had tried to call because the news wasn't good. The Shiites hadn't come to the meeting and the Maronite ...

'Charbel?'

'Yes, Charbel. His brother doesn't want him to cross the demarcation line.'

'Does he have to?'

Silence at the other end.

'What do you mean, does he have to? Everyone except him lives in West Beirut or in the southern suburbs. Even Nakad has left the mountains for Hamra.

'Nakad?'

'The Druze. His family has moved in across the street from the Cavalier hotel. No way that eight of us will cross the demarcation line to meet up with one person!'

'What can we do?'

'No idea. His family doesn't even want me to let you speak to him on the phone. I think his brother won't allow him to spend time with Muslims. You see?'

I saw. Of course. But I didn't understand. Sam had told me there had been a first meeting in town after he left. A first read-through. He described it to me just as Imane had told him, with laughter and the smell of tea. But this meeting had never happened. The Palestinian admitted it. She had made up the rehearsal to avoid adding to Sam's pain. Ever since he had been hospitalized, his actress had spared him what she could. She hid bad news and embellished the tiniest progress. She knew the Armenian and the Chaldean. She had also met with the Druze, and claimed that all the others had come, too. Another evening she had spoken to Ismene by phone. This distant conversation had become an important moment for Sam. He had imagined Antigone and her sister reciting their lines in the street, applauded by a group of laughing children. She told me that the Shiite who was supposed to play the page had realized how small his role was. Four lines at the end. Eleven words. He and his brothers weren't sure if they were still game. They would represent half the Muslims in Lebanon. They wanted guarantees if they were going to participate. Was that all? No. The actress playing Ismene had used the Sophocles version to rehearse. Three months for nothing. And no one had heard from 'The Nurse' for weeks.

I was stunned. Except for the agreement in principle that the Palestinian Liberation Organization had given Sam, nothing was real. Nothing had ever been real. Sam's dream existed on thirty notebook pages. The phone receiver was hurting my ear. Imane was breathing.

'Are you still there?'

I was there, yes. Standing, then sitting, before collapsing.

'And you, Imane, where are you in all this?'

'Me, I'm ready,' Antigone replied.

Aurora entered with Louise, back from crèche. I was getting off the phone.

'That was Beirut,' I said.

'And?'

'They're ready. Just waiting for me.' I was a good liar.

'You know, I think I'm a little envious,' my wife said.

I smiled. My stomach was full of sand.

* * *

'Did you speak to Imane?'

Sam was staring at the ceiling. I was shaking with anger. At the desk, a nurse had asked where I was going. I didn't answer. In the corridor, another nurse told me I had no business being there. That visiting hours were over. I kept walking. She blocked my way. I pushed her. My hand on her shoulder, to move her away. A doctor came out of the break room. He was tall, young, his hair prematurely grey.

'This man has no right to be here!' the nurse cried.

I turned to the doctor. He was calm. Unafraid.

'Are you a family member?'

I exploded.

'His family? You want to know where his family is? Dead, all dead! Exterminated in Auschwitz, his family. You understand what I'm saying?'

'Calm down.'

A nurse emerged from another room, a finger to her lips. 'Too much noise.'

'I am asking if you are a family member, if you have an important reason to disturb a hospital at this hour.'

The doctor was eyeing me. I stood facing him. I put my hands in my pockets to keep them calm. My anger was beginning to melt away. I was sorry for the look on my face, my words, my late-night threats. The corridor was quiet. The women were afraid, the man stood his ground. I was sorry. I had rushed out of the house. Sam had to know the truth. Now. Right now. He had to know that his *Antigone* was in ruins. That his actors had never existed. If I went to Beirut, it would be to put an end to it. To apologize for Sam, and for myself, to everyone involved: the actors, the associations, the institutions, to explain that Samuel Akounis was giving up the project. Imane had lied. He needed to know. I had raced down the street, into the Metro, into the hospital foyer, down the corridor, breathless. I wanted my friend's eyes, his hands in mine, even here, with the noise of his heart, the suction of the tubes, his laboured breathing, the smell of disinfectant, the rancid odour of his agony. I had to tell him the truth.

'I am his family. He has no one else.'

'Who are you talking about?' the doctor asked.

'The myositis room,' the nurse answered.

The doctor looked at his watch, his wrist raised to the name badge on his chest.

Dr. E. Cohen.

Then he observed me. I lowered my head, read his name.

'I'll give you fifteen minutes.' The doctor smiled.

'Did you speak to Imane?'

I sat down, tucked my hands under my thighs. I nodded. I was upset by my own stupidity. My heart racing, I could feel the nurses' fear in my body.

'Did she tell you about the rehearsal?'

I answered vaguely, mechanically.

The rehearsal? Yes, of course. But not all the details. Just part of it. The line was bad, the connection with Lebanon. And I had called late.

Sam tilted his head. I hadn't turned on the light in the room. There was only the blue night light. His eyes were probing me. So I answered.

'The Christian had trouble crossing the demarcation line because of his brother, but he made it. He arrived late, in the middle of the read-through.'

Sam's expression. Open-mouthed, his lips dry.

'And?'

'Imane told me it was amazing. Haemon, Ismene, the Nurse and Eurydice, all of them stood up and hugged Creon.'

Sam smiled. His voice entombed.

'You see, George. The theatre at peace, war everywhere else.'

I nodded. I was crushing my hands. He closed his eyes.

'It can be done. I knew it.'

I told him the actors knew their lines, except for Ismene, perhaps, who recited hers as if she were in an ancient production, draping her body in somewhat ridiculous poses. The Shiites had finally accepted their small roles and played along. Eurydice knitted an endless scarf.

A smile from Sam.

'Imane told me that the Nurse was good, very sweet, totally natural. Creon also was fantastic.'

'And Antigone?'

'She's ready. That's all she said.'

'When do you leave?'

'Next week.'

I spoke without thinking. Sam turned slowly away from me, towards the wall.

'Take the envelope on the table, and the record. The sealed pouch in the bag is to share between Imane and Yassine, her brother. I promised them.'

And he fell asleep.

The corridor was deserted. I passed the nurses' room. I walked towards the elevator. The doctor stepped out with files in his hand.

'Were you able to talk to him?'

I nodded. Words failed me.

'I want to apologize.'

'For?'

'Auschwitz.'

He looked at me, his face unreadable.

'Say that to the nurses. You hurt them.'

I didn't have the courage to turn back.

'Would you rather a Cohen apologize for you?'

I went back to the door of the nurses' room. They didn't stir from their seats. I stood in the doorway, my own burden. One looked up, the other kept writing in a file.

I apologized. I wanted to explain my rage, my pain, my fear of losing my friend, Antigone, Beirut, the war waiting for me. But I couldn't get the words out.

'I'm sorry. It was stupid and unfair.'

The youngest one nodded her head. The other looked up at me.

'Forgive me,' I muttered.

And I fled.

* * *

In the envelope Sam had given me, there were addresses. The French Embassy in Beirut, the residence of the Greek ambassador, phone numbers, direct lines to the consuls, the cultural centres, the associations. And more obscure things, like the names of militias, their contact numbers, ways to reach the Lebanese authorities.

Sam had attached five passes to the list. Laminated cards with my name on them. One was in Arabic and French, with the green cedar tree in a red circle and the stylized cross of the Lebanese Forces. Another featured a blue globe overlaid with the pen and pickaxe of the socialist Druze. There was a pass from the Lebanese Army, a laissez-passer issued by Amal, the Shiite militia, and one from the Palestinian Fatah. On each document I was making a silly face. Crossing my eyes, curling my lips. I was astonished. The photos Sam had asked for. Aurora was right. He'd planned this years ago.

I wanted to wake her up to tell her. I couldn't bring myself to do it. She was sleeping peacefully. We would have plenty of time to bad-mouth our friend. Louise must have cried during the night. Her mother had nestled her into my place in the bed. I watched them. Aurora slept on her side, as always, her hands folded under her cheek. My daughter lay on her back, her mouth open. I stroked her forehead with one finger. She twitched like someone shaking off a summer fly. Then she turned over, pressed against her mother. My daughter's back, my wife's back, my friend's back. As if they were leaving me, one by one. I left the light off. Sam had given me his church candles.

'Darkness is winning,' he had said.

I lit two ivory-coloured candles. I put Sam's album on the record player. The *Requiem*, *opus 9* by Maurice Duruflé. I wasn't familiar with that composer. I liked Mozart, like everyone. Fauré, like some. Jacques Mauduit, like very few others, though he had written a mass for Ronsard's funeral. Sam had made me tremble with the mourners' Kaddish. He had also given me the *Requiem* composed by Dmitri Kabalevsky, 'in memory of those who lost their lives in the struggle against fascism'. But apart from a few notes overheard during visits with my friend, I had never listened to the prayer he had reserved for me.

The recording was made in 1959. Hélène Bouvier singing, Duruflé himself conducting the Lamoureux orchestra. I sat down in the half-light. Listened to the *Requiem*. The *Introit*, in waves of modern chorus. The *Kyrie*, *Sanctus*, the *Pie Jesu* that Sam offered to Antigone. I did what he did. Ten times I lifted the turntable stylus and replayed the her chrystalline voice. Wine, fatigue, the stress of the hospital, the shock of the photos, the fear of tomorrow. I let the solemnity of the moment fill the room. Swaying with the soft flame of the candles, my eyes half-closed, my fists clenched so tight it hurt my palms. Then I opened *Antigone*. I read through my tears.

ANTIGONE

> Poor Creon. With my nails broken and covered in dirt, and the bruises your guards made on my arms, with my fear twisting my stomach, I am queen.

I listened to the *Requiem*. Men's voices replied to the women's. I still had the pouch for Imane and her brother in my pocket. Sam's gift was in a small clear bag, sealed with a black rubber band. Twenty grams of brown dust, somewhere between poorly sifted flour and minuscule gravel. I wanted to open it, I didn't dare. Samuel Akounis, a Jewish Holocaust escapee and Greek fighter had given me this nameless powder for a young actress from Shatila and a Palestinian fighter. I owed it to myself to honour his promise without asking questions.

10

MARWAN

'Yorgos?'

The man walked towards me, his arms wide open. I shook my head.

'Sorry, no. My name is George and I am French.'

Marwan burst out laughing.

'Like George al-Hakim Habache, the Palestinian terrorist?'

He had my photo, looked at it briefly, then extended his hand.

'I got your name wrong. Sorry. But since Samuel sent you, *ahlan wa sahlan*! You have found a family here and a land.'

He was crushing my fingers.

'I am Marwan, your driver.'

I must have looked odd. Shaken, perhaps. Tired, anxious, already in a rush to get it over with. For the entire drive I kept asking myself what I was doing there.

'Do you know if the museum crossing is open?' my seat-mate had asked me in the plane.

No, I didn't know.

'And the Ring? I heard you could cross there yesterday morning.'

The Ring? What Ring?

She was a Christian from Achrafieh, wondering how to cross the line.

'I'm Druze,' Marwan smiled.

He had found me on the tarmac when I deplaned. With one motion he pulled me out of the line of passengers so I would follow him. We came to a door guarded by a soldier. Or a militiaman. I don't know. The man wore a headband over his long hair, an army jacket and jeans. His assault rifle hung over his shoulder, barrel down, behind him. Marwan shook his hand. The other man opened the door. We were at the baggage claim.

'Give me your passport and get your bag.'

I handed my passport to the Lebanese man. Absolute trust. And no other choice. Sam had described his driver as a prince. In his sixties, handsome, tall, slender, with an angular face, grey hair, a moustache and an old scar from the edge of his mouth to his right temple. That's what I saw first. Then his outstretched hand. His smile. And his rolling accent, which ornamented phrases by modulating the last vowel. There are men like that. At first glance, first touch, something is sealed. It doesn't have a name, or a reason, nothing tangible. It's instinct, murmuring to follow his steps.

Marwan handed me my passport, stamped. His car was parked in front of the airport, on a pavement. A black Mercedes covered in ochre dust. The sea on one side of us, tall buildings in fog, mountains in the distance. A freshness of spring. He got behind the wheel. Looked me over.

'Shall we travel together?'

I said yes. Of course. I was there for two weeks and I had no one but him.

He pulled a pistol from his waistband. He removed the magazine and handed it to me. I hesitated. Then I took it. It was empty.

'Open your other hand.'

He slipped eight bullets into my palm.

'Do you know how to load?'

I said yes. Vaguely. I'd done it twice at a friend's house when we wanted to play war. I looked out the window. There were passers-by. I covered my hands with my jacket. I was shaking.

'You can do that without looking? A real pro, I say!'

Marwan laughed again. A warm, resonant good humour, freely offered.

The spring was tight. It took all my strength to load the bullets. One made a scratching sound, wouldn't go in. Metal on metal. It popped out, hitting me in the thumb. It was 10 February 1982. An hour after I arrived in Beirut to save *Antigone*, I was loading the Tokarev of a laughing Druze.

Marwan had set me up for two weeks at the Cavalier Hotel, in the centre of Beirut. The establishment was Druze, run by Druzes, and my host lived one street from my bed. The night I arrived, we talked money. He had to, and he did. Sam had worked things out famously. My room, my meals, my travel, all paid for by an Association of Artistic Action, under the rubric of the Ministry of Culture and Foreign Affairs. Everything, including the actors' costs, their meals and transportation, lodging in case the line was closed. Marwan was paid by the month, secretly, by an official at the Greek Embassy who had experienced the prisons of the Colonels.

But sometimes Sam added a little something, the driver said, smiling.

A wife, four children, two cars to feed. The Mercedes 280SL that he had brought to the airport to pick me up and a 1972 red-and-white Toyota Corolla patched from bullet hole to bullet hole amassed over the past five years.

In the envelope Sam had slipped Lebanese pounds and dollars, the country's other currency. I could call a name at the French Consulate. It was this contact who had organized Sam's medical repatriation to Paris.

'Money won't be your problem,' Marwan said.

He served me a light-coloured tea made from orange blossoms. I was in his living room, on the wide couch. He had taken the armchair. Nakad, his oldest son, was sitting on the armrest. Others stood in the doorway. He was smoking. In a gilded frame, two men who looked like him. His brother? His father? He laughed out loud, repeating my question to his wife who had just come in. The children laughed, too.

'This one is Kamal Jumblatt and the other is Walid Bey, his son. Kamal was a father to all of us. He was assassinated by the Syrians in 1977.'

His cup in the air, Marwan offered a toast in their honour.

'And Walid?'

'Not quite his equal, but still our leader.'

'The leader of the Lebanese?'

Another laugh from Marwan. Translation. Outbursts of joy from the children.

'Of the Druzes! You are in Druze country here, you need to start learning!'

They were heterodox Muslims, children of Ismael and Shiism. And the only ones with a soul and a beating heart. I smiled.

'How's that, the only ones? And the others?'

He frowned.

'Executioners, slaves, thieves. Not human beings.'

Nakad nodded, one finger raised. The young man spoke French with elegance.

'The Druze are proud and fair,' said the son, with a smile.

His mother had brought us bread, hummus, tabbouleh and yoghurt with garlic. She pushed the children into the hallway. And Nakad with them. Marwan stood. He took two glasses and a bottle from a sideboard.

'Arak?'

I knew ouzo. Sam had introduced me to its Lebanese cousin, an anise-based liqueur that had to be drowned in water.

'Druzes drink alcohol?'

He laughed.

'No. But I smoke and I drink.'

With a slow motion, he cut a strip of pita bread to plunge into the chickpea purée.

'You might say I have my own doctrine, even more secret than our religion's.'

I had a burning question.

'Why did you say that money wouldn't be the problem? What is the problem?'

He emptied his glass, tapped it on the wooden tabletop.

'I had this conversation a hundred times with Samuel. Lebanon is struggling for everything. We have to fight for school notebooks, for electricity, water, bread, to patch holes in battered roads. You come here from France with a play and all the doors open for you. You snap your fingers and ministries invite you in.'

'And that bothers you?'

I blanched. That was too quick. Think before speaking. I wasn't in a lecture hall surrounded by friends. Or trying to provoke an adversary over something silly. I was in Beirut, in the home of an armed Druze who was offering me protection and aid.

Marwan didn't react.

'It doesn't bother me, no. I just believe that Samuel and you are thinking more of yourselves than of our people. In fact, I've never understood what your theatre was coming to do in our country. Peace? That will take far more. An hour's entertainment? Thanks, but no thanks.'

He served himself another drink.

'Sam is dying.'

I couldn't think of anything else to say. Marwan looked at me. His head was cocked to one side, as if he were reading something inside me.

'You weren't part of the project at the beginning, were you?'

'No. He asked me to take his place a month ago.'

'Why you?'

'Maybe because there wasn't anyone else.'

A young girl entered, carrying a plate of small cakes.

'So you're doing this for him?'

'I'm doing it for him.'

He ran his fingers through his child's hair tenderly as she removed our plates.

'Are you Jewish?'

I searched for his eyes. He wasn't looking at me.

'Why?'

'Like Samuel, I mean.'

'No.'

Marwan bit into a sweet.

'So why does he trust you?'

'We were militants together, did theatre together. He was best man at my wedding and he's the godfather of my child.'

'He's a brother to you?'

Brother. I preferred this word to all others. I nodded my head without saying it aloud. Brother, that's what he was. My brother had just surrendered his task and asked me to take over for him.

'Did he explain the situation to you?'

No. A little. Not much. There was some shooting at the demarcation line, skirmishes in the south, tension in the north. I knew the actors had never met. That one of them hadn't even risked crossing to the west for the rehearsal. And the others were reluctant to take the first step.

Marwan approved.

'What's your plan, then?'

I had thought about it a lot. On this first trip, I wanted to meet the actors separately and give them each a copy of *Antigone*. Sam had typed out the play on stencils, then mimeographed it, the way we made our leaflets. But I wanted them to have a book in their hands. Before I left, I bought ten copies of an edition that came out in 1975. In each book I had inserted a photo of Jean Anouilh and a copy of his dedication letter to Samuel.

'Who do you want to start with?'

I wanted to meet Imane. I had talked to her on the phone, she said she was ready. I had a sense she could be a guide for me. And it was she, the small, thin girl. Without her, nothing could happen. She was the foundation and the beginning.

Next, I wanted to hear from Charbel. To ask him whether he really agreed to act, or if it was all just a pipe dream. The answers I got from Antigone and Creon would dictate my next steps. If they accepted, I would move ahead. I would go meet the Shiites first; they were integral to the symbolic community. I was counting on Marwan for the Druze. Talking about peace with a Catholic and survival with an Armenian didn't seem totally insurmountable. I had decided to meet them last.

My host thought about it. He asked if I had passes for the militias. If the actors knew I had arrived. If I had their names, their correct addresses. Sam had only been to Achrafieh, to see how the Christian would react.

'You haven't seen anyone else? The Palestinian?' I asked.

'Once, but here. Not in Shatila.'

'You'll be able to drive me everywhere?'

'Yes. That's what I'm paid for.'

He took me back to my hotel. Just one street, a corner, a few dozen metres. In the dark, men were filling bags with sand. Shots in the distance. I startled. My first sounds of war. Wood cracking, the harsh echo of metal throughout the city.

'Who's shooting?'

Marwan extended his hand to me in the entryway.

'It's Lebanon shooting Lebanon.'

I pulled out Sam's notebook to write for him. I had trouble falling asleep. I was a bit lost. At the airport, Marwan had a brotherly laugh. This evening, he was distant. He was going to help me half-heartedly. I was convinced. A wary driver, nothing more. Maybe even hostile. I was relying on a man who hadn't expected me. This theatre production was our dream, not his. For the first time, I imagined myself going back to Paris hanging my head. The war was too powerful for us. In the night, salvos of gunshots rang out.

Antigone was forced against a wall, executed by the entire city.

11

IMANE

The street was narrow, full of holes, flooded in some places. Cars, small vans, handcarts, horns honking for no reason, stalls of fruit, cigarettes and dubious perfumes. Everything here was like Beirut, but poorer, sadder and more confused. Marwan drove in silence. He didn't like Palestinians. He had told me in no uncertain terms. On breeze-block walls, faded posters celebrated martyrs. Men holding rifles, posing before their death against a backdrop of sun. On the rear dashboard and below the windshield of his car, the Druze had arranged strips cut from a keffiyeh. He had stopped before entering the Shatila camp to set them out, in full view, haphazardly, like a man who'd taken off his head-covering to drive. The artifice fooled no one. It was a pledge of good will. I was tense, watchful. My driver didn't have a weapon on his knees. I never found out whether the ritual he put me through at the airport was to illustrate a real threat, a way of including me, or a hazing.

The sight gripped my heart. For the first time in my life, a real Palestinian flag. A torn rag, hanging from the iron railing of a balcony. I had no words for this place. Not a neighbourhood, or city, or shanty town, or ghetto, but a bit of each. A monotonous bowel of small grey buildings, battered alleyways, peeling walls, raw cement, one-eyed windows, corrugated metal, meagre shops with their metal grilles gaping open. Wires crisscrossed the sky, hundreds of them, hung from one window to another, rooftop to rooftop, running through the streets, some at eye level. In several alleyways the network of cables was so thick it had the weight of night. On terraces, barbed wire strung with bits of cloth. Scraps of paper, fragments of plastic, balls flattened or forgotten by the wind. We drove with the windows open. The air was unhealthy, putrid, heavy as rotten fruit. Everywhere, at intersections, piles of rubbish slowly burning out. Fire injected a sickening grey smoke to the fermented smells. Barefoot children waded in this soup. They ran behind our red-and-white car, laughing. Marwan scattered them with a wave of his hand. He was on edge. His body tensed.

'Fedayeen,' my driver muttered.

Three petrol drums blocked the road. They'd been filled with cement and decorated with a colour portrait of Yasser Arafat. Seated on one of them, a man with an assault rifle between his legs. He stood up, his finger on the trigger. Two other men sat on plastic chairs against a wall. The first raised his hand. He was wearing a scarf. He pulled it up to his eyes. Marwan stopped the car and turned off the engine. He smiled at the fighter, stuck his head out the window. I knew that smile. A gesture of fear, of worry, a smile that meant hands in the air. The Palestinian signalled us to get out of the car.

'Your pass,' my friend whispered.

I put my hand in my jacket. He stopped me.

'First get out. No brusque movements.'

The street was empty. The Druze spoke. The Palestinian didn't answer. He made him open the boot, the glove box. One fighter walked around the car, another patted down Marwan, then me. The Druze was still talking. He filled the silence of the others. He laughed at something, pointed at me.

'Your pass. Hand it over!'

I pulled out my five passes, in a fan, like a poker player holds his cards. Marwan's eyes widened. He was shaking. He shrugged his shoulders, apologized mutely, open-handed, imploring the Palestinian to forgive him. The man in the keffiyeh lowered his scarf. He burst out laughing. He had round glasses, a few days' growth of beard. He looked like a student, not a militiaman. His comrade took my cards. All of them. He spread them out on the hood of the car. The others joined in his laughter. The Lebanese army, the Druze progressive socialist party, the Christian militias, the Shiite Amal Movement and the Fatah. The fighter took the last one, two fists, their rifles crossed, a grenade between them and a map of Palestine in the background. He waved the pass like a rattle.

'You speak English?'

A little, I answered. Like everyone. Marwan stood beside me. His distressed look leapt from one face to the other. He left no space between us. I felt him against me. We were one. That day, I was reassured forever. My Druze didn't approve of the play. He had hosted me without fully trusting me, but he would keep his word to Samuel Akounis. He didn't like Antigone, but he respected her.

The Fedayeen showed me the Fatah Movement pass. He was still smiling.

'This is the wild card. The only one!' he said in English.

I shook my head. I didn't understand.

'It's the joker,' Marwan murmured, still looking the fighter in the eyes.

'Joker! Yes! You understand joker? Arafat is the joker!'

Joker? I nodded my head with a wan smile. Yes, I understood. Of course. The only card that can save you. A Palestinian had picked up all the others. He was about to tear them up. My Druze spoke again. He talked, talked, pointed to his car, his passenger, his heart. I heard him say *Antigone*. I think. The Fedayeen looked at his chief. He nodded, with an indulgent look. The one holding my cards gave them back to me.

'*Ahlan wa sahlan!*' the Palestinian called out, adjusting his keffiyeh.

The phrase my Druze said at the airport. I had a new family and another new land. One after the other, the fighters extended their hands to me. I offered both of mine to them. I had been afraid. I realized it as life came back to me. My heart, almost inaudible, renewed its beat. My lips were parched. The bottom one cracked when I smiled. Marwan was in the car, I was still thanking the Fedayeen. I almost told them that in France we had supported them. Told them about our demonstrations, our fights with Zionists, their flag painted on the pavements of Paris. Marwan honked. He was calling me back. He was right. My joy looked too much like panic. I was humiliating him.

'*Yallah shabab!*' the Palestinian called out.

Go ahead. Drive. Welcome to Shatila.

We stayed on the main street, then turned by the hospital. Marwan was ashen, his mouth half open. His hands shook on the steering wheel. He watched his rearview mirror. At an empty patch of land, he stopped, raising a cloud of grey dust. He opened the hood.

'Get out, George.'

Shielded from the road by a wall, he held out his hand.

'Give me your passes.'

He looked around us. 'When you arrive at one camp, all the others are enemies. Understand?' I understood. 'If a militiaman asks you for a pass, it's the one for his movement that you pull out. And no others. Understood?'

I nodded.

'So you can't keep them together. You have to put them in different pockets.'

'And how do I remember which is which?'

A Toyota pickup passed noisily in the street. Marwan darted under the hood, as if he were checking the engine. There were three armed Palestinian fighters in the back of the pickup with a heavy machine gun.

The Druze stood back up. 'Don't lie to me. Who do you support?'

I looked at him without understanding.

'Forget that I'm Druze. You understand who's in this war?'

I fumbled my words, babbled. I didn't know. I was here for peace, not for war. I talked about *Antigone*. After the Palestinian barricade, my driver was ambushing me. Once again, I was lost.

'Answer me, George. It's important. The Phalangists? The Christians?'

I shook my head. Not them, no. In 1975 the Black Rats had left Assas to join them, to fight against the Lebanese left and the Palestinians.

'The Palestinians,' I said.

Marwan shrugged his shoulders. He pulled out the Fatah card from my deck.

'Arafat? Then you put him on your heart. That way, you'll remember.'

He slipped the card into the left front pocket of my shirt.

He showed me the Druze card.

'You pay me? So put Jumblatt where your wallet goes. Right front pocket.'

His smiles from earlier began to reemerge.

'The Lebanese Army? In your passport. It's an official document. You can take it out anywhere. No one will hold it against you.'

There were still the Shiites of the Amal Movement and the Christian militias.

'Those two, you sit on them, okay?'

A burst of gunfire in the distance. Two more, closer. I froze. He didn't.

'For you, the Lebanese Christians are fascists? Extreme right rear.'

'Amal, left rear?'

Marwan held out the remaining pass, laughing.

'*Yallah*! You're making your Antigone wait.'

* * *

Imane raised her white headscarf, letting a few wild strands escape. I was watching her silently when she caught my eye. I looked away. She smiled at my discomfort.

There were about fifty of us in the dark, seated on breeze blocks between two damaged buildings. An empty strip of land transformed for an hour into a theatre. No stage. An outline scratched in the dust. The Palestinian sat at the end of the row, beside me. Her hand hid her lips. She was translating the poet Mahmoud Darwish, after each speaker finished a line.

'Write it down! I'm an Arab. I work in the quarry with my companions in pain. And I have eight young children ...'

The actors were children. Five had come from Sabra, the others lived in Shatila.

'I am their teacher,' Imane had told me.

I found her beautiful a second time. Too beautiful not to think about it. Taller than I imagined, and younger. She was wearing a black party dress with red and green embroidery. Her accent was different from others around her, strong and melodic. She had chosen the text in September and staged it with the schoolchildren. They had rehearsed for several months before the performance. In the small gathering, there were parents and friends. Many held flashlights that they pointed at the stage like pocket projectors. Marwan had left. We had agreed on a return time. When we arrived, the Palestinian woman had looked at the Druze without extending her hand. He touched his heart with his fingertips.

When Imane wasn't translating, she was mouthing the children's lines. *'My grandfather was a farmer. A being without value or ancestors. My house, a guardian's hovel.'*

'She lives directly across the street from Pierre the dentist,' Sam had said.

At the entrance to Shatila, I could just ask for his office and follow the pointing fingers that replied. I had let her know I was coming. Imane had prepared a tray of tea. We sipped it outside, standing in the narrow street. She did not invite me in. A low house with bars. Everything was rundown. A corrugated metal roof reinforced with plastic tarps, two cardboard windowpanes. The walls were scabbed. I didn't see her mother. Her father didn't come out. I saw him in the shadows of the room. Two small girls were laughing in the doorway.

'Yassine,' a young man introduced himself behind me.

It was the Palestinian with the round glasses who had been laughing at the barricade earlier, holding my passes. Imane's older brother had a sweet face and a quiet look.

'So it was you? The Frenchman from the theatre?'

Yes, I was that Frenchman. He looked at me. He spoke poor English.

'And you've come to make peace in Lebanon?'

He wasn't kidding. He wanted to understand. I smiled.

'I just want to give adversaries an opportunity to talk to each other.'

'Enemies.'

'If you prefer.'

'Talking to each other by reciting a text that isn't theirs, that's the goal?'

He checked the strap of his assault rifle.

'It's a form of respite?'

I liked that word. I said yes. Theatre as respite.

When we finished our tea, Imane handed me a flashlight. We walked through the narrow streets in its glow. I caught glimpses of her graceful shadow. She had wanted me to come that night to hear *Identity*, written by Mahmoud Darwish in 1964. We would talk about *Antigone* another time. She wanted to see me before listening to me.

I shivered in the darkness. Two coal fires had been lit on each side of a stage outlined by the children's backpacks. From time to time, the sound of a shot in the distance broke through a line. I was the only one startled. The children acted out their parts, Imane translated. I studied their faces by firelight. Women, men, old, white-bearded men. Three fighters leaning against a wall, their weapons on the ground. Earlier, a Palestinian leader had come with Yassine to greet me. His hand in mine, he said the play was a beautiful idea. I was relieved. At least one man knew what I had come to do in this country. That night, I wasn't in Lebanon, or in Beirut, not even in Shatila. I was in a land of exile. An airless strip of earth between two grey walls.

A low sky striped with electric wires. I opened Sam's notebook. I wrote everything down for him. A few words on the majesty of the faces. On the hardness of some looks. About Imane's hair, her pale hands, her astonishing beauty. At her first smile, I knew she would be Antigone.

'Write this down! At the top of the first page. That I have no …'

The little girl couldn't remember.

'No hate for men,' Imane whispered in Arabic.

The girl flashed apologetic smiles to the audience. Seeking her mother, Imane, words to come to her rescue.

'No hate for men,' Imane repeated.

'No hate for …' the child mumbled.

The teacher stood up. Her student held out her arms. Eight years old, maybe, seeking refuge. Imane sat down with her in the gravel.

'May I assail no one,' the Palestinian woman recited.

She whispered into the child's ear.

'But if I go hungry, I eat the flesh of my usurper,' the child repeated.

Imane stood up, thrusting her arms skyward. All the children stood, fists on their hips.

'Beware! Beware!'

Then they gathered around their teacher.

'Beware of my fury!' Antigone screamed. Before bowing.

I stood, surrounded by applause and the women's ululations. The children pulled rice from their pockets and threw it at us. From windows, from terraces, shadows commended this exhilaration.

And then everyone scattered abruptly.

'Safety issues,' Imane explained.

The Fedayeen waved everyone out of the area. Yassine was clapping his hands. A community split back into families dispersed across the camp.

Marwan was on the other side of the street, in his car, with the lights out.

'Can we meet tomorrow?'

Imane nodded.

'I think so,' she answered.

My heart was racing. It was a work meeting. I felt like I was stealing a kiss. We would meet outside the camp, in a café downtown. She didn't want the stern looks from her brother, or her sisters' laughter. I held out a shaking hand. Men walked by. She turned away.

* * *

'First, cross to the East. You have to convince Charbel's brother the way Sam managed to convince mine.'

I was drinking a beer. Imane hadn't touched her soda.

'On the demarcation line, across from the yellow house, there's a cinema in ruins. That's where he wanted to stage *Antigone*.'

I snuck glances at Imane. Using her glass, she swept away the moist circles on the wooden table. She'd kept her head bowed since the beginning of our meeting,

'What's the yellow house?'

Now the Palestinian looked up. She seemed surprised.

'The Barakat building, if you want to know.'

I didn't want anything. Just to understand. And she explained, slowly, her voice steady.

'Once you get past the Ring, the expressway, you reach the Sodeco intersection, which marks the entry to Achrafieh, the Christian sector. The yellow house is there. It's a strategic outpost. From its three stories, the Phalangists control the entire sector. There are snipers at every window. If you arrive without warning, you die.'

'And the old cinema?'

'On the other side, on Damas Street. Not East or West, in the middle.'

'Sam told me about it.'

'He wanted to reach out to the militias for a three-hour truce. With one actor from each camp, he said it was possible.'

'Did you believe him?'

'No,' Imane answered.

Then she turned.

'But if the Christians accept, we're set.'

'And the Druze? The Shiites? The Palestinians?'

'The Fatah agreed. The Druze will follow.'

'And the Shiites?'

'They'll need to be convinced. They are liars, but Sam was hopeful.'

'The Shiites are liars?'

She shrugged, with a motion that said, *of course*.

'Their dogma allows it.'

'Is this the Palestinian talking?'

'It's the Sunni.'

I gulped down my beer. It was bitter. My head was spinning. A twenty-year-old girl was explaining to me that to get onstage, I had to make a pact between warring forces. It was a minefield. Sam had cleared the way with the authorities and the Palestinians, but not with the other fighters. First, the official stamps, then getting the weapons lowered.

'I can get a written commitment from the Fatah?'

She smiled.

'The Palestinian authorization is the only thing Sam managed to get.'

'But I have no written proof.'

'Is my word enough or do you want to ask Arafat?'

I was tense. I apologized. Through the café window I could see Marwan's car. His face turned towards us.

'Palestinians are snakes,' he had said. Don't put your hand out. They bite.'

This time, however, Imane took the hand I extended, holding the small clear pouch wrapped in foil. She kept my hand in hers, with Sam's gift, undaunted by the passers-by haunting the pavements.

'He remembered,' Antigone muttered.

She smiled. She lowered her eyes.

'It's land from Jaffa,' Imane whispered. She closed her fist around the little bag.

'A piece of Palestine to share with my brother.'

I had ten more days. We decided to meet again the day before I left. I already felt it in my chest.

12

JOSEPH-BOUTROS

'On the way there, I need you to be quiet,' Marwan said.

He explained that we would be in the open for eight minutes. In mortal danger. That we'd be in the sights of every sniper in the city. First, of the Shiites and the Nasseriens who occupied the Murr tower. A four-storey building that was under construction when war abandoned it to the combatants. After that, rifles will track us as we pass Serail, into Canon Square. You never know what a finger on a trigger will do. When we arrive at the Sodeco intersection, we risk becoming targets for Christian snipers. The ones watching from the Rizk tower overlooking Achrafieh, and the ones guarding the yellow house. Marwan put his hand on my shoulder.

'What did the Kataeb say, exactly?'

'Charbel's brother?'

'Yes. What did he say?'

'He said he didn't control everything.'

'He told you that himself on the phone?'

'Yes.'

'But he didn't say you couldn't come?'

'No. In fact, he told me to get to Sodeco before eight.'

Marwan kicked the front tyre of his car. He tied a piece of white cloth to the antenna, and to each of the door handles. He was breathing hard. Talking to himself in Arabic. With pointless gestures of anger.

'I'm too old for this,' Marwan said as he opened the door for me.

He chugged down a full bottle of water, told me again to stay silent throughout the trip. Only he would speak.

'I don't want you to even breathe. I am alone in the car, you understand?'

'Why?'

He looked at me.

'I don't want to remember that you are there. Risking his own life is enough for any man.'

He sat in the front, ordered me to lie down in the back, on the floor between his seat and mine.

'But why now?'

He slapped his steering wheel with both hands.

'*Astaghfirullah!* God, forgive me.'

He leapt out of the car. Slammed the door and walked away from me.

'Marwan!'

I shouted. I blamed myself. He stopped in the middle of the street. Then turned around without a word. He came back. I immediately lay down the way he wanted. He got in. He didn't start the car. Him, me, silence. And then he prayed softly. A few words, his hands clutching the wooden rosary that hung from his rearview mirror. He took it down, put it into the glove box. Then he hunched down in his seat, protected by the dashboard, his face barely above the wheel.

The street was empty. It was daybreak. We moved slowly. Then faster, to the expressway overpass. Once on the Ring, the car flew. It felt like a plane taking off. I shut my eyes. We were riding in a red coffin, an offering to every bullet in the city. I panicked. My friend should have repainted his car for war, the colour of asphalt, of nothing.

'Murr Tower,' the Druze said under his breath.

I opened my eyes, raised my body slightly. The building was on the right, rectangular, immense against the sky. Its windows of death were watching us. I clenched my fists. I waited. Not a shot. Only the sound of the engine.

'We made it through,' Marwan muttered.

A quick burst of gunfire. Far away, near us. I don't know. More. Longer gaps between shots.

'*Mourabitoun!*' growled the Druze.

Nasseriens. They picked us as a target. Four violent blows. The car was hit. It skidded.

'May God protect us!'

Marwan accelerated, swerving from side to side in tight loops. More hits. A whistling. Sound from a movie, the burning wasp described in books. The rear window shattered. Rain of glass. I grabbed two cushions off the seat to cover my head.

'We're in the sights of the Rizk tower.'

I was expecting another salvo. But nothing. The engine was screaming. We exited the Ring as two cars entered, horns blaring. And an ambulance screaming. Marwan slowed down.

'Sodeco intersection.'

He stopped the car. Parked on a pavement reclaimed by weeds, his head thrown back. Two taxi drivers were there, squatting on their heels.

'You can get out, George.'

Then he walked around the car, shaking his head. He frowned. A colleague joined him. Three bullets had pierced the boot. Two others had worked over the hood. One impact on my door. The wasp had entered from the left, exited through the window. It had crossed the rear seat just above me. Marwan inspected the tyres, the headlights, the engine.

'I'll wait for you until eight o'clock tomorrow morning.'

'You're not coming?'

The Druze looked at me with a smile.

'You want me dead?'

He lit a cigarette offered by one of the drivers.

'How do I get there from here?'

'Take this taxi.'

The other driver asked me to pay in advance. In dollars. Marwan turned his back to me. He opened a bag of bread. He was shaking. My teeth were chattering. We had ridden some distance with death.

I got out of the taxi with my hands up, my bag hanging from its strap on my arm. Two Phalangists had been hidden behind blocks of concrete, protected by the carcass of a blistered bus. One of them yelled to the taxi to free up the intersection. Then signalled me to approach. Ordered me to kneel about ten metres from him. To cross my hands behind my head. He walked heavily towards me, his assault rifle ready to fire. On his sleeve, a cedar tree with two swords. His friend kept his gun on me, his elbows on a sandbag. An order yelled in the distance. A shout. Shots in bursts.

'*Shu baddak?*'

'Français! French!'

The Christian approached. He raised his hand, gesturing with his fingers.

'Passport!'

He was young, a riding helmet on his head, his face smeared with green and brown. Instinctively, I reached into my shirt pocket and pulled out the Palestinian pass. I saw it emerge in my hand. A nightmare. The two armed fists, the grenade, the flag. I was sick. Out with one blow. I was going to die with my mouth wide open. I dropped the document. The Phalangist armed his M16 as he called for reinforcement. I tore the back pocket of my trousers. I held out the right pass to him. He hit me in the face, ripped the document from my hand, crushing the other under his boot. He examined my photo, my name. Then he snatched up the crushed Fatah card and threw it in my face.

'Eat!'

He spoke French. I looked at him. Him, the gold cross that hung from his neck. I spread my hands. I didn't understand. The Lebanese leapt at me, grabbed me by the hair, pulled me backwards, the barrel of his rifle against my temple.

'Eat your shit!'

He pushed me forward. I fell. I was on all fours. My mind went blank. Nothing. Not a word. Not an image. Not a thought. I was an empty man. I heard but I no longer functioned. I had left my fears on the side of peace. The threats, the anguish, the frightening moments from before the war, assuaged by this absurd order. Eating paper would be my death. I couldn't feel my fingers. The pain in my knee had stayed behind in Paris. My heart was on pause. I picked up the pass. I tore it in two, then four, then eight. I was buying time. In the photo I was cross-eyed, laughing. I put the first piece in my mouth, rolled up like a cigarette. Don't chew. Don't eat. Swallow fast and raw. The second one was harder. I should have been afraid, or ashamed, or ashamed of being afraid. Nothing. I imagined myself rising, powerful, standing up to him like Joseph Boczov, tearing this man's heart out with my teeth. But I was eating my pâté without a shred of dignity, my knees in the dust, like a dog. The cardboard wouldn't go down. It stuck to the roof of my mouth, to my tongue, it was crumbling, it refused my body. The gravel dust scraped my throat. I coughed. There were two more pieces of Palestine to betray.

The militiaman spat on the ground.

'Go on. *Bas, khalas*!'

I stood up, my hands on my head. The Christian had pulled a two-way radio from his bag. He gave my name. I understood the word 'French'. We walked towards the Green Line. Vegetation had overrun the deserted neighbourhood. Taken advantage of the absence of men, invaded everything. Seized disembowelled streets, embankments, sand. Brambles streamed from torn balconies. A pine tree born of asphalt leaned against a wall. Shrubs, thorned weeds, giant ferns, ficus occupied the centre of the intersection. The pavements looked like tormented hillsides. Along the walls, markings with skulls, warnings that everything was mined. Directly across the street, a superb yellow three-storey house. The Barakat building in war lace. On surrounding streets, two Lebanese Forces jeeps, a machine gun mounted on a pickup. To cross the plaza littered with shell-casings and debris, we ran. Them in front, me behind. I no longer amused them. A man was waiting for me in the pockmarked doorway, behind a concrete wall. Army jacket, sunglasses, black beret, a pistol tucked in his belt. He smiled broadly to greet me, descending the gutted stairway. This house was not a war ruin. It *was* war. From the balcony to the ground, the fighting had hammered it like copperplate. Not a centimetre was intact. Everywhere on its fragile columns, its balconies, its Roman windows, the pointillist bursts of gunfire, holes of precision marksmanship, scrapes of grenades, ripping of rockets, scars torn by mortars. In the rising sun, the rubble of an ancient arena.

The man looked down at his watch. 'Ten past eight. My men held you up, I'm sorry.'

'They humiliated me.'

Life was coming back. Working its way into my body.

'They're bulls and you waved the red cape.'

'You knew I would come. I trusted you.'

Still the same smile.

'But you were right. And you are still alive.'

He extended his hand to me.

'Joseph-Boutros, Charbel's brother.'

I followed him through the covered entryway. Then into the courtyard. The building was a labyrinth of enormous empty rooms, ravaged by gunfire. A majestic palace. When they passed the gaping windows, the fighters lowered their heads. They had piled sandbags up to the ceiling.

'Your permit is until midnight?'

The brother spoke to me without turning around. He crossed through rooms, slipped between holes in the walls.

'I have to be outside at 8 am.'

He stopped, turned to face me.

'Who is it?'

'Who what?'

'Your driver, who is it?'

I hesitated. It was pointless.

'A Druze.'

The Christian kept walking.

'There's been a nasty smell since you got here.'

He laughed. The militiamen were silent. Some of them sat against the wall, others lay on mattresses. A mix of military jackets, camouflage trousers, leather jackets. A man walked by in a green duffle coat. Another wore a Lebanese Army helmet. We walked beside iron railings, climbed the stairs. I ran my hand over a chipped mosaic.

'Art deco,' the militiaman said. 'Astonishing, isn't it? There are floor tiles from the 1930s, paintings, wooden archways, remnants of marble columns. It's one of the most beautiful buildings in Beirut. Construction began in 1924 and ended in 1932. It was destroyed in two months.'

He opened a mangled door to let me through. The room was dark. The windows were walled off with breeze blocks. Electric wires had been ripped out of the walls, leaving gaping trenches. He sat in the armchair, gestured for me to take the sagging couch. Carefully, he placed his pistol on the low table. A U.S. Army Colt 45, so well polished it was parade-ready. He had decorated its grip with a shining square of ivory emblazoned with the Phalangists' cedar tree. In this room, like everywhere else, the floor was littered with rubble, papers, leftover food. Newspapers covered the walls.

The door opened. A young man stuck his head in.

'Tea? Coffee?' my host offered.

Joseph-Boutros lit a cigarette.

'Or alcohol, if you prefer. We're not at your Muslim buddy's house here.'

I was thirsty. I asked for water. My lip had been bleeding since the Ring.

'So, let's see. Before we begin, I have a question.'

He slid his weapon under the seat cushion.

'Are you Christian?'

I shrugged.

'Baptized.'

The Maronite shook his head. He didn't like my answer.

'What do Western Christians hold against Lebanese Christians?'

'I don't understand.'

'Can you explain what you don't like about us?'

'Who, "you"?'

'You, the baptized, in France and elsewhere. What did we do to you?'

I drank. He looked at me without rancour. He wanted to know.

'You're the ones who invented "Palestino-progressives" and all that nonsense, aren't you? What is it you believe, in Paris? That this is a fight between the right and the left, here, like at your university? You are at university, right?'

'I'm going to be a history professor.'

The Phalangist laughed.

'A student at your age? That's perfect. I'm your student and you're going to teach me, okay? So, do you really believe that the Palestinians, the Shiites and the others are democrats? And we, what are we? Nazis? Is that the story, professor?'

He drank down his coffee in one gulp, set the glass on the floor with a bang.

'Do you know what happened at Damour in 1976? Hundreds of Christians were murdered and dismembered by your progressive friends. Did you know that?'

'And at Karantina? And at Tel al-Zaatar? How many Palestinians were killed by Christians?' I finished my water. 'I'm here to talk about your brother, not about your war.'

The Phalangist looked at me closely.

'Do you have children?'

'Louise, a daughter.'

'All right, so listen carefully to what I'm about to tell you, mister intellectual. Here, we fight for values that you share …'

'I don't think so.'

He raised his hand to stop me.

'Let me speak. We're on the western front. On the front line. And, you see, every time I go up to my post on the roof, every time I fire my weapon, it's Louise I defend.'

'You can't say that.'

'Then what? When they burn our churches and massacre our villages, there are Louises bleeding all over our pavements.'

'You are part of the massacres here!'

'May the massacres cease!'

He stood abruptly. I feared he was leaving the room. He turned away from me, put his hands against the wall, spread his legs. He was stretching. Turning his head, raising his knees to his chin, first one, then the other.

'Between Mecca, Moscow and Arafat, your Louise has a beautiful future.'

I was quiet. Smells of cooking rose up the stairway. I told myself I should leave. Nothing was working. This guy was toying with a Frenchman before he went back to his butchery. I was his entertainment. I got to my feet.

'Tell me about *Antigone*.' A calm voice. He was studying me, his back to the wall, stretching his arms over his head. I opened my bag.

'*Antigone* was written by …'

'Stop, I know that. Tell me about your project.'

I took a deep breath. This is it. Here, now, right now. Everything I had created in my head, in my gut. Everything I had written, practised, prepared for the actors, this was the moment. I thought the Phalangist would be the last one to hear me out. He was the first to listen. So I told him about Anouilh. About Samuel, my pledge. I explained that my friend's idea was to steal two hours from the war, souls from each camp. He was listening, I think. Stretching on the floor, looking at me from time to time.

'Why Lebanon?'

'For Damour and Karantina, exactly.'

'Both of them?'

'Suffering to suffering.'

A Maronite soldier entered the room carrying a tray. Bread, a purée of fava beans and a bowl of tabbouleh. There were two plates. I was his guest. We ate in silence, in the airless storage room. We sat on the floor, facing each other. The chatter of a radio beyond the door. Footsteps in the stairway. Two shots from the terrace. Laughter. A barracks in the middle of a Roman theatre.

Joseph-Boutros got up.

'For Charbel, I'll give you my answer before morning. I know he's crazy about this project. But it isn't up to him to decide the fate of the Green Line.'

I stood.

'How will you let me know?'

'I'll tell you myself. You are staying.'

He made his way towards the door. I asked his back,

'What will I do?'

'I'll keep you here. You'll be staying up all night, so rest this afternoon.'

* * *

'*Abu Ammar?* Let's go! *Yallah!*'

I was asleep. A soldier had put a blanket over me while I slept. It was cold.

The first few days, gunshots woke me up. Then they reassured me. I didn't like the hypocrisy of silence.

'*Yallah!*'

A Phalangist was laughing, shaking me. He had called me Abu Ammar, the nom de guerre of Yasser Arafat. The story of me swallowing the Palestinian document had made the rounds. Startled awake, I pulled open my bag. Checked everything. Passport, dollars.

We crossed to the other side of the yellow house, behind the well of light that the architect had envisioned. After climbing two flights of battered stairs, I reached the snipers' stronghold. Not a single wall of the Barakat building was immune to the war, but here, in this room fortified by the militiamen, not a trace. No bullet holes, no scratches, nothing. They had built a wall that reached the ceiling, a rampart of rubble. Imperfectly, heavy-handedly. The large stones were not aligned. They vomited their mortar towards the floor. In this fortress, almost two metres thick, the warrior architects had cut three rectangular medieval-style arrow slits where they could set weapons and ammunition. The gun was slid into the arrow slit, which opened onto an old window or a hole in the wall surrounded by sandbags. From the street, no one would suspect a killer was there.

When I arrived, Joseph-Boutros was reloading his rifle. His face was blackened with soot.

'*Ahlan wa sahlan!*' The Phalangist smiled as I entered.

I had a new land, a new family.

He was in charge of a wall with seven firing posts. Their position swept Damas Street. Two slits in doors, two window openings, plus two more firing axes near the balcony's colonnade. He squatted to greet me. He was different. Smiling, almost elegant. One elbow against the outer wall, his head against the inner edge of the arrow slit, with two other snipers.

'This is Kim, and Robert.'

I shook their hands.

'Tomorrow, Tarzan and Katol will relieve them. And Begin will take over for me.'

'Begin? Like the Israeli?'

I speak the truth, my soul will fly away in one minute, Begin had written on the hallway wall.

'Yes. And Tarzan, like the monkey,' Robert laughed.

In the bunkered room, there were just three of them, water bottles at their feet and a thermos of coffee. Outside, nightfall hesitated. It was the cruel time of day.

'France has some good ones, you know? This is from your country ...'

The Christian showed me his rifle, its blonde wood stock, its mounted scope.

'Let me introduce you to my friend the FR-F1. Bipod, pistol grip, night-vision scope, all the modern conveniences. And it's accurate at 800 metres. Enough to see what's coming.'

He turned back to his post. The other two were waiting for dark.

'So, George, listen closely now. George. Yes?'

I nodded.

He slapped his thigh with one hand, the way you call a dog.

'Right here, this is your spot. At my feet. You stay seated, with your back to the wall. Okay?'

'I have a choice?'

The sound of a spring retracting. Rounds sliding into the magazine.

'Not really, no. But I'll explain. I want your arm and your shoulder against my leg. I want to feel them every second. Got it?'

'Why?'

'It's a thing I do. I want to feel life beside me.'

'That's usually my spot,' Kim interjected without turning around.

Clatter of the breech. He held out cotton for my ears.

'One more thing. I fire, you stay quiet. You don't ask questions. Not to me, or the others. Especially if the guy is on the mat.'

'I sit on the right or the left?'

'If you want to eat burning shell-casings, on the right.'

I sat down heavily to his left. The Christian moved closer. Pressed against me. I felt his heat.

'You have everything? Water, patience?'

'I have everything.'

In a corner of the room, a flashlight, its glass painted blue. Daylight was fading. I watched the backs of the fighters, their legs spread, unmoving. I pressed against Charbel's brother. He pressed against me. I breathed softly. I thought about Marwan, who was sleeping in his car. About Imane, dreaming behind barred windows. About Sam's heart, beeping in the hospital room. About Louise, who took my place in the bed. About Aurora. I was in Beirut. In the depths of war. It was terrible and vertiginous. Both. I didn't come for that. It wasn't the mandate Sam had given me. The pistol of a Druze, the rifle of a Christian. I was consorting with metal, not the human heart.

Robert and Kim fired almost as one. The shock was violent. The room became an echo chamber, the firing slot returned fire, smoke, gunpowder. The tinkling of casings on the tiles. One of them rolled near my shoe. It was smoking. I had never seen battle close up. Street fights, violence, anger, but not the death of men. I felt the leg of the Christian tense up. Then tremble. His shaking swept through my body. I held him up with all my strength. I contained him. After applauding Palestine, I was joining the opposite camp.

He fired three shots. Insanely violent. The recoil slammed his shoulder, his torso, his legs, my neck, my shoulder, my arm. The copper of the casings hit the wall. I hadn't put in the cotton. My ears were whistling. I winced. The air was unbreathable acidic powder. The sniper's leg quieted. Resolidified. Joseph-Boutros moved away from me. I let him decide how far. Everything had fallen. Darkness, silence. Outside, others were firing. I could see our facade in their scopes. Night was taking over. We were nothing but shadows, stroked by the blue of the blind light.

I wondered what my snipers saw. A car headlight? A poorly closed curtain that betrayed a living room? An imprudent cigarette passed from hand to hand?

It was frightening. Deeply disturbing. At one point I told myself I had experienced more in five days than in my entire life. And that no kiss from Louise would ever measure up to the little Palestinian girl, retrieving the words of a poet as she raised her fist in the air. I shook my head. Literally. Shook it to scatter what it contained. I was ashamed. I could leave for home tomorrow, let this go, return to peacetime, fast. A smile from Louise and Aurora's caress were the things in the world that made me alive. And I repeated that to myself. And I was no longer very sure of that. Then I was truly afraid, for the first time since I arrived. Not fear of the men who were killing, or for the dying. Fear of myself.

'George?'

I raised my head.

'Do you know Victor Hugo?'

My jaw fell open. The Phalangist adjusted his weapon, his gaze lost in nightfall. He had glued a Virgin to the stock of his rifle. Blue-veiled, hands folded, somewhere between suffering and glee.

'You know Hugo?'

I pressed my elbow lightly against his thigh to say yes.

'*Demain, dès l'aube, à l'heure où blanchit la campagne,*

Je partirai. Vois-tu, je sais que tu m'attends,' the killer recited.

It was my turn to tremble. My whole body. I couldn't hold back. I cried. Too bad. This time I felt his leg come to my aid. I knew my shaking pulsed through him. That my secret tears traveled up his arm, to his hand, to his finger poised on the trigger guard.

J'irai par la forêt, j'irai par la montagne.
Je ne puis demeurer loin de toi plus longtemps.
Je marcherai les yeux fixés sur mes pensées,
Sans rien voir au-dehors, sans entendre aucun bruit,
Seul, inconnu, le dos courbé, les mains croisées,
Triste, et le jour pour moi sera comme la nuit ...

And then he took the shot. Twice. A third, right after. This time without shaking, without me feeling it come. His body was stiff with war. My tears had no power over it. Neither did Aurora's beauty, Louise's frailty, or my fear. He shot at the city, on the wind's breath. He shot the glimmers of hope, the sadness of men. He shot me, all of us. He shot the gold of the falling night, the bouquet of green holly and heather in bloom.

13

NABIL, NIMER, HUSSEIN AND KHADIJAH

The next morning, Marwan seated me majestically, beside him in the front seat. And we took the Mercedes, a sign that the drive would be calm. He drove with the windows open, the songs of Farid al-Atrache on his lips. We had left in darkness so we could cross Saida at first light. Marwan didn't like south Lebanon, but he respected it. When Beirut flared up, Druzes and Shiites often fought shoulder to shoulder. The alliance might shift locally overnight, over a disputed parking space or a glance askance, but the leaders held their troops together. Leaving Saida, we took the road to Nabatieh, in the heart of the Shiite realm. Creon's guards lived there, and Eurydice. We were still in Lebanon, with one foot in Iran. More religious than the Amal Movement, which it deemed corrupt, Islamic Amal wanted to install a republic of mullahs in the Land of the Cedars. Marwan explained all this, tapping his temple with his forefinger. The father of our three young actors was an important cleric in this movement in Nabatieh. Without his assent, the young people could do nothing. Certainly not appear in a theatrical performance. The religious leaders had had a copy of *Antigone* in their hands for months. They had studied it. And wished to give us their answer in person. Marwan did not think it would earn their blessing. He said this trip would probably be our last. And their refusal would sound the bell for my departure.

He had thought the same thing about the Phalangists. When I crossed back over the line, leaving the yellow house, he greeted me with the solemn look of someone who had predicted defeat. He went slack-jawed when he heard that Joseph-Boutros had agreed, laughing,

'You're giving my little brother a chance to bury a young Palestinian woman alive?'

The Lebanese Forces consented to lower their weapons. Four hours this week for the actors to meet, and three hours on Friday, 1 October 1982, for the only performance. It was the feast day of Saint Thérèse of the Child Jesus. And the Christians chose this themselves. The ceasefire would be local, centred around the Barakat building. It wasn't a military truce, or a political act, just a humanitarian gesture.

'Like letting stretcher-bearers pass after battle,' Joseph-Boutros had explained.

The Christian couldn't refuse two hours of grace. He had read *Antigone*, found the young woman's insistence on death laughable, vain, without reason or goal. He said her blind stubbornness defied common sense. He approved of his younger brother becoming the powerful Creon. The one who led the city, who was feared by his people, who worked in the interest of all, who kept his head high, escaped dishonour.

'It's a little more complicated than that,' I answered.

The militiaman looked at me with a smile.

'That reading works for me. And I'd like it to work for you, too.'

Driving back west, Marwan muttered in Arabic the whole way. Not a single shot saluted our departure or greeted our return. The red car was a white flag, as if all the killers along the line had passed the word.

That evening the Druze seemed annoyed. The foolishness continued. Better still, it was taking shape. Palestinians, Christians. I think he was counting on the Shiites to put *Antigone* on the first flight back.

All I had seen of Lebanon was the city. Suddenly, at the foot of dry hills and olive trees, pine forests stretched to the horizon. I thought we should have gone outside Beirut to perform *Antigone*. Offer the young, rebellious girl something besides a bombed-out theatre. The beauty of this land, the torment of this sky. A performance under the autumn stars instead of for men in ruins.

'It's beautiful, isn't it?' Marwan asked.

He read my silence. He said Shouf was even more moving. Waterfalls, mountains, cedars, the women and men of Aley, their hearts of stone and honey. I leaned against the window. We had left the war on the other side of the line. I imagined Aurora and Louise running down this hill, laughing. I wished they were there with me, in the car. Just for a moment. Long enough for the small lake, the child on his donkey who raised his hand to us. Enough time for the man seated on the side of the road. And for the royal eagle.

We arrived in Nabatieh with the winter sun. Men from Islamic Amal led us through the city to its eastern outskirts. A low house covered with sandbags. Once again, Marwan would stay near the car. I worried about his solitude. But he said he preferred silence to certain meetings. As soon as I left for my rendezvous, he would get behind the wheel and read, or sleep, or listen to the radio for hours. His car was a second home. He brought water, bread, coffee. He could withstand a siege without taking his hands off the wheel.

'You will be received by Sheik Mamâar al-Sadeq, the father of your actors. The uncle will also be present,' Marwan explained.

He recommended I remove my shoes at the doorway, not be the first to extend my hand, not to look the man in the eye and not to ask any questions, just to answer. I was 'haram', impure. I must not taint him. Once more I felt fear fill my throat. I had to rehearse, reassure myself. I was delivering a message that was not my own. I was defending a project I had not begun, I was carrying out the final wishes of a dying man. And for him, this man, this friend, this brother, I was willing to take every risk.

I took off my shoes. At the door, two bearded men armed with assault rifles. Long white kameez, caps of the pious, sombre faces. One of them searched me, patted me down. Under my arms, my sleeves, my belt, my back, my belly, my crotch, my buttocks, my legs, one at a time, my ankles, the soles of my feet. I had my back to the house, my hands in the air. In the car, Marwan was stretching, his arms spread. I wanted to smile. He didn't even glance in my direction.

The room was small, covered in rugs and cushions. No table, no chairs. A window blocked by a green curtain. On the wall, along with a sura framed in gold and a tapestry of Mecca, a photo of the Iraqi mausoleum of Imam Ali, in Najaf. A guard entered with a lawn chair. He set it down facing the sightless window. And then I waited. An hour, two. I don't know how long. At first I was sitting cross-legged, then almost lying down because of my knee, the shooting pain. When the sheik entered, the bearded man motioned for me to stand. Three other men followed him in, two young men with dark looks and a fat man who sat on the floor, in a corner. The religious official took his place in the armchair. A very old man, using a cane. He sat with his back to me.

'You are here because I desired it.'

I shivered. He spoke difficult English. And addressed the wall.

'My brother Hassan and I – may God bless this – have spoken at length about your play.'

I watched the fat man. He nodded his head.

'He is against this project. He believes that an actor enacting a resemblance is a miscreant. To play a role is to be false, to lie. This is akin to sin. He assumes that one who imitates a group will be viewed as being part of that group.'

Hassan watched me closely. No expression crossed his face. He understood his brother's words and listened to my face. He looked into the depths of me for a reply.

'I have not read your play, but Nabil, my eldest, read it for me. He said, on the contrary, that a play is exempt from slander. That it neither represents the Prophet – prayers and blessings be upon him – or his messengers. That a play does not lack respect for his great companions. And also that it does not insult Islam. That it does not harbour any nudity, or insult, or other taint.'

The sheik took a handkerchief from his sleeve and wiped his eyes. 'My sons told me that their role as guards would be to stay close to their leader, to protect him like a father and to ensure that his authority is respected. They explained that a young woman defied him. That by challenging him, she had disrespected divine law and that their well-guided caliph put an end to her arrogance.'

The old man fell silent. He turned slightly, looking at the floor.

'Isn't that right?'

I looked at Hassan, at the guards. They were no help to me.

'Isn't it?'

The brother urged me to respond, nodding his head. The slim thread of my voice.

'That's exactly right, Sheik Mamâar al-Sadeq.'

Silence. He turned back to face the wall. *Antigone,* abstracted by some, purloined by others, and me, meekly nodding my head.

'And the role of the old woman, what is that? Why does she knit?'

Find an answer. Gather myself together.

'She's the wife of the caliph. She is very pious and spends her days making warm clothing for the city's poor.'

Silence, again.

'That's zakat. Alms for the indigent,' the religious leader said in a low voice.

More silence.

'*Radi Allahu anha*. May God be pleased with her.'

At the beginning of the conversation, I felt like laughing. This man talking to a curtain, the others sniffing me out like a pack of dogs following a buck. And then the steel of the rifles, the soft voice, the words chosen with care. I was almost calm, my hands hidden under my thighs. After Anouilh revised by the Christians, an Anouilh transformed by Shiites. Creon, an old war-weary man who wants only peace for his people. Creon who tries until the very end to save his niece. Creon who does what it takes to uphold the law. Creon becomes a Phalangist on one side of the line, an enlightened caliph on the other. My head filled with strange music. Somewhere between entrapment and betrayal. The guards didn't take their eyes off me. They stood against the wall. Hassan was praying, or passing the time, stroking prayer beads of black stone. I thought of Charles Maurras. There, in that room thick with faith. Sam had loaned me a book by Maurras that described Antigone as a submissive young girl, obeying laws consistent with the laws of God, of man, and the city. 'Who violates these laws, who defies them all? Creon!' Maurras had written in 1948. For him, the edict of Creon was not legal because it was not promulgated by Zeus. In Maurras' writing, Antigone was a 'Virgin-mother of Order.' And Creon? 'He is the anarchist. He, and only he!'

Sam laughed about that book. It also irritated him. Maurras erected a monument to Sophocles; Akounis built an altar for Anouilh.

'These are the kinds of differences that breed the left and the right,' said my friend.

He believed that, when compared to the many interpretations this drama provokes, politics and the economy expressed very little of the differences between us. And here, sitting on a prayer rug, on the other side of the world, with a bothersome hole in my sock, I nodded my head religiously at the idea of a hysterical Antigone quite fortunately countered by a wise ruler.

The sheik tapped his cane. His brother helped him up. He did not glance my way.

'That you chose Friday for the performance is a good thing.'

Then he left the room, dragging his leg as I did. I found myself alone, standing, pins and needles flashing pain from my foot to my hip. The front door was wide open. In the yard, three young men were waiting, seated on the low wall, with an old woman veiled in black. The oldest of the three boys smiled at me. A magnificent, disarming smile. The joy of the conqueror. He moved towards me, holding out both hands.

'Hello, George, I am Nabil. The guard and the messenger.'

I faltered. I nearly threw myself into his arms. He was a handsome young man, about twenty-five, in jeans and a sleeveless undershirt. He took his brother by the hand.

'And this is Nimer, who will also be the page.'

The third one approached me, his hands extended like his brothers'.

'Hussein. I'm only a guard, but I'm here, too.'

He was the youngest. He's the one who did it. He put his arms around me. He was laughing. His brothers, too. We did a happy dance outside the sinister mausoleum.

'*Ahlan wa salan!*'

It was dizzying. I had another land and another family. Day after day, men offered me a piece of their country.

Marwan had gotten out of his car. Leaning against the door, he was smiling. The accursed Frenchman had persuaded a Shiite dignitary. It never occurred to him that I was the one who had backed down.

'Khadijah,' Nabil said, introducing the woman.

I was about to reach out my hand. A second more and I would have greeted her with a kiss, the French way. Hussein halted my hand mid-motion. On the other side of the street, Marwan sank his head into his hands.

It was 18 February 1982. I had set the meeting for the 24th, the day before my departure. The Phalangists, the Palestinians and the Shiites had accepted that it take place from 8 am until noon, at the Beaufort, the abandoned theatre on the line.

I practically ran to the car, turning around three times to my hosts, my arms in the air. The old woman was watching me. With one hand she held her scarf just below her eyes. From the second floor, a silhouette observed my departure.

'All that's left is to convince the Druze actor,' I said, taking my seat in the freezing car.

'The Druze actor?' Marwan repeated.

'Do you know where to find him?'

He started the car with a smile.

'My son? At home, I hope.'

14

HAEMON

I watched Marwan. Secretly, in profile, the way I watched him in the car. But this time he feared neither bullets nor bombs. He wasn't on a death-riddled road or navigating a hostile alley. He was home, a Druze prince. He was smoking, a cigarette wedged between his middle and ring fingers. His wife was there. I didn't know her first name. He introduced her to me, saying, 'My wife.'

She came and went with pastries, tea and white coffee.

My host had invited some friends, about ten people. They sat in a circle in the living room, on the couch, a few chairs and cushions on the rug. Most of them were dressed in black, a round white cap on their heads. Islam considered these men apostate. They refused to recognize the Prophet, or Sharia. Their religion had no liturgy, no place of worship.

Marwan had left his armchair for me. He waited for the guests to arrive, embrace one another at the doorway, and then he stood up. He spoke in Arabic. Gravely, his eyes narrowed. He wasn't asking any questions. Or expecting answers. He spoke with the authority of what must be said.

Then he sat down. And Nakad entered. Frail and elegant.

He wore traditional clothing: sarouel pants, the crotch mid-thigh, and a tarboosh wrapped in a white turban. He strode to the middle of the room. He looked at us, astonished, as if he had just noticed us. He faced his father, bowed, looking first at his father, then at me.

'Haemon,' Nakad said.

The Druze was going to recite the first lines of his text. He lowered his head, raised it. He coughed. Took a deep breath.

'You know that I forgave you even as you slammed the door. Your perfume lingered, and I had already forgiven you. Who did you steal it from, that perfume?'

I stood abruptly.

'From Ismene,' I answered.

The young man was surprised. And then he smiled. He continued.

'And the lipstick, the powder, the pretty dress?'

'Ismene.'

'And why, for what occasion, had you made yourself so beautiful?'

I was facing him. He was supposed to put his arms around Antigone. So he had to put his arms around me. I guided him. He opened his arms and I took refuge there. Murmurs in the room. Marwan said something in Arabic. Nakad froze.

'My father is explaining to the others that you are playing the role of the woman.'

I nodded to him.

'Don't worry about that. Go back to your text.'

He paused, took a breath.

'For what occasion had you made yourself so beautiful?'

'I'll tell you. Oh, my darling, I was so silly. An entire evening wasted. A beautiful evening ...'

Marwan was translating for his friends. He was uncomfortable. His son had his arms around a man, a stranger under his roof.

'We will have other evenings, Antigone.'

'Perhaps not.'

I withdrew slowly from his embrace. Nakad stood with his arms open. And I applauded. I walked around the room, clapping, looking at each of Marwan's guests. And they all stood. Marwan first, encouraging the others. And then his companions. And his wife, behind the door, and the hidden children. Nakad recited his text poorly, but he had mastered it. I shook his hand, one way of undoing the effect of the hug.

'You learned your role by heart?'

He took three steps back.

'Antigone! Antigone! Help!'

And he took off his turban.

'Isn't that my last line?'

I nodded. First my Antigone, now my Haemon existed.

Marwan couldn't see what made this play interesting, but he had offered up his son. I was deeply moved by this revelation. My friend had his back to me. He was explaining to his guests that a woman would play my role. That the kiss would thus be normal. And also that his son's character was a man in love, courageous, noble, who preferred to die with his beloved rather than live without her.

Haemon was a fighter, a resistant who took a stand against the tyrant who oppressed his people. He explained that Nakad had the best role, the greatest of all. That he embodied the example of hope, of life. That in this play he would die for love of liberty and justice. And also for the love of a woman, as beautiful as the women of their mountains. He said that his son played the Druze. The only one among them with a soul and a beating heat.

I put my hand on his shoulder.

15

SIMONE

I was the first to arrive at the theatre on Wednesday, 24 February 1982, at 7 am. Sixty minutes before the ceasefire. The Ring was deserted, the killers asleep. Marwan had driven without a word. He was enraged. He had begged me not to try anything outside the pact. He swore that the rifles would not sleep before the agreed-upon time. But I needed this clandestine dawn. I needed to be alone in the theatre, to walk alone on the stage, do the voice check alone. So he consented to drive me.

About a hundred metres from the Sodeco intersection, the Druze told me to get out of the car. And he left me there, at the line. A deserted street in a time of rubble. In every direction, grey buildings destroyed by machine-gun fire, twisted metal beams, hills of concrete assailed by weeds. He left me with my hands in the air, a strip of white cloth tied around one arm.

After three steps, I froze. A harsh shout behind me. Another, right in front of me. Men's voices, an echo. A threat among the silent stones. Day was breaking. I was in Joseph-Boutros' sights. In the scope of the militiaman of the Risk tower. In the sights of the Shiite on Damas Street. I knew that fingers were hesitating, stroking the curved steel of the trigger. Never in my life had I felt so mortal. My head high, my mouth open, I walked forward like one surrendering. I stumbled into the war. I watched the windows. I stepped over decorative reliefs bruised by flying steel. I advanced step by step through broken glass. I had stopped breathing. I stared at the lunar facade of the Beaufort theatre across the street. I was struggling. I showed neither fear nor hostility. I was one of the dim shadows that rifles tire of following.

I entered the building from the west side of the Line. Everything was ransacked and superb. No doors. A hole in the facade, blasted open by an RPG. The sign swung above the floor, hanging from electric wires. Only three walls. The fourth had been blown out. An explosion had torn off the roof. It was a sky-topped arena, a theatre open to lions. Bullets could rip a path to the heart of each actor. Four rows of seats had been spared by munitions. They were covered in velvet and grey dust. The other seats were crushed under roofbeams. The movie screen had been torn, but the set was there, just as Sam had promised, intact, in a corner of the stage.

'You'll be amazed when you see it,' he had told me.

He had misrepresented nothing. I could hardly breathe. My leg quit on me. I sat on a pile of stones to contemplate the set. Three Corinthian columns, upright on their pedestals, with crowns of acanthus leaves. They were plaster, dyed a worn rose colour, imitation porphyria. The stage designer had carved them with care. He had sculpted a frieze of vegetables on the cornice and worn down the high relief just as time would have.

'You'll see, it's the temple of Zeus,' the Greek had said with a smile.

A fourth column lay on the ground, intentionally broken, across a flight of stairs that led to a trompe-l'oeil door.

Sam had spent an hour in the theatre, sitting almost where I sat, without authorization from the militias, studying this abbreviated peristyle. Marwan had told him about it. In the early days of this civil war, a Cypriot theatre group had been rehearsing Aristophanes' *Lysistrata*. The story of the beautiful Athenian woman who proposes that her sisters and the wives of Sparta refuse the act of love to their husbands as long as they remain at war. When the first tracer bullets flew over the building, workmen were installing the set. The entire stage was meant to be surrounded by columns, but fighting stopped the show. The actors, the set designer and his men fled the building under gunfire. Like the captain of a ship, the director refused to leave the stage. Lebanese soldiers had to drag him out of the building by force. The press reported that he went half-mad. That he struggled against them, crying in rage and distress, that he screamed the words of Lysistrata, 'To stop the war, refuse yourselves to your husbands!' into the streets. The reporter from *L'Orient-Le Jour* faithfully transcribed his words. That's all Beirut heard of the play.

The theatre had no windows. Mortar shells had made it their work to create windows everywhere, opening doors and carving out terraces. But the set had been spared. Shells of every calibre had hit the back wall. Some had pocked the grey stucco steps, two columns had been grazed. I stood up. I ran my fingers over the first one, barely speckled with shrapnel. With one hand on the column's glazed flutes, I knew that Lysistrata offered its glory to Creon. These columns, these three steps, would be the palace of his pride.

I pulled out Sam's notebook, my pen. He had asked me not to call him, ever. He wanted me to write. To write everything. My impression, my fears, the beautiful and the ugliest things. He didn't want a distant voice over the phone. So I wrote.

To dress this set, I would need a red drape across the back, from the tympanum to the base of the columns. One that would cover part of the stage, die at the actors' feet. This space would hold the power. Creon, Antigone, Haemon, Ismene, Eurydice, the guards would each have their place, seated on the steps, immobile when the curtain rose and light blasted into the rubble.

In one corner of the stage, a mortar shell had ploughed through everything. Ripped away carpet, parquet, concrete, exposing the red earth beneath. Its trajectory flowed all the way to the front row of seats, leaving a sinister pile, the sand and dirt that would be the site of Antigone's forfeit. There, at the spectator's feet, she would dig her own grave by offering a sepulchre for her disavowed brother.

Daylight found me. I raised my eyes to the sky. It was almost 8 o'clock. I was numb with cold. I climbed the battered stairs to the stage. I examined the theatre, the soiled seats. The ceiling scattered across the floor.

'You'll need to sweep up a bit,' Sam had said.

I didn't think so. I wanted to preserve the debris of this world. I imagined Antigone covered with dust. And Creon in his palace of wind.

I put on Sam's kippah. He wanted the Chorus to be played with a head-covering, to honour his people. Whether it was Sam or me was unimportant. His father's skullcap should mingle with the keffiyeh, turban, fez, the cross and the crescent. So that Salonika would be there, too, in this place, on that same night, in front of everyone.

'You will be the Jew,' he had said to me.

I replied that I wasn't brave enough. A velvet cap doesn't make a man Jewish.

'You ask too many questions. A character is a character. This is how I see the Chorus, and you are the one who must become it.'

'The Chorus is partly the observer, the one watching. Aren't you worried about being perceived as the Jew making remarks about the plot, as an outsider?' Imane had asked him.

'Would you prefer he do it as an insider?'

I never knew what had happened between the two of them. But something had happened. He spoke of her with emotion, she of him with sadness. In one photo, she's looking at the camera, and he's looking at her, with an ardour that is unmistakable. This image is unusual, shot inside a room. Imane has her arm in his, laughing. She's not wearing a veil.

'Mr Samuel?'

A white-haired woman entered the hall through a break in the stone, both hands loaded with bags. She wore a white armband.

I quickly removed the kippah, gripping it in my hand.

'I am Simone, Mr Samuel.'

'My name is George, madam.'

She looked me over with suspicion.

'So you're not Samuel.'

I said no. Explained that he was ill. She extended her hand to me.

'There's no reason to be ashamed of your religion, you know.'

I put the kippah in my pocket.

'It's just a theatre prop, nothing else.'

She observed me with a smile. Then looked around.

'I was the usher in this theatre in 1975.'

She was wearing a gold cross and a grey coat.

'Joseph-Boutros sent me,' she said.

I nodded.

'He assured me that on the day of the play I might be useful.'

An usher. I thought about Victor Hugo recited by a murderer. About the absurdity of war. We were going to perform Anouilh crushed in ruins, with an usher taking care of us. Who would greet the spectator at the door. Would escort him to his seat among the bruised stones, shell casings and broken glass.

'You'll be at the east entrance?' I asked.

'Yes, at the Sodeco door.'

She explained that we would need someone at the west entrance to greet those arriving from the other camp. That she couldn't manage both. Then she put her canvas bags in a corner. She went up to the front row, covered a seat with a piece of cloth and sat down without a word, covering her legs with a light blanket.

The public could not attend this meeting, the combatants had agreed. Only the actors and I had the right to enter the theatre. When I looked at her, Simone smiled. She raised her arm and waved her hand, revealing her armband, the signal agreed on by both camps for our gathering.

'Don't worry, they know I'm here.'

And she opened her bag and drank a bottle of water.

Her presence bothered me yet reassured me. This woman was completely at home. She acted like she owned the place. So I decided to be her guest. I sat down in the seat next to her, facing the desolate stage. She had taken out her embroidery, an unusual design with tones of blue, along with needles and thread. Two people lost in a fog of frost. One facing away, the other looking towards us. The face was a white blur.

'Do you know Elie Kanaan?' Simone asked me.

No. I didn't know him.

'He's one of the greatest painters in our country,' she went on without looking up from her work.

She worked using a running stitch, lending her thread to the grace of the design.

'I was inspired by one of his paintings. Two women waiting. Waiting for who knows what.'

'In your opinion?'

She stitched and stitched, tightly, pushing up her glasses each time they slid.

'What are they waiting for? Other than death, I have no idea.'

Simone would have made a beautiful Eurydice, bent over her tapestry, without a glance beyond its frame.

'Why death?'

'Because one leaves life no other way.'

She sewed. I re-read the lines of the Chorus.

'Death took my grandson. He was in Damour in February 1976.'

She looked up.

'You know about Damour?'

I nodded.

'But not Elie Kanaan?

'But not Elie Kanaan.'

'For a moment there I thought you knew nothing about us.'

'I know what happened at Damour.'

'No. Don't say that. You don't know. No one knows what a massacre is. They only talk about the blood of the dead, never the laughter of the assassins. They don't see their eyes at the moment they kill. They don't hear them chanting victory on their way home. They don't talk about their wives, who brandish their bloodied shirts on balcony after balcony, like rows of flags.

Simone worked her blues patiently. She attacked the upper right corner, a dark night that paled towards the sea, to azure, then royal blue, then paler, to white.

'His name was Maroun. He was our angel. His throat was slit.'

I watched the needle, the wool. I wondered if the others would come.

'He was with the Lebanese Forces?'

Simone raised her needle and shook her head.

'He was eighteen months old, Mr George.'

A young man entered the theatre at that exact moment, rescuing me from drowning and too many wrong words. He came from the east. Two armed Phalangists accompanied him. They stayed at the doorway.

'Noon,' the Christian said before they turned to leave.

As I stood to greet him, I kissed Simone's shoulder. She was surprised. I found no other gesture to express compassion.

Creon was the first of my troupe. He approached me, unsmiling.

'Charbel.'

He shook my hand like a man who fears nothing. He was what his photo had shown. Tall, hardened and disquieting, yet with the eyes of a child. We'd need talcum powder for the hair, pencil to darken around the eyes, the pallor of a sovereign.

'Thank you for what you have done.'

'What I've done?'

'Coming to the Barakat house to convince my brother.'

He kept my hand in his.

'You were courageous.'

Then he inspected the hall wordlessly, hands in his pockets, turning slowly on his heels.

'You've been here before?'

He spat on the ground.

'No one's been in here for seven years.'

He went up to the seats, walked along the walls, stumbled on a beam. He made his way to the stage like a runner checking the course, walking with long strides from one side to the other. Instinctively he recognized his palace. The steps, the colonnades, the torn parquet floor.

'We could hang a curtain here,' Creon conjectured, pointing at the pockmarked wall.

'That's the plan,' I answered.

He looked at me. He smiled for the first time. He sat on the edge of the stage, his feet dangling in the air. He checked his watch.

'The Progressivists are late,' Charbel joked.

Simone laughed. The young man greeted her with a raised hand, the way an actor thanks his audience. Then he pulled a copy of *Antigone* from his khaki jacket and began reading to himself.

Imane arrived from the west, a white scarf over her forehead. Ismene and the Nurse entered the ruin with my Antigone. The Palestinian knew them both, the Chaldean and the Armenian. I had made her my messenger. In less than two hours they had agreed to appear on stage. As soon as she walked in, Imane took off her armband. She was tense. Charbel noticed her action and removed his own. I did the same, slipped the strip of fabric into my pocket. And the two actresses copied us. We left the war at the door of our theatre.

Simone rose when the three women entered. The usher was greeting them.

The Christian came down from the stage, wiping his hand on his trousers. Greeting him, I'd felt sweat chilling his palm. Like his brother, the sweat of emotion. Imane and Charbel were face to face. They had recognized each other instinctively as Antigone and Creon. Without me introducing them, the two actors knew.

'Charbel,' the Christian spoke, his hand on his heart.

'Imane,' the Palestinian said, extending hers.

The young man shook his head with a smile. He accepted the tendered hand.

'Pardon me. I didn't think a Sunni would shake a man's hand.'

'I didn't know a Phalangist would ask forgiveness,' Imane replied.

'I'm a Maronite, not a Phalangist.'

Imane introduced me to Yevgenia the Armenian and Madeleine the Chaldean.

'You can shake their hands,' she told Charbel.

'You are the pride of Oedipus,' the boy interjected.

Imane smiled. Then breathed in, tense, her hands curled to fists at her sides. She lowered her head, searching deep within herself for an expression that was not her own. Charbel understood what the young woman was doing. He imitated her. I stopped breathing. The girl raised her head. The boy opened different eyes. The moment was magnificent. Two actors taking the measure of each other. Not Christian or Sunni or Lebanese or Palestinian. Two characters. Antigone and Creon. She taunted him. He defied her. She would go as far as her own death. He would go as far as killing her. They stood motionless, their bodies arched forward, towards each other, holding each other's gaze, wordless. Simone clasped her hand to her mouth. The other women froze in place. Suddenly, Imane burst out laughing.

'That's a good start,' the Christian smiled.

'You started without me?'

Nakad had slipped through an opening in the west wall, breaking the spell. Marwan's son was dressed like a young man of his times. Vexing his father a bit, I had explained that Haemon could not play Antigone's fiancé wearing the traditional baggy pants.

'Then no one will know he's a Druze?'

I compromised. I had agreed to the tarboosh with the turban.

Right after he came in, the Shiites entered from Damas street. This time, Imane did not extend her hand. They introduced themselves timidly, one after the other. And also the old woman, who remained behind them.

'We have bottles of water and blankets,' Simone called out to them.

I rubbed my hands together. I didn't expect it to be so cold. It was daylight. A pale sun encouraged the sky. I looked at my troupe. They were all there. And all looking at me.

'I suggest we get on stage, and address each other informally.'

Reaching into my bag, I pulled out the large photo of the dress rehearsal of *Antigone* at the Théâtre de l'Atelier in Paris, on 4 February 1944. This image was my stage plan. I seated Antigone alone, at the far left side of the stage. Creon sat in the middle, in a seat torn from its row. Next to him, the page took his place. Haemon, Ismene and the Nurse each stood on a step, from bottom to top. I had found a comfortable chair for old Eurydice. The two guards stood towards the back of the stage, beneath the columns. I had them pass the photo around as Simone offered everyone blankets.

'A gift from the Christians of Mount Lebanon,' Charbel commented.

'Very touching,' Nakad answered.

Except for the two Shiites, all my actors spoke fluent French. Nimer and Hussein had difficulty, resorting to Arabic for a recalcitrant word. But Nabil, their half-brother, had spent part of his childhood in Belgium.

'That dress rehearsal and this meeting have much in common.'

My voice was shaking. My hands, too. I was moved. Imane helped me with her eyes.

'Today is 24 February. The photo was taken on the fourth of this same month, thirty-eight years ago.'

The old Shiite disappeared under the Phalangist blanket.

'Are you cold? They were cold, too. That night, the male actors wore tuxedos and the women, ball gowns, but they had sweaters and ski pants under their costumes.

Jean Davy, who played Creon, wore his dress coat. The audience was shivering. And you know why?'

'Because it was winter,' Nakad answered.

'Because it was war.'

I looked at my actors one after the other.

'That's two things in common.'

I told them about it. The unheated theatre, the lighting rigged with a set of mirrors to reflect daylight onto the stage. The air-raid alerts, the audience heading down into shelters two, three, four times during the play.

'Anouilh hadn't managed to negotiate a truce?' Nakad inquired.

'My brother wasn't there to help him,' Charbel responded with a smile.

'*Ma khalas!* That's enough!' Imane interrupted.

Nakad rolled his eyes spitefully. Charbel raised a hand. Two schoolboys.

I pulled a folded paper from my pocket. Over several days, even though I hadn't quite believed it would happen, I had scripted today's meeting as carefully as I could. I had to get back on schedule. Not let the young men take over. Within these walls, I wanted no more Imane, Charbel or Nakad. Only Antigone, Creon and Haemon had the right to breathe.

'First and foremost, I bring you the fraternal greeting of Samuel Akounis, my friend and brother. Some of you know him well, others not. That doesn't matter. You all know who he is.'

The actors were looking at me, protected by their blankets. Only Imane had relinquished hers, folded next to her.

'This play is him. It's his idea. It's his life. He chose all of you, and he chose me. Always remember that he is with us. Even trapped in his hospital bed, he remains your director. This play will be dedicated to your country, to peace, and to Samuel Akounis.'

'Are you also a Jew?'

I was expecting this question, but not from Imane. Simone was watching me.

'No.'

'Are you a Christian?' Charbel intoned.

'I am French.'

'Can you say, "no, I am only French"?'

'I am also French.'

Charbel crossed his arms, looking self-satisfied.

'Why this interrogation?'

It was Madeline, the Nurse, who asked the question. She continued.

'When we arrived here, we took off our armbands. I propose that we also leave our religions behind, our names, our camps. We are actors.'

The woman stood. She was older than the others.

'I am the Nurse. I have taken care of Ismene and Antigone since they were babies. I love them both, equally. That's all.'

'I am Ismene,' the Armenian began, following her lead. 'I am pretty and shallow. I don't have my sister's courage, her strength, or her faith. And I love life.'

Applause from all the others.

I sat down on a stair. I let them go on. I felt feverish.

'I am Haemon. And I am not Druze,' Nakad said, smiling.

He put the white fez on his head, rolling the turban slowly around it. A whistle of admiration, some laughter.

'I am the son of Creon and I am in love with Antigone. We will soon be married. I am ready to die for her. In fact, I will die for her.'

Applause.

Nabil stood next. He spoke for his brothers, his fists clenched in front of him.

'We are Creon's guards. We protect his law. The questions that men ask themselves are not ours. We carry out our orders to earn higher rank. If we must kill for that, we will kill.'

A moment of awkward silence, then a shy clap. Nabil's expression, his voice and his gestures had spoken of issues beyond Thebes.

Simone passed among us with cups of water and sandwiches. I wrote in Sam's notebook. This day was brimming with content. I had to make sure none of it was lost, I had to get it all down.

Khadijah motioned, raising her hand to speak. She said a few words, holding her veil with her other hand. An embarrassed look from Nabil.

'My aunt says she is here because Sheik Mamâar al-Sadeq asked her to come.'

'Did she realize she was going to be in a play?'

The young man translated my question. She replied meekly. And all the actors burst out laughing.

'She knows she has to knit sweaters for us.'

I turned to Nabil.

'Will you translate for me?'

The guard approached Eurydice. And I spoke.

'You are the wife of Creon. During the entire play, you knit sweaters for the poor of Thebes. Since your son dies because of your husband, you will kill yourself.'

More laughter. The old Shiite said she didn't want to die. She said no one had the right to kill themselves. That I hadn't dared to say all that when I had come to ask permission from the religious authorities.

She took the blanket off her knees. She stood with a sigh.

The three brothers stood also.

'She wants to leave,' Nabil proclaimed.

I walked over to her. My heart stopped. A driver was coming to pick them up after this meeting to take them back to Nabatieh. I had paid for the trip. There was no one waiting outside. Without these four actors, the play couldn't happen. Nabil was still translating, in a low and serious voice. I explained that we don't see Eurydice's death. That she doesn't kill herself in front of us. It was the Chorus, it was I, who told Creon. All she had to do was knit. Nothing else. I spoke, she answered. She said that to play a woman who kills herself was to become that woman. It was tricking others by taking on an appearance that was not one's own. It was an insult to God.

I inhaled all the air around me. I closed my eyes.

'Eurydice will not die. Translate!'

I blurted that out, surprised at my own words. Nabil looked at me.

'I tell her that?'

'Eurydice will not die, tell her.'

'And Antigone makes it out alive, too?' Charbel teased.

I waved him off brusquely.

'Everything in its own time.'

'My aunt wants your word on this,' the Shiite claimed.

'She has it.'

'No, you have to say it to her face.'

The old woman looked at me with fear in her eyes. I bowed down, looking right at her, holding her gaze. She raised her veil.

'Madam, I give you my word of honour that Eurydice, wife of Creon and mother of Haemon, will not take her own life.'

While her nephew translated, she watched my lips without understanding my words. When I bowed a second time, she nodded and sat back down in her chair, with her nephew's help.

I didn't dare meet Imane's laughing eyes, but I felt her gaze on me. I consulted my notes the way a lost traveller reads a map upside down. I had just betrayed Anouilh to avoid displeasing a devotee of Ali, cousin and son-in-law of the Prophet. I had to interrupt the silence that followed. I looked to Imane for help. But it was Charbel who came to my rescue.

'My name is Creon. I am King of Thebes. I had two nephews, Eteocles and Polynices, both dead for no reason in an absurd fight. They were hooligans, condemned men who had each tried to assassinate their father, Oedipus. To preserve my family's honour, I lied to my people. I told them Polynices was a good-for-nothing and Eteocles a fine man. For Eteocles I organized national funeral honours. I refused even a sepulchre for Polynices, threatening death to whoever tried to bury him.'

I applauded Charbel. I was moved by Joseph-Boutros' brother. He had read the play. He had understood the stakes. And, most importantly, he left it to Imane to explain her own role.

'My name is Imane. I am Palestinian. My ancestors lived in Jaffa. I am going to play the role of Antigone, the one who says no. Who refuses orders, directions, advice. She who does not wrap herself in a blanket as the others do. Who does not answer questions as the others do. Who wants her brother to be buried in the earth and not abandoned to the dogs. Who will scrape the ground with her nails to cover his body as ritual demands. Who will say to the king, to her uncle, to Creon, this weak man, that she does not fear him. Who will refuse to conceal the truth from the people of Thebes. Who will scream that it is she, Antigone, Imane the Palestinian, who wanted to bury her brother in his native soil. She who will refuse her own happiness with Haemon. Life with all the others. And who will choose death over disloyalty.'

Nothing, this time. Not a sound in the wounded room. Imane stood still. Head high, scowling, her mouth slightly open, she was shivering. That's when Charbel moved towards her. He picked up the blanket from the ground and covered her shoulders with the gift that she did not want.

'I am not a Phalangist,' the young Christian repeated.

She pulled the blanket around her. She smiled at me, so I applauded. I stood up from the bottom step and congratulated my actors. All of them. One after the other. I praised their temerity. No warrior hidden behind a rifle sight, nowhere in the city, would ever have their courage. I loved them as though the curtain had just fallen, hiding the audience that hailed our triumph.

* * *

In February 1944, on the evening of the dress rehearsal, a deadly silenced followed the final words of the Chorus. 'One minute, maybe two,' the actors said. An eternity without a sound from the audience, not a cough, not a squeaking chair. Devastated, assembled behind the curtain, the actors whispered to each other. Some of them had tears in their eyes. No one had believed in this play.

'Twenty performances, that will take us to the end of the world,' Anouilh had said.

'Only if they happen,' his director replied.

After the war, the playwright explained that the idea of adapting *Antigone* had come to him in the summer of 1941, when he first saw the red Nazi posters on the walls of Paris. On 27 August, in Versailles, the worker Paul Collet, aged twenty-one, had opened fire on Pierre Laval and Marcel Déat, henchmen for the collaborators. The same day, in retaliation, five hostages arrested for participating in a Communist demonstration were executed by firing squad at Mont Valérien. Roger-Henry Nogarède, Alfred Ottino, André Sigonney, Raymond Justice and Jean-Louis Rapinat. The youngest was twenty years old, the oldest only thirty-four. And when he saw the announcement of their execution, the word *'Bekanntmachung'* in black letters on blood, Jean Anouilh remembered the little rebel girl put to death for having thrown a grain of dust on an iron-fisted law. Like her, Collett had acted alone. Absolutely, on his own initiative. Tortured at rue de Saussaies by the Gestapo, he gave up nothing but his own name.

The writer then modernized Sophocles' drama, risking everything. When German censors gave him the green light, the underground press went wild, denouncing a play that encouraged collaboration. To them, Creon opposing Antigone was Montoire versus the Resistance. Revolt crushed by law. Others, the large majority, saw the opposite – Antigone as the incarnation of refusal. By offering up her life, she condemned Creon to the solitude of lost men. Her death would be his downfall. She transformed his realm into a hotbed of rage. She decimated the family of the executioner, leaving him alone, with three guards who would soon kill him, after praising the first man to offer them a bribe.

In the shadows behind the curtain, everyone thought the same thing. This play should never have been staged. The terrible impression that a wall now separated them from the audience. The fourth wall. It truly existed. In concrete, in steel, snuffing out the barest breath of life. Letting nothing in from beyond it. Leaving them alone on stage, abandoned. As if the theatre had abruptly closed in on them. A roof, four ramparts. For one full minute, they felt walled in.

And then the audience started screaming and shouting. With intense joy, filled with tears and 'bravos'. The curtain rose. It was chaos. People were standing on their seats, their arms in the air, to applaud Antigone the rebel even louder.

At the time of that ovation in the Théâtre de l'Atelier, the twenty-two men on the other Red Poster, the one of Missak Manouchian, Joseph Boczov and his foreign comrades had been detained by the Nazis for nearly three months. Seventeen days later, on 21 February 1944, they fell before a firing squad. 'I don't know why I'm dying,' Antigone said. 'I am dying as a soldier of the French Liberation Army,' Manouchian answered her.

* * *

That's when Hussein began to speak. Slowly, in Arabic. The page, looking straight at me. Khadijah, the old Shiite, nodded her head and clapped her hands slowly, to encourage him, the way one does at a children's play.

'Hussein says he doesn't agree. That the Palestinian has broken our agreement.'

Nabil was translating. Imane stared at him, her eyes blazing.

'My brother says that he came because this woman is Antigone. He understood that she was acting out the big scene of Antigone defying the law for us, but here, being more than the role is not an option. Otherwise, he also must revert to his real identity.'

The page was speaking. I hadn't recognized the toughness behind the mask of his child-like face.

'My name is Hussein Al-Sadeq,' said his brother. 'My life is threatened by Palestinian Wahhabites, who claim the land of my ancestors as their own, a "Fatah-land". They behave like conquering invaders, threatening our fathers, leaving our restaurants without paying, not waiting in line, stealing our cars and our bread. If Arafat accuses Israel of stealing Palestine from him, I accuse the Palestinians of moving into a country that is not their own.'

The old Shiite was still clapping with the rhythm of her grand-nephew's words.

'So let's stop this, please. I said I was the page of Creon, not the son of a humiliated people. Imane is only Antigone. If she is here, it's because she took refuge in the theatre, not because she lives in a refugee camp. That's why my brother and I came. We all wear the masks of tragedy. They make it possible for us to be together. If we take them off, we put our armbands back on, and the war.'

Everything stopped. Total silence. We were back in the ruins.

'Imane?'

The Palestinian gave me a look. She shrugged her narrow shoulders.

'I am Antigone. It is Antigone who is here today.'

I nodded to her respectfully. I took a breath.

'Thank you both.'

Then I clapped my hands, like a schoolmaster setting off the clamour of the end of class. The Christian militiamen were at the door. Marwan kept his eye on us through a hole in the wall. The old Shiite stroked her nephew's forehead. Simone kissed my hands. Imane gathered her things, isolated and tense. All this was so fragile. My head was spinning. One wrong word, or gesture, or expression and everyone goes back to war.

I passed my notebook around so that everyone with a phone could add their number, and I gave them mine. They could call me any time.

'We've finished our introductions. First rehearsal on Friday 4 June, somewhere easier to get to. That's in four months. Basically, tomorrow. So learn your lines. Thank you, everyone. *Chokrane*. And good luck between now and then …'

16

ESHKOL COHEN

Aurora and Louise were waiting beyond the sliding doors of the airport. It wasn't my wife or my daughter that I was coming back to, it was my entire life. From before. I felt it. I had sensed it as I boarded the plane that would take me back to their peace. Flying over Beirut, my forehead pressed to the window, I was overcome by grief. I no longer understood why I was going back. Why I wasn't staying, helping all of them rehearse. Showing them gestures, expressions. Crossing the line for Charbel, the countryside for Nabil, correcting Nakad who declaimed with great sighs, finding quiet refuge in Imane's smile. I had no reason to allow myself a truce. I was wasting time. To counter those thoughts, I told myself I was coming back for Sam.

My stomach was in knots the entire flight. I looked at the photo I always carried. Aurora and me, our daughter between us. I loved these people's smiles. The father, the mother, the child. They seemed both familiar and foreign. The father, especially. He was sparkling with happiness, his two forever women. His world limited by the boundaries of their skin. He was coming back from afar. He had felt the leather of life, its harshness, its vulnerable passions, and walked away. Those two smiles sufficed to fuel his own. A family, a job, an apartment, a car, love to give, to take, the sweetness of the long shadows of summer nights. After fighting for so long, side by side with others, hoping together, suffering together, he had left the fight without a word. Certain the world would go on without him. He had forgotten his own rage. His fist had become an open palm. I ran my finger across my face as a father, over my wife's eyes, my child's hair. I'd cut the photo into an oval to fit in my wallet. It already looked like a memory. In my hand, those three people looked like the portraits in chipped frames forgotten on tombstones. Like the eternal smiles that mask the dead.

Aurora was wearing the red dress I liked. Louise had a butterfly painted on her cheek. In the car they were humming.

'Mama, Papa,' Louise babbled, kicking her feet.

'Papa came home,' crooned her mother, one hand on the wheel, the other on my thigh.

I tapped the beat with one finger, smiling. I didn't speak.

'Tell me everything about Beirut,' Aurora had asked.

'It's hard. But I'll get there. Let's talk about something else for now.'

With my backpack on, I had said only that. Aurora had looked me in the eye. No. She didn't want to talk about anything else. It was the first time that life had separated us. She had been afraid, for herself, for Louise, for me, the first day and every day that followed. She had wondered what state the war would leave me in. So she demanded to know everything. To hear it all. She wanted me to tell her about the actors and the city. She wanted Antigone, the theatre, the Green Line, the colour of the sky. To take me back, she had to know what I had left behind. She was hungry for Imane, Charbel, all the others. She wanted to feed on me. Since my departure, she'd taught her classes, protected our child, kept vigil through her difficult nights. She'd gone to the market, bought milk, mineral water. She'd sought out Sunday activities in the winter sun. She'd spent time with her mother, a few friends. She'd watched my war on television. She'd scoured headlines for the word 'Beirut'. She had waited all this time, waited. She had counted the hours, the days, hardly slept. She'd been wracked with worry. A pink pityriasis marked her worried skin from the nape of her neck to her waist, colouring her chest and her back. She'd imagined me dead. Or unfaithful. Leaving her for someone else, a combatant with no children, no bus to take or half-baguette to pick up on a normal evening. Loving that stranger as I had loved her the first night we met. My feminist, my warrior, my Breton. She woke up numb, hating me for having succumbed. Lying on the ground with my arms splayed, or in other arms, not hers. Either way, in the morning I was lost to her.

'Papa came home,' my wife crooned.

She watched me out of the corner of her eye. Something was wrong. She could tell. I sought Marwan's hands, on his steering wheel. The Druze rosary missing from the rearview mirror. And the music, the tension, the Ring, the line closing in. Even distant gunfire. Imane, I missed her too. I opened my window to breathe in the winter air. My wife's voice, strained.

'You have a child in the back seat, remember?'

I remembered. I rolled up the window and closed my eyes.

* * *

When Doctor Cohen saw me in the corridor, he came to greet me, his hand like a smile.

'So here's the man who's going to end the war in Lebanon?'

Sam had told him. *Antigone,* to be performed unarmed in a city where other hands strangled. I walked with him past the nurses' station, lowering my head again. Before he opened the door to the room, the doctor looked at me. My pallor, my anxiety.

'Sam has lost ground, but he's fighting.'

He was asleep. He looked dead. His face was yellow. The tip of his nose, his chin, some of his fingers were almost black. His breathing sounded like the heavy bellows of a forge. His entire body was pierced with tubes. My leg was shaking. I was freezing.

The doctor stood behind me.

'Can he hear me?'

'Yes, of course. You'll be able to speak to him.'

I leaned over him.

'Sam?'

The man put his hand on my shoulder.

'Wait until he wakes up.'

He pulled up a chair for me, then left the room, closing the door quietly behind him. So I sat down, my knees against the bed frame. My friend had lost weight. A metal armature rose above his chest to support the weight of the blanket and the sheet. On the bedside table, *Libération* announced Lebanese rockets had struck Israel. A strand of amber *komboloi* lay on the newspaper. A Greek rosary for my Jewish friend. Another visitor who had done what he could. I smiled. Sam was dreaming. He moaned softly with every breath, as if the air were wounding him. He had a phlegmy cough. The heart monitor accelerated madly, sounding out his pulse. He inhaled violently, like someone on the verge of drowning. He moved his hand, his finger imprisoned by the pulse monitor. And then he opened his eyes, slowly. Without moving his head, he looked at the ceiling, the wall, the window. When his gaze landed on me, he hesitated. He was lost. His eyes met mine without greeting them. I raised a hand, as one would on a railway platform.

'*Ahlan wa sahlam*, Sam.'

He smiled. Then closed his eyes. When he came back, I found a trace of him. My Sam, my Greek, my brother. I leaned over him. In his eyes there was sadness and silence. He was contemplating something beyond this room. He was watching death at work.

'Tell me.'

It wasn't a voice, barely a sigh.

He focused on me from afar.

So I told him. I took his notebook from my pocket and I read, I mimed, I recreated every gesture, every colour, every smell. A nurse came in to rearrange his pillows. He wasn't quite sitting up or entirely lying down. He looked at me. He smiled. Opened his mouth for a question that wouldn't come. I told him about Marwan, crossing the line, Nabathieh and the Shiite brothers, the fortress of Joseph-Boutros, the killer at the Sodeco intersection. I described the theatre, our theatre. I introduced him to Simone, to her slaughtered child, the ghosts of Damour. I imitated Sheik Mamâar al-Sadeq, turning my back brusquely to speak only to the wall. I acted out Khadijah's fear of Eurydice's suicide. I declaimed Haemon in Nakad's voice, playing the role of his life. And he looked at me like a child at play. His eyes sparkled, laughed, enjoying it all.

'And Imane?'

The same breath of a voice.

I talked about Shatila, about Mahmoud Darwish, the children reciting such beauty surrounded by garbage.

'But Imane? Imane, did you see her?'

I think I blushed. I managed to say a few words. She would be a very beautiful Antigone. She was more refined than the others, more intelligent, eager for life.

Sam kept looking at me. I stopped talking. He waited. And then a slight shrug of his shoulders. A weariness.

'Does Aurora know?'

'Aurora?'

I answered too quickly, confused. Aurora? There's nothing for Aurora to know. There is nothing to know, anyway. After our rehearsal, I took her home to Shatila. So what? What harm was there in having taken her hand in the dark? I simply told her that her presence was moving.

'The French are sensitive to emotion?' she had asked me.

'Yes,' I answered, 'Not all, but some.'

'And what does that mean, to be moving? Explain it.'

I told her what I knew about her. Her elegance with the children, among the actors. I told her that her face was sad and beautiful. Her expression. I told her that her hands were very pale.

'Are you married?'

Yes. To a loving woman. And also that I had a child. A little girl who laughed out loud.

'Then you must not speak of my face, my expression, or my hands,' Imane had replied.

I withdrew mine, still between her fingers.

'Don't play around with her, or with any of them,' Sam murmured.

He was exhausted. He closed his eyes.

'I set up your meeting with Antigone, not with Imane.'

I was furious with him. There was no reason for reproach. Nothing had happened. I was also furious with myself. The Palestinian's face leaned over mine day and night. She haunted my every hour. I felt like I was cheating.

'Swear to me,' Samuel said, his eyes closed.

I came even closer, my mouth a breath from his lips.

'Swear to me to perform Antigone, to commit to whatever it takes.'

I put my forehead to his, closed my eyes. I took his face, his closed eyes, in my hands.

'I swear to you, Samuel.'

He fell asleep. I left. I leaned against the wall in the corridor. The doctor was waiting near the lift. He moved slowly away from its doors.

'Coffee?'

We left the hospital. He would finish his shift with a house call. He led me across the street, to a nondescript café. I followed him. I don't know why. I had promised Aurora I'd come straight home, that I wouldn't be gone long, because of Louise's winter cough. But I had to atone. I had been obscene with this doctor about Auschwitz, and with the nurses. I had behaved badly and I was paying the price. As we sat by the window, I wondered if he would speak, or if I should.

'We aren't here to lie to each other, right?'

I nodded as I ordered a beer. He ordered a green tea.

'It's reached your friend's liver and his bones. His lungs, his head, his stomach, his ribs and his spine. His bones have become his enemy. We do what we can to keep him comfortable, but morphine doesn't solve everything.'

'Do you have a time frame?'

The doctor looked up.

'Of deliverance?'

I nodded. Deliverance. I would never have come up with that word.

'I don't know. Before the end of the year.'

I looked at him. He sipped his tea, looking towards the hospital.

'Why drag me into a bar to tell me that?'

Doctor Cohen smiled.

'Because that's not all.'

He and Sam had talked a lot. The Greek and the Tunisian. Before foundering, my friend had told him about his life. Salonica, the resistance against the Colonels, his hopes for Palestine, the way a dying man soothes his memories. Week by week, over time, he had become his confidant. And the doctor, his confessor.

Doctor Cohen had also opened up. As a young Zionist, he had joined the ranks of the Betar. And had a wound as a reminder of this commitment. Sam was responsible for that, and I also. The two men had figured that out by chance. That's what he wanted to tell me when he led me across the street.

One evening in April 1974, as a medical student, he had taken part in a demonstration supporting Tsahal, at the Palais de la Mutualité in Paris. On the pavement, in front of the doorway, leftists had painted a large Palestinian flag. The paint was barely dry when he and his comrades arrived to secure the area. The paint cans had been abandoned near a tree, along with the brushes and gloves. That was eight years ago, and the doctor still felt the disgust viscerally. The night before, nine children had been slaughtered at Kiryat Shmona by a Palestinian commando.

'I sat on the pavement for a long time, looking at that flag. I dipped my fingers in the four colours. The black, the green, the white, the red.'

I was looking at the doctor. He avoided my eyes.

'I wondered how it was possible. How men could have painted over the blood of those children.

I wasn't angry. I felt no hate either. I simply could not understand.'

I remembered Samuel, alone among us, imploring us, our conscience.

'I tried to imagine the faces of those people, their voices, their lives. I wondered what they would feel, seeing this sacrilege.'

I was at a loss for words.

'We did that as a reminder of the suffering of a people.'

He looked at me.

'On a day when the other people were dying?'

I think I shrugged my shoulders. A gesture of disdain that I detest.

'We didn't think of it that way.'

'When you were painting the flag, Samuel was holding his father's kippah.'

'Palestine had nothing to do with the annihilation of the Jews of Salonica.'

The doctor lowered his head. 'I know. But you had something to do with the annihilation of nine children.'

I wanted to get up. Doctor Cohen put his hand on my arm.

'It's good, what you're doing in Beirut. Connecting the factions in a shared dream of peace, it's just and it's good. I wanted to tell you that.'

I had the impression he was breaking into our secret.

'And also to tell you that I am relieved. I know now that the people who painted that flag are capable of understanding the pain of others.'

He stood, leaving money between our glasses.

'You have a daughter? Louise, isn't that her name?'

I nodded.

'May God spare you from this, but if the war throws a dead child in your path, mourn it. And honour the martyrs of Kiryat Shmona, please.'

The doctor smiled. He held out his hand. I stood up to take it. Louise filled my heart, and her easy laughter. I held Maroun there, too, Simone's grandson, whose throat was slit at Damour. And the schoolchildren of Shatila reciting exile. There was still much more space to fill.

'Do you promise me?'

'I promise, doctor.'

'And I will pray for your little girl.'

Slowly, the doctor pulled on his winter coat. He was changed, relieved. Taller than at the hospital, more regal, more handsome, too. He hadn't forgiven me, but he had listened. And a golden light followed his movement.

17

THE CHORUS

On 4 June 1982, at noon, my actors took their seats around an oval table covered with a textured white paper tablecloth. In exchange for an ad in the play's programme, and its logo on the publicity posters, the Greek Cultural Centre had given us a large room for the weekend, in a dilapidated building in the Bir Hassan neighbourhood. On one wall, a poster of the Temple of Zeus signalled a welcome to the characters of *Antigone*. Running water had returned to the western part of the city just yesterday, after being cut off for several days. Electricity, too. Imane was at home here. To come to this Friday morning rehearsal, she only had to cross the airport road.

The Shiite actors had arrived the night before. They had spent the night with relatives in Jnah, near the stadium. Marwan had driven me and Nakad, who practised his lines aloud all the way there. Yevgenia and Madeleine came together, as usual. Ismene, coquette, had pulled her hair up, letting a few strands escape across her forehead. The Nurse wore a simple flowered top. I had asked each actor to bring a prop. The Druze had brought his fez in a plastic bag. Imane hid her red hair under a black-and-white keffiyeh.

Seeing the Palestinian disguised as a Fedayeen, Charbel scowled. The previous night, a Palestinian commando had tried to assassinate the Israeli ambassador in London.

'Is this to celebrate that?' the young man snarled.

'It's not a flag, it's a scarf,' Imane replied.

'I should have worn my brother's army jacket, then we'd be even.'

The Christian was in a bad mood. It had been risky for him to cross the line alone at the museum passage. I took over.

'What object did you bring, Charbel?'

The young man had wrapped a silver-handled cane in newspaper. It was also a sword.

'The weakness and all-powerful nature of Creon,' Charbel announced, leaning on it like a harangued old man.

The guards had brought nothing, but each of them had grown a moustache. Exactly the same width, to the edge of a well-groomed goatee.

'It's more discreet than a uniform and it gives the three guards a consistent look,' Nabil explained with a smile. 'But it's not to look Shiite.'

Imane shot him a piercing look. The incident wasn't over yet.

Before we began, I asked them to write down the dates of our next meetings. After these three days of reading, we would meet here again on the 17th, 18th and 19th of September. From Friday to Sunday, since Friday was a public holiday. Then again on the 24th and 25th. The 26th would be the dress rehearsal, closed to the public, in this room. And our one and only performance on 1 October, as planned. We could not rehearse at the Beaufort theatre beforehand. It wasn't safe. Fortunately, the room we were reading in was nearly the same size as the stage. So our rehearsals would be in close to real conditions. We had very little time. I was aware that in another life we would have needed ten times as many meetings, but the war gave us only this opportunity. And we couldn't afford to waste it.

All the actors wrote down the dates on paper. Except Imane. She had scribbled them on the palm of her hand.

'Any questions?'

Yevgenia the Armenian raised her hand.

'I didn't dare ask, but why *Antigone*?'

I was organizing my papers. I stopped.

'Why *Antigone*? What do you mean?

'Lebanon is a country at war and we are not gathered around a text that speaks of peace. No one tries to help anyone and everyone dies at the end, right?'

Imane clapped and laughed.

'It's a play about dignity,' Charbel answered.

'Whose dignity? Creon's or Antigone's?' Nabil asked the question.

I was both happy and somewhat disconcerted by this exchange. I thought this conversation had happened with Sam, that the subject of why had been dealt with. Imane read this text as a call to rebellion. Nakad saw in it a proof of love. Nabil and Nimer interpreted *Antigone* as emblematic of cities deserted by God. For Madeleine,

Anouilh revealed the isolating force of power and the fragility of adolescence.

'Antigone is a girl with no cause but herself,' Hussain cackled in Arabic.

Imane was incensed. Also Nakad, her stage lover. Everyone started talking at once. I raised my arms.

'Samuel loves this text because it was written in the darkest hours of our history. When everything was lost. Each of you can find some strength in that.'

The Nurse nodded. Imane also agreed. I spoke.

'And I, I love the lesson of tragedy that this play offers, the distance it keeps from the banality of drama. Remember what the Chorus teaches us about tragedy. It says that tragedy is clear, calm and straightforward. In drama, with its hordes of innocents, traitors, avengers, it becomes horribly complicated to die. One struggles because one hopes to evade it. That's utilitarian, ignoble. And if one cannot, and succumbs, it's almost by accident. In tragedy, that struggle is pointless. There's no hope. None of the vile hope that ruins everything. Because there's nothing else to try. Tragedy is for kings.'

Nabil smiled. Nimer translated for Hussein, who was having trouble understanding. The Shiites had come without Khadijah, who found it unnecessary to rehearse her stitches – knit, then purl – for three days.

Charbel opened his book. Imane did the same, then Nakad and the others. I noticed all of them had underlined lines, marked paragraphs, turned down pages. They had worked. I had, too. I read a brief introduction.

'And so, I am the Chorus. I come from Ancient Greece. I am what Anouilh retained of Sophocles. I am on the sidelines. I am the narrator. I introduce the characters, I talk about events, I anticipate what's to come. I am both the messenger of death and the voice of reason. I will walk among you but you will pay no attention to me. You speak to the other characters and I speak to the audience. I am the only one to break the fourth wall. The only one to accept the fictional nature of my role. The only one to shatter the illusion. The audience sees me, the actors ignore me. I am on the stage, but marginally. Don't look at me when I speak my lines. Speak at your cue, then freeze. Samuel worked with two technicians who will come from France to set up a follow spot. The character who is speaking has the spotlight. As soon as he finishes, he is a pillar of salt. He remains standing or sits in the shadow. When the curtain rises, you are all there. And at the end, you will be there. The audience must think of chess pieces. They are immobile, then they move, from square to square, propelled by the Chorus and destiny.'

Nakad looked at me, moving his lips. His heart kept telling him he must be Haemon. Imane gazed skyward. Charbel was writing.

'Let's get started. We'll go quickly around the table.'

I asked each of them to tell us briefly about their experience in theatre. And to read a line from the text that best revealed their characters.

Madeleine went first. A Christian from the west, forty years old. For ten years she had taught theatre at the Chaldean Daughters of Mary school. Her repertoire at the school was primarily biblical. Once, only once, she had betrayed the Holy Scriptures by playing Dorine in *Tartuffe*. She blushed as she made this admission.

'Go on, Madeleine.'

'Well, it's near the beginning, when the Nurse surprises Antigone, barefoot, in the morning. The girl has been out all night. She had only gone to honour her brother's corpse, but the Nurse thinks she's secretly met with a boy.'

Madeleine looked at us. She was the first to read, both nervous and proud. She opened her book. She ran her finger along the lines.

THE NURSE

> Act crazy! Act crazy! I know that song. I was a girl before you. And not an easy one either. Hard-headed like you. Where have you been, naughty girl?

Nabil was twenty-eight years old. He and Nimer had acted in a troupe that performed the Iranian rituals of Ta'ziyeh theatre, devoted to the martyrdom of the Iman Hussein, grandson of Mohammed, assassinated in 680 along with seventy-two members of his family. The two brothers played Hussein's companions and died tirelessly alongside him. They acted in their family circle and in village gatherings at the time of Ashura, the bloody holy day that commemorates the massacre.

'Nabil? Which passage did you choose?'

'It's when the guard tells Creon that Polynices' body has been disturbed during the night. He's very afraid of the king. He is careful to avoid blame.

THE GUARD

> The body, chief. Someone has covered it. Oh! Not very much. They didn't have time with us nearby. Just a little dirt ... But enough to hide it from the vultures.

Ismene wanted to become a psychologist. Behavioural problems in war interested her. She had noticed that militia members feared ceasefires, not combat. The young woman had studied classical theatre in high school, then at university. Two years ago, for the Christmas celebration at the French Cultural Centre, she had played the daughter of Minos, King of Crete, in Anouilh's *Léocadia.* Ismene chose lines from the moment she seeks to join Antigone, to share her torment. And gets scolded for it by her sister.

Nakad had never acted. He had joined the group with Marwan's help, when the Druze actor from Shouf deserted the project. Haemon did not read any lines. He preferred to act out his death with high drama, miming the words of the Messenger announcing it to the public. He thrust an imaginary sword into his belly with the ardour of a silent movie. With both hands, and his eyes rolled back.

Charbel had always dreamt of being a movie actor. His heroes were James Coburn and Clint Eastwood. He had often imagined himself next to one or the other of them in a wide, deserted street in the American West, his fingers around the ivoried grip of a Colt. As a child he practised different expressions in the mirror, ones he saw in close-ups in Italian films. And he said more. It was the first time the young Christian actually spoke about himself. He did it without holding back, accepting the others' laugher. And then he recited his favourite moment, when the king tries to offer Antigone her happiness instead of death. Happiness, a poor word. And once again, Charbel left an opening for Imane. So she stood. She took off her keffiyeh, unwrapping her hair, to everyone's astonishment. Nabil turned away. Hussein and Nimer didn't lower their eyes.

'I've never really done any theatre. But I have taught many children to perform Palestinian poetry adapted into little plays, spoken, sung and acted out. In our play, I like the exchange between Creon and Antigone. He claims he will do everything to save her, but he will do nothing. They are truly at war. He asks her to understand the role of a king. She answers him.'

ANTIGONE

> I don't want to understand. That's good for you. I am here for something else, not to understand. I am here to refuse you and to die.

Imane sat down. Charbel was frowning.

And I felt like Sam had smiled.

I wished he could have been there with us.

'There are very few stage directions in Anouilh's text. It's daunting. He lets you choose your gestures and expressions. It's an opportunity. Take advantage of that.'

Madeleine raised her hand. She was chewing her pencil.

'It would be easier for me with some direction. I don't know what the others think, but some insight into our characters doesn't seem like too much to ask.'

'The guard, for instance, he doesn't seem at all serious. He's totally out of sync with the plot. Is he an idiot, or what?'

I looked at Nabil, Madeleine, Imane, who was nodding her head.

'Okay. Just one comment for each of you.'

I picked up my notes.

'Nabil, yes. You are right and wrong. The guard is not stupid, just totally invested in his job. When he delivers his long tirade at Antigone, who's about to die, and talks about his promotion, his salary, the advantages of being in the king's guard over being a sergeant in the Army, he plunges the scene into the absurd. It's Boulevard theatre colliding with tragedy. This disconnect has a huge comic effect. You act like a bureaucrat looking forward to his vacation, doing his job just well enough, checking his watch and wondering what Mama has made for dinner.'

Nabil's beautiful smile. He was writing everything down.

'The strength of your character is that nothing gets to him. Work, work. He's a bit of a wimp, a scaredy-cat, a little of everything you must hate, no?'

'A composite role, they call it,' Imane suggested, laughing.

'Exactly. Now, let's talk about your Antigone. She is young, passionate, dishevelled. Many actresses play her as half-crazed, tensing up, jiggling a leg or tapping a foot like a child. There is some of that in her, but that's not all. Antigone's not crazy, she's strong. She's the one who says no. Her refusal of happiness must be both incomprehensible and seductive. She wants everything, right now, or nothing, ever again. Antigone embodies our courage, but also our obstinance and our ruin.'

This time Imane was writing. Without looking at her paper, her eyes fixed on mine. And the harder she looked at me the more I knew she understood every word.

'And Creon? The bastard Imane believes he is, or a hero?' Charbel queried.

I told him that I didn't know. No one had ever known. Every actor had to figure out which Creon knocked at his door. I told him that he, Charbel, could inhabit this king however he wanted to.

Charbel replied that his Creon does everything he can to save Antigone. He loves her. He protects her. He wants to understand her, but she refuses his proffered hand. He believes her death is pointless. He hates this personal pathos. He hates the pride of this little Oedipus. He will go as far as he can to keep her from dying. In vain. She will not die because of him, but in spite of him.

Imane was perplexed. It was to Antigone that Charbel had spoken.

'You have the great role!' she claimed, just as the first plane passed.

Two windows were open. It was 3.11 pm. A terrible screaming. Stupor. Everyone froze, before throwing themselves under the table without a word. They reacted instinctively, sought shelter. I was the only one still sitting in my chair, staring at the ceiling. I almost stood up. Nabil pulled me down by my trouser leg, shouting. A second plane, a third. I fell off my chair as the windows exploded.

'The Jews!' Nakad screamed.

Nabil and Hussein turned the table onto its side to make a shield. Madeleine bumped into something. Her nose was bleeding.

'We have to get out. I want out of here!'

Charbel held her, crouched beside her.

'Calm down. We don't know what's happening. Let's stay together.'

Hussein was piling up the chairs.

'Don't look! Close your eyes!' Imane shouted at me in French.

The others had abandoned my language. They were screaming in Arabic. I lay on the floor, my hands over my head. Yevgenia lay pressed against me. She was sobbing, Ismene's hair streaming over her doll-like face. Madeleine was crying too, holding her nose with both hands. His back to the window, hands raised skyward, Nabil was on his knees, praying. Beirut was under attack. I repeated this sentence in my head as I struggled to grasp its meaning. Planes flashed over the city. They were bombing the capital of Lebanon. It was beyond belief, disgusting and enormous. I was at war. For real this time. I kept my eyes shut. I was shaking. Not in fear, or surprise, or rage, or hatred of anything. Just the terrible shock, repeated, the immense turmoil, raw, pure violence, steel in every direction, fire, smoke, sirens awakened one after another, insane car horns, screams from the street, explosions, again, again, again. My soul had collided with torn concrete. My skin, my bones, my life, violently soldered to the city. No one saw it happen. Surrounded by their shouts, I was smiling. I thought about Joseph-Boutros and his childhood gun. His shot in the dark, the squeal of a grey mouse. I thought about the snipers at the Ring, at the Rizk tower, about all the snipers thrown against a wall at this moment. I thought about the loud bangs of Parisian tear-gas grenades, the blasts of fireworks on Bastille Day, of thunder, lightning, all those too-human sounds. I gnawed the inside of my cheeks, I opened my mouth wide, snapped it shut with a ripping sound. My stomach churned, risen into my throat. My leg launched cries of its own rage. I had never heard that. Never. War. That was the sound. Before the shouts of men, the spilled blood, the graves, before the infinite tears that drench cities, the destroyed homes, the frightened hordes, war was an uproar loud enough to break skulls, crush eyes, tighten throats until air gives out. A fierce joy ploughed through me. I was ashamed. I wasn't afraid. I was ashamed. I was in hell. I was fine. Terribly fine. I was ashamed. I would never exchange this fright for the silence of before. I was tragic, drunk on gunpowder, cold, my body pierced with pain. My ears must have been bleeding. Nimer vomited. In his corner, without a word. No one went to his aid. No one came to mine. A bomb had hit our house. Or the one next to ours. A block of wall fell from a floor above us, breaking off our balcony.

Nabil stood in the black dust. He gave a sharp order. Then he opened the door into the hall, holding a chair on his back.

'Let's get out of here. Go!' the Shiite yelled.

I grabbed my open bag. I ran like the others. Then I stopped. *Antigone* was scattered across the floor. Books everywhere, folded, wrinkled, thrown into the plaster and rubble, along with notes, pencils, bags. I grabbed Imane's copy. It was covered in blue paper, decorated with a flower studded with thorns. The building was struck a second time.

'They are bombing the stadium!' Nakad shouted.

When I reached the street, there were only three of us left. Imane, Charbel and I. The others had fled towards Mar Elias. I saw Nabil from behind, with his chair, a protective shell. Ismene and her nurse ran towards the hospital. Nimer spat at the sky from the top of a promontory, screaming at the murderers.

'To Shatila!' Imane shouted.

'You want to die?'

Charbel pointed towards the columns of black smoke rising from the camp. Everything was burning. Two planes flew over us, diving towards the stadium. Marwan had told me it was a munitions depot for the PLO, and a training camp. It was in flames. The concrete was burning. Sabra, Shatila, the southern suburbs were devoured. The Palestinians were firing back, along with the Nasseriens, the Communists. Their rocket-launchers resounded all around us. They sprayed the sky with rage and ammunition. Right behind us, towards Burj al-Barajneh, the whistling bursts of missile launches. A pickup with a weapon mount roared past us. In the back, pressed against the side rail, a fighter shooting the clouds with a heavy machine gun. All around us, cars abandoned in the middle of streets, their headlights crazed, doors wide open. Charbel started running towards the UNESCO building. He stopped. Came back towards us. More planes. He threw himself into a corner, against a wall. Imane pulled me under an archway. The Israelis were hitting elsewhere, father away. The Christian threw himself against me, extended his hand.

'Farewell, George.'

I looked at him.

'Goodbye, you mean.'

He smiled sadly. Imane offered her hand to him.

'Farewell, Charbel.'

She hesitated for a moment. He, too. They looked at each other. Drew closer. They might have hugged, I think, had they been alone. But I was one onlooker too many. I hadn't realized what a handsome couple they made. They weren't Antigone and Creon any more, just a girl and a boy, two kids of our time. They didn't kiss. They could have. They should have. For a long time, I was unhappy about that, for her, for him, and for myself.

'Good luck, little sister,' the Christian said to her before he ran off.

'May God protect you,' the Palestinian called out as he crossed the street.

He raised his hand, swallowed by grey smoke. And then we stood there like that, Antigone without her king and the Chorus without his script. Standing next to a wall, watching a sky shredded by blinding decoys. Marwan wouldn't come. I imagined him stuck in the chaos of downtown, yelling Nakad's name, breaking his horn. A mother ran on the pavement across the street from us, a child in her arms. The sheet wrapped around it hung like a shroud. From an archway, men called to her. She squeezed in with them. I thought of Aurora, listening to the radio. About her skin, inflamed with worry. I saw Louise. Her smile, her hand waving a big hello, her princess hair. I saw her in the middle of this street. Ripped away from peace, from hot chocolate, from the ribbons on her dress. A young woman approached us. I saw blood streaming down her arm, her coat torn, one side of her face black with soot. Her eyes wide, blank. Her hair in clumps of dust. She screamed in Arabic, stopped, ran again.

'The PLO hospital was hit. There are victims, wounded, dead,' Imane translated.

'The PLO hospital?'

'The Gaza hospital, in Sabra.'

She tried to stop the news-bearer, but the other woman pulled away. Ran like a madwoman, calling for help.

'I'm going back to Shatila, they'll need me.'

Imane took off running. She left me standing there with my open briefcase in my hand.

'Wait! I'll come with you!'

She yelled without turning around, 'You have no business there!'

'Or here!'

I followed her. She slowed down. We walked through the rubble to the camp. I wasn't afraid. I moved through the panicked streets like a sleepwalker, a prisoner of the smoke, the deafening noise, the frenzied atmosphere. We passed the wounded, the lost, plaintive cohorts. A woman cried over her dead, kneeling next to him. A street merchant lay stretched out under his cart, his vegetables scattered in water from the disembowelled sewers. Facades were sliding, torn from buildings, dragging coloured curtains, bedsheets, life from before. Imane looked at me in disbelief. She was worried. She glanced up at the sky and kept looking back at my face. She stopped suddenly.

'Is something wrong, George?'

She put her hand on my chest to make me stand still.

'Why are you asking?'

'Because you are laughing.'

* * *

She threw herself to the ground. I didn't move. A bomb exploded ten streets away. Then another. A white light to rip your eyes out, intense beams in all directions, angels' hair striping the sky, falling in thick columns like rolling clouds buffeted by wind.

'It's the Gaza hospital. They're hitting the hospital again,' Imane muttered.

She scrambled back up. She ran, bareheaded. Her keffiyeh lay on the floor of our rehearsal room.

'Imane!'

A nurse in a green smock, across the street. She ran, too. The entire camp, rushing to the hospital. She shouted over the pandemonium.

'She says there are phosphorus bombs!'

The two women pushed through the crowd to make their way into the building. I followed, my leg trailing behind me. Women, men, children everywhere, flowing in all directions.

'We need hands, George! Follow us!'

I followed Imane into a stairwell crowded with nurses carrying stretchers into the basements, with the wounded, sheets, IVs. We entered a room of sick children. On the floor, blue mattresses with white flowers, woven wicker beds. Two wounded newly arrived, five or six years old. They'd been hit on the beach near the main road. The little girl's arm was torn off. It lay beside her leg, sliced meat in rags of skin. Her brother was coated in white cream, his burnt skin in tatters, torn away in long strips like old wallpaper.

'Take the little girl!' Imane cued me.

I bent over her. She wasn't crying. I slid my arms under her body. I lifted her. She weighed nothing. Her arm fell from the stretcher with a soft thud. I stood there, holding her against me, immobile.

'Down to the shelters! Move!'

Medical staff carried mattresses. One man carried a baby in a crib. I wedged the wounded girl against my chest, her cheek against mine. She moaned softly. Closed her eyes. Her hair smelled charred, and her clothes, her breath, her burning skin, as if fire was still eating her. I reached out to grab the dead arm. A bracelet of beads around the small wrist. I saw Louise, a princess in her mirror, her shiny plastic crown. I heard Louise, her voice, her morning songs. It was Louise I carried across the hospital room. I made my way down the stairs with her, bumped by rushing shoulders, exasperated elbows, the cries of others, distorted faces, open wounds, tears. Imane was in front of me. She carried the boy like an offering. I held up my child, heart to heart, one hand clasped around her cold wrist, its stranded arm knocking against my thigh.

Refugees streamed in from everywhere. A doctor took the child from my arms in the chaos, in the middle of the corridor. He looked at my bare hands.

'Disinfect yourself. Don't touch your eyes or your mouth.'

And then he left, with my burden in his arms, his skinny legs each taking their longest strides. Imane had disappeared. I didn't know what to do.

'Are you a journalist?' a nurse asked.

I said no. I almost answered theatre director.

'Journalists have to see this!'

And he left, too. Everyone in every direction. They each had a role. I didn't. I was lost. I was no longer an actor of anything. I had become useless, a spectator. I was in the way, in the middle of the hall, pushed past by the living, the dying and the dead. I watched a nurse in the corner of one room. She had seated a dozen children against a wall. Most had torn clothing, bare feet. None were wounded. Their faces were black with soot. She asked them to hold hands. They formed a silent circle, craning their necks in search of a familiar face. They were orphans. I could tell by the adults' gestures. The way they stroked a head as they passed. Made a reassuring face. I understood as I watched the doctor who crouched down to hand out chewing gum to them. I would have liked to be that doctor or that child. To be part of this compassion or this pain.

'George?'

Imane was coming towards me, two jerrycans in her hands.

'The water pipes behind the building were hit. Go get some water, please.'

I didn't answer. Didn't even look at the Palestinian. Just the two blue containers. I had a task at last. I dropped my briefcase and ran towards the exit. Dozens of people were going for water, containers in hand. Next, they would need candles, bandages, bread, and hope. For Imane, for the wounded children, the orphans, the suffering, the frightened, the prostrate, the lost, the crying, I was ready to run back and forth until the end of time. I reached the street. I ran between the scattered stones, following the cohort of thirst. I rounded the corner of the building.

And then the air ripped apart. Howl of metal. Collision with fire. A white flash, painful, immense. I was inhaled. A hole tried to suck me in. My heart was swallowed by the blast of air. It broke my ribs like a birdcage. It swept out of my chest. Rolled into the dust. I let go of the jerrycans. I covered my eyes with my hands so they wouldn't be ripped out. I closed my mouth instead of opening it. My lungs burst into flames. My face. My ears. My palms were soldered to my cheeks. I was thrown backwards. The ground slid, and my legs. I thrashed my arms to escape the abyss. I smelled like grilled pork. Like Sunday chicken that my mother plucked, over the fire. I was sizzling. My eyes had melted, light was exploding behind my eyelids. It flashed as it pierced my forehead, my temples, the back of my neck. My nostrils had closed. I wasn't breathing. I crashed onto my back. Without protecting the nape of my neck, my heels, my elbows. My leg ripped itself apart. My hip. I vomited out my intestines. An endless snake making its way to the waterhole the crevasse created.

I was lifted up. Carried as though in triumph. Voices all around me. Men, women. Sharp orders. I was thrown over a shoulder, then a back. Laid onto a stretcher. Carried, feet up, head down, my hands stuck to my face. I was burning. I was literally on fire. Like a limb thrown onto a hearth. I tried to open my eyes, I screamed. Someone threw sand onto the coals, cut through the flames with a razor. I recognized the noises of the hospital, the dragging footsteps, the moans, the shouts from person to person, the smell, disinfectant and sweat. The stretcher was set on the ground, bumping my head.

'George! My God!'

Imane. Nothing could hurt me any more. I felt her hand on mine. She slowly pulled it away from my cheek.

'My God!'

A voice in Arabic. A man.

'They're going to wash your eyes. You understand, George? They're going to clean your eyes.'

The man lifted my other hand off my face. He was more brutal. He and Imane held me. Someone drowned my closed eyelids for several minutes. Enormous pain.

My eyes all sand, needles, crushed glass. A taste of sea on my lips. Circling flies. I was going to lose my life.

'It's all right. It's a saline solution,' Imane murmured.

They stood me up. They were taking off my clothes.

'Everything is drenched in it. We have to get these off.'

I was holding Imane's hand. I was breaking Antigone's.

'How will I be able to cry?'

I didn't say it. I thought it. How do you cry without your eyes?

'Careful, the doctor is going to open your eyelids.'

Another man's voice, irritated. A brusque movement. A curt order.

'No, he's not going to open them. We have to keep washing. We'll move to the operating room.'

'Is it really bad?' My first words as a blind man.

Silence from Imane.

'Please tell me.'

Imane asked some questions in Arabic. The man answered her. She translated one of every dozen words, her hand crushed in mine.

'You are burnt. You have eyelid lacerations. They don't know if you have shrapnel in the corneas. Whether there are lesions.'

The same man's voice. Imane translated.

'Try and open your eyes.'

Impossible. Nausea. Headache. Two fingers forced them open. Intense pain.

'That's good.'

Total darkness.

'Move your eyes, left, then right, the serum must go everywhere.'

A voice in Arabic.

'What is he saying?'

'Nothing.'

'Imane!'

'He's looking. He's checking to see if the cornea was burnt. If the eye was perforated, or the orbital bone broken, or the eyeball ruptured.'

'He hasn't found anything?'

'He's looking.'

The voice. The translation.

'Have you had a tetanus vaccine?'

What did I know? Yes, no, maybe? A flu shot? I had lost my eyes. I was in a bombed hospital, a lifetime away from home, on the floor, surrounded by orphans, my head shredded with pain. I will never see again. Ever. My eyes had been eaten. They dripped down my cheeks like broken eggs, the white, the yellow, the shell that scratched.

'Calm down, George.'

The voice. The translation.

'You have bruising on your eyelids, but no deformity of the pupil.'

I let go of her hand.

'I don't understand anything, Imane. Stop.'

'You ask me to translate, I translate.'

I tried to raise myself up on my elbows. I fell back. I was bare except for underwear, without shoes or socks. I was ashamed of my body offered up that way. Someone put a blanket over my legs.

'Am I going to lose my eyes? Just ask him that!'

Imane's voice. Her halting question. Then the man's answer.

'We always have two eyes too many.'

* * *

All night I lay in the corridor of the Gaza hospital, surrounded by moaning. Bandages protecting the burns on my arms, my forehead and my cheeks, kept moist with frequent applications of saline solution. Since I was scheduled for surgery, I was fasting. I was hooked up to an IV. I thought about Sam. Him on his bed, me on my stretcher. I had given Aurora's number to Imane. She had to reassure her. A minor wound that kept me far from her. My eyes were sealed off. First by ocular bandages, then two cardboard shells attached with adhesive. In the evening, the doctors had argued about what kind of protection to use. Imane translated what I could hear. The pain was subsiding. That wasn't a good sign. Terrible pain could signal a benign wound. A slight tickling sensation, a deep lesion. Nothing corresponded to what I thought. I had tiny bits of shrapnel in my cornea. A fragment of wood had been blown into my right eye socket. I was on antibiotics. I was taking pills for nausea and vomiting. They were drawing blood and fluids to test. Flushing my eyes with water, again and again. Once, I heard the word 'evisceration'. It was a British voice. Foreign doctors were helping out their Palestinian colleagues. And then Imane spoke of tweezers, like for removing a splinter. Of stitches, of sutures to sew the eye back together.

On 5 June, while the doctors were deep in my cornea, Israeli planes flew over the city. Imane told me they had bombed Nabatieh, Damour, Beaufort castle. They had blasted the bridges in the south of the country. I thought of Nabil, of Nimer, of Hussein, of Creon's guards. I envisioned old Khadijah, Eurydice worried about taking her own life. Imane swore that the surgeon had done his work well. Glass dust, wood ash, iron shavings. He had retrieved materials to rebuild the hospital from my eye. Antigone had spent a long time responding to Aurora's tears. She had tried to reassure her. Had sworn to Aurora that I spoke only of her. And our child.

The evening of the second day, Yassine came to my bedside. Imane's brother took my hand. I was surprised by this gesture. He thanked me for the soil from Jaffa. Imane would look after his part of the treasure. It would be safer in their home in Shatila than in a fighter's vest. His sister had poured Sam's gift into a gilded purse, then attached it to the key of their ancestral home, on top of the clock in her room. That key had opened their family home in Jaffa in February 1948, the night of the expulsion. It would open it again the morning of the great return. Imane and Yassine had even sworn to each other to spread the soil in the reclaimed garden once they reached it.

He explained that Beirut was cut off from the world. The airport had been bombed. To get out of the country, I would have to cross the Green Line, reach the Christian port of Jounieh and make my way to Cyprus.

'And our play?'

I said we had little time left, just a handful of rehearsals, that we would have to find everyone. That we had scattered without setting our next meeting. That the 1 October date still stood. That it was too late to stop now. That everyone agreed. The Shiites, the Christians, the Palestinians. That it was too late to turn back.

'It's too late to turn back, Yassine.'

My eyes burnt with tears. I grasped his arm with both hands.

'You understand? We can't stop now!'

He understood, yes. Of course he understood. And he would even come to the theatre to watch. Alone. Or with his comrades in arms. He would leave his rifle at the door, with the other weapons. He would try to get a good seat, in the front row. Could I made that happen?

I stopped breathing. I recognized that voice. It was lying. It was the voice that the dying hear. The voice that talks about days to come, about a summer that will never be, about so many things to do together. It's the voice that forces a smile to keep from crying, the voice that dresses up death, that hums, that soothes, that warms the heart. It's the voice that closes the curtains, then the door, then the casket. It's the voice that no longer believes a single word of life.

'And I would like to be in the front row when you open the door of your ancestral home. Can you make that happen?'

I shouldn't have. It was sickening and unfair. I wanted to ask forgiveness. Yassine didn't give me time. He leaned over, one hand on my arm. I felt his breath near my eyes, this brotherly pressure.

'You'll be the one who turns the key in the lock, my friend.'

And then he stood up. Imane approached. Her voice just above us.

'George?'

Imane had taken her brother's place. I crossed my arms on my chest. Since my pain had eased, we kept our hands to ourselves. I stunk of sweat, garbage, fire. I was in a tunnel of moans and cries. They gave me a shot to put me under. I went to sleep with Antigone. She spent the night near me, lying on a blanket beside me.

In the morning, she changed my bandages. She no longer even tried to reassure me. She sponged my infected sap, my shredded skin. Around us, men talked loudly. A woman was crying. Outside, the street crackled with sounds of automatic gunfire.

'What's going on?'

'The Israelis have invaded Lebanon,' Imane replied.

'How are they going to make me die?' Antigone asked me.

The Blue Helmets had scattered in disarray. Tyre was surrounded, Nabatieh, Hasbaya. The Rashidieh camp had been bombed. Tanks had already made it past Saida. The Beirut airport no longer existed.

'The planes will be back. We have to evacuate you.'

I protested in vain. I said I would stay here, in this corridor of death. That it was my place. That no one could force me out. But Yassine had made his decision. And Imane agreed.

In the early afternoon, Marwan came to pick me up at the hospital. He gathered my belongings, retrieved my briefcase. He was getting me out of there. I refused to take a step. So Yassine and my Druze brother carried me to the car, holding me under the armpits and dragging my feet. It could have been a kidnapping, but I wasn't crying out. They put me in the back seat, lying on blankets, a pillow under my head. Imane spoke to Marwan. She was giving instructions. He didn't answer. What courage he had had to come so far. Into the depths of Shatila's rage, to recover his Frenchman. I was on my back in the heat, locked in my new darkness, the pain, all these unfamiliar sounds. Imane leaned over me.

'Thank you for what you did.'

'I did nothing.'

'You gave me Antigone's strength.'

'Ridiculous.'

'Figure it out.'

She put her hand on my forehead. Then she shut the door, the way one shuts the door on a sick child. Marwan got into the front. He honked to free up the road.

'You're going to rest,' said a soft voice.

I startled.

'Nakad?'

'Hello, George.'

Haemon was there, with us. He reached his arm between the seats to squeeze my thigh. Danger was receding.

'You're going to eat, sleep and go back to France brand new,' his father added.

The car wasn't avoiding the holes in the road. It was leaving the camp like someone running away.

'Where are we going?'

'To Aley, to our home in the mountains,' Marwan answered.

His voice, deep, steady, beautiful.

'*Ahlan wa sahlan*,' I said.

I think they might have smiled. I hoped so. The son, the father. I had just told them that in my heart, too, they had a family and a land.

18

NAKAD

After Imane's hands, Nakad offered me his. With infinite gentleness, he washed my eyes morning and evening, changing my bandages like an elderly doctor. A week after my arrival in Shouf, I tried to remove the shells that protected my eyes. Light entered like a bayonet, crushing my temples and the base of my skull.

'You have your whole life to see,' Nakad repeated.

When he brought me tea or white coffee, Haemon recited a few lines. Sometimes even in the voice of Antigone. Every three days the young man shaved me. It was both unsettling and solemn. He pinched my nostrils between his thumb and his index finger, raised my chin, put two fingers below my ear to slightly turn my face.

One night, Nakad brought me a mirror. It hurt to see my reflection. The whites of my eyes were bloody, a brown halo biting into the pupil, the right iris spotted, distorted by a greyish patch. Every time I closed my eyelids, they dragged burning sand. I had lost some light, but I had kept my eyes.

We were far from everything. Nakad was my messenger. He told me that at Nabatieh, the Shiites had greeted the Israelis with bread and thrown rice on their tanks. The

Jewish State's army even authorized them to keep their weapons and their positions. Because both considered Palestine an enemy.

I was lost. I thought about my guards. About Nabil, Hussein, Nimer, who said they were ready to die defending their borders. I imagined old Khadijah, raising her hand to greet the star of David.

The Druzes were not fighting the Israelis either. When I asked him why, Marwan made a vague gesture. He explained that his enemies were the Phalangists, Christians in the Shouf and Metn regions. That they had to take back every inch of land from them with their teeth once Tsahal withdrew. He had said *Tsahal.* It was the first time I heard a Hebrew word from a Lebanese mouth.

On 13 June Beirut was surrounded. Louise had a serious purulent otitis, a sore throat and a sinus infection. The Israelis had joined forces with the Christian militias. The doctor had just left Aurora when I managed to get a call through to her. The capital of Lebanon was bombed by air, sea and land artillery. My daughter had been put on antibiotics for ten days.

'She keeps calling out for her daddy,' her mother had told me.

I knew. I called out for her, too, saying her name under my breath each time the pain came back.

One evening I was walking down a street in the village with Nakad. I was holding his arm, like an old man. He told me about the war. He was the voice of it. Beirut had no water, no electricity, nothing. Some Shiites had created the Hezbollah movement to return to the fight.

'After the Syrians, the Iranians are joining in,' he had said.

I listened. My head ached from not understanding anything anymore.

'We'll never perform *Antigone*, Nakad.'

I sat next to him on a boulder at the edge of the road.

'Can you see the cedar trees from here?' the young man asked.

He pointed towards the summit of the mountain. I blinked. I saw them. A dozen of them, like a triumphant flock. The sky grumbled with storm.

'And further away? The village, over there, can you see it?'

I saw it, yes. I looked at its faraway lights through my tears. I listened to the silence of peace. I was enraged to be there. Shatila had been bombed again and again. I thought about Imane. I imagined her in a basement, gathering children under her veil. I thought about Charbel, watching the Israeli soldiers pass. About Joseph-Boutros, who must have shown them his shining Colt with a laugh.

The previous night, the Israelis had combed through our mountain. And then they entered Aley. I was with Nakad when the first vehicle passed. In Beirut, their planes dropped flyers ordering civilians to leave the city. Here, they drank peacefully at the fountain, their rifles propped against the edge of the well. When villagers approached, the soldiers smiled. Hands were extended. Lebanese civilians and Israeli soldiers spoke the same language.

'They are Druze,' Nakad whispered.

I saw Marwan again. His discomfort, his irritated gesture at the idea of fighting the invader. I understood. Israel was occupying Shouf with his blood brothers.

* * *

All of July was bombed. The planes passed over us to crush Beirut. Arafat had called for resistance

'He'll negotiate his own departure,' Marwan predicted.

I hadn't believed him.

Every morning he left for the capital. He had become the driver for three French journalists. They paid him cash, in dollars. In just a few days, the Druze had earned enough to buy himself a used Mercedes.

He returned at the end of each week with important news. His house in Hamra was intact, and my hotel hadn't suffered. One August evening, he came back shaking. He had never seen such a deluge of iron. His car's boot was riddled with holes. Right in front of him, a driver had been hit in the throat.

As he described this, his wife left the room. She didn't want to picture the tall towers lying down. She refused to hear the children crying. She feared the crazed shadows that haunted the mountain road. That night Marwan didn't sleep. He told me he was too old. That he was very tired. He stayed outside, in front of the house, sitting on a chair, his cigarette shielded from the wind by the palm of his hand. I joined him after dinner. We sat like that, two wounded men, in silence.

'There will be nothing left of us,' my Druze muttered.

Louise was doing better, but she was still coughing. The doctor had scheduled tests for the following week. I had spoken to her on the phone.

'Nakad, the line's working!' A neighbour had shouted.

He spent his days trying to reach his children in London, tapping the phone in search of a dial tone. We ran to his door. The receiver was off the hook, on the table. I shook as I dialled my number. Aurora was beside herself. She talked too fast. Wanted to know everything. My eyes, the bombs. When was I coming home? But when? I must have some idea? I asked her to put Louise on, quickly, now. We were about to get cut off.

'Talk to me, it's Papa.'

A bird sound. From a cartoon. A duck high in a tree. I didn't understand a word.

'Say hello, it's Papa,' Aurora repeated.

A laugh. A gurgling. A mouse squeak. A tiny voice, splintered by the crackling line. I collapsed into the chair. I repeated, 'My love, my love, my love.' I didn't know any other words. Again, her little frog laugh. A sound of skin against the mouthpiece, breathing too close. A big cough. And then nothing. No dial tone, no beeping, just the sound of my blood. I looked at the dead receiver. The neighbour tapped it several times. He shrugged in dismay. I felt Nakad's hand on my shoulder. I didn't thank our host. I was like a blind man. I let myself be guided out of the room, out of that house. I dragged my leg along the dirt road, led by Antigone's fiancé. I didn't want to see any more, to look at anything. I kept my eyes closed until I got to my room. I lay down on my bed. I asked Nakad to leave. I wanted to go back to Beirut, cross the line at the museum, get to the port of Jounieh, take the first boat, set foot on Cyprus, board a plane, glue my face to the window, arrive in Paris. I wanted my wife, my daughter, I wanted my bedroom, my bed, fresh bread, a hot shower, a glass of white wine. I wanted to be carried, whisked away, rescued. I fell asleep with my clothes on, and my shoes, a pillow crushed over my eyes.

* * *

When Marwan returned from Beirut, he blasted his horn. Loud and long. He got out of his car, did a little dance.

'The Palestinians are gone, far away! The Syrians, too. It's over.'

Arafat and his group were sailing towards Tunisia, Sanaa and Aden, with their light weapons. Marwan was at the port. He told us how they fired salvos into the air as if they had won the battle. I thought about Yassine. He must have been on the boat. I hoped that Imane hadn't gone with him.

'Did they take the women and the children?'

My friend had seen only fighters. The women cheered them on, but had not gone to sea.

That evening Marwan washed my eyes himself. By the light of the yellow lamp, he asked me to look to the right, then the left. He was pleased with my progress. Wiping my cheek, he counted the mornings to come. It was 31 August. In about two weeks' time, he would drive me back down. He had set up a taxi to take me across the Green Line.

He couldn't take that on. But the man was trustworthy, an Armenian, Christian like me.

I slept like a dead man. That night and every other night. I'd grown accustomed to the silence of the mountain. The evening of 13 September, Nakad joined me on the terrace. He talked to me about *Antigone*. He said everything was still possible. He was still there. And Imane, too, probably. Finding Charbel would be child's play. And the Shiites really wanted to perform. I looked at Haemon. I didn't know any more. He said that after this ordeal the play would be even more beautiful, even more necessary. I studied the mountain. I thought about our theatre, our pact, the weapons we had lowered. All that seemed like another era. Nakad hesitated. Then he put his hand on my arm.

'I like you very much, George.'

I smiled. Me, too.

'But me, I love you,' he repeated.

The young Druze looked at the ground. He seemed frightened by his words. I had neither the gestures nor the voice. I looked at him, his eyes in flight, his hair tousled by the wind. I should have put a hand on his shoulder. Moved closer. Or talked to him. I couldn't leave him alone with this confession. I couldn't.

'You're right. We're going to keep going with *Antigone*,' I cooed.

He raised his head.

'We still have two months. It's doable.'

He looked at me closely. His eyes sought mine.

'I told everyone we'd rehearse on the 17th, 18th, and 19th of September, but that was cutting it close because I was going back to Paris. We could still meet on the 24th and 25th, as planned, couldn't we?'

He was smiling. A magnificent smile, kind-hearted, infinitely sweet. He kept his eyes on mine. I talked fast. Too fast. I lined up dates, numbers, names, hurling the words out, fully engaged. He let go of my arm.

'So, dress rehearsal the 26th of September? And performance on October 1st, as agreed.'

We wouldn't change the schedule. We mustn't. Because once we started changing dates, we might as well change plays while we were at it. I laughed. An affected chuckle, loud, forced. Imane would handle contacting the Nurse and Ismene. I would call Nabil and Charbel once everything was set up. They'd better not let me down now, or it would be war! The same stupid laugh. A tear of sweat ran down my back. I kept talking. About the poster we had to make, the invitations, the projectors. The same pathetic hiccup.

Nakad breathed in. He looked at me again. Put his hand on my thigh.

'Everything's fine, George. Don't worry.'

And then he stood up. Spread his arms. He stretched, facing the black mountains. I felt like an actor without a script, without a gesture, without elegance or beauty.

'Don't tell my father about it, okay?'

I nodded briskly.

Nakad was still smiling.

'No matter what happens to us, we'll perform *Antigone*. And I'll be your Haemon.'

He looked at me.

'You know why?'

I shook my head.

'Because a Druze believes in reincarnation.'

* * *

'My son's name is Nakad, not Molière. I will not let him die on a stage like a puppet,' Marwan said, driving back towards Beirut.

We were heading down the mountain in his old red car. He drove slowly, avoiding the potholes. He was tense, anxious and angry. Two days earlier, the president of the Lebanese Republic, leader of the Phalangists, Bashir Gemayel, had been assassinated in the centre of the Christian quarter. In retaliation, the Israelis had invaded West Beirut and taken up positions around the unarmed Palestinian camps. Marwan feared a terrible vengeance would sweep down on the country.

My eyes were painful, but my bandages were gone, along with the shells that covered them, and the moist bandages. Just dark glasses to protect myself from the summer light. I hadn't lost my eyes.

'Molière died at home, Marwan.'

'I don't care. He died wearing a costume, not as a man.'

'Your son is a man, you know that. And he's a good actor.'

Marwan frowned, raised his chin. His proud expression.

He had hung his rosary on the rearview mirror and turned off the radio. He was afraid for me, I knew it. He looked at me.

'You think Nakad is a good actor?'

'He's the most beautiful Haemon I could hope for.'

'I am just asking if he's acting it right.'

'It's his heart that speaks. You saw that, didn't you?'

Marwan nodded. His son recited his lines to Antigone the way a man offers a woman his love and his life. It's true. He agreed. But he added that the war had caught up with us. And that it had opened his eyes. What had been possible before the Israeli invasion on 6 June was no longer.

'You don't like theatre.'

He laughed.

'I am talking to you about Lebanon.'

'And you don't like actors.'

He glanced at me.

'Not yours, no. What you tried to do has no more meaning today. You mixed brothers with enemies for nothing.'

'To build a dream together.'

'But what dream? They recite your text but they know perfectly well it's not reality.'

'It's not my text.'

'That doesn't change anything. Real life is not in your lines.'

'They're not my lines, they're Jean Anouilh's.'

The Druze laughed, letting go of the wheel. He slapped his thighs with both hands.

'*Anta majnoon!*'

He repeated that I was out of my mind. Anouilh or not, it didn't matter. I didn't understand the situation. The country was on its knees when I flew in from Paris in a Harlequin coat. He said peace isn't made with a powdered clown's face. When a country is counting its dead, ten kids on the stage of a broken-down theatre no longer made any sense. He almost regretted having taken me in and helping me. He said putting on this play was pure vanity.

'Another Jew idea!'

I was shaken.

'You have no right to talk about Sam like that.'

Marwan slid down in his seat. He stared at the road with his angry look.

'I have much respect for Samuel Akounis,' the Druze told me.

I looked away. Turned my back to him. He was scolding.

'You know I did all of this as much for him as for you, so stop!'

I didn't answer. My eyes were burning. My head throbbed.

'I'm sorry,' he muttered.

He lowered his window, took a deep breath.

'A European doesn't hear the same words we do. Do you understand that?'

No, I didn't understand. I didn't want to understand.

'And if I say "it's another idea from a Greek dreamer", does that work for you?'

I didn't answer.

'Look at me, George. I've been part of this story for two years. And for seven months I have protected you like a son. I even loaned Nakad to your comedy.'

'It's not a comedy, it's a tragedy.'

'Comedy, tragedy, whatever you say! But now that your friend is going to die, and Israelis are in Beirut, and everyone is shooting at everyone, I say all this must stop. You cannot stage *Antigone,* do you understand? It's over, George. No one is above war. There's no tragedy here now except this war.'

I turned back to him. I looked at him. His face, his brushy hair, his grey moustache, the old scar working across his cheek. His lips had disappeared. His eyes, half-closed. On the wheel, his knuckles were white.

'I'm sorry, too, Marwan.'

He blinked his eyes. He smiled, barely.

'I know war. It seeks out men everywhere. Even in the wings of a theatre. In a month, all your actors will have joined up.'

'Maybe. But before that, they'll be at the rehearsal.'

He shrugged his shoulders.

'No, George. My son won't come.'

'He'll be there October 1st for the performance. You promised him.'

'I promised that a long time ago. But nothing is up to us any more.'

On his hospital bed, I had sworn to Samuel that *Antigone* would be performed, whatever it took. But today, without him, I was no longer sure of anything.

'A dog is always a dog, George. Even raised by sheep. Your actors are not actors, they are soldiers. You don't know it, but war remembers.'

We entered Beirut on Friday, 17 September 1982. Darkness was falling. The weather had calmed.

Israeli tanks were making risky manoeuvres at downtown intersections, between fruit carts and bread vendors.

19

ANTIGONE

A child. He sat against the wall. In a blue coat, with sandals on his feet. He had dried spit around his lips, a web of brown blood that reached his chin and closed eyes. Another boy lay next to him, his stomach looted by a cloud of flies. A dog was there, too, on its side, its legs stiff, crushed against the child's legs. I leaned against an open door.

Marwan had awakened me in the night. I was asleep in his living room. I felt his presence without him speaking or touching me. He crouched down, his face close to mine.

'George, something's happening in the camps.'

Just those words. Not a single word more. I looked at him. He had dressed in the dark. I got up without taking my eyes off him. I had never seen him in shadows. I thought of the messenger of my *Antigone*, the man who announces the end of time.

I pulled on my trousers, my shirt. I asked no questions. Something was happening, and that's all. My Druze had a serious voice, slow movements, a tormented expression. He went to the window without turning on a light, put his hand on the glass, on his forehead, his tall body anxious.

A man was waiting in the living room. Jacket open, a pistol in his waistband. He stood as I approached, greeted me with a nod of his head. I had seen this Druze before. He was in a corner of the room when Nakad played Haemon. At the moment I took him in my arms, we exchanged a look, he and I. He seemed to be the only one not wondering what two men were doing in the middle of the room, hugging and reciting strange words. He had applauded at the end of our performance and shaken my hand before he left.

'Anouilh is a Druze,' he had said under his breath at the doorway.

I had been surprised at this phrase, uttered in the middle of the ritual goodbye. The others put their hands on their hearts, but he touched mine. I had noticed the socialist insignia he wore on his lapel, the pen and pickaxe in a triangle, also the five-pointed star tattooed between his thumb and index finger. That evening he'd offered me a smile of complicity.

But this night his face told me nothing.

The three of us got into the red car. The streets were deserted. When we reached the sea, near Mar Elias, Marwan parked. He got out of the vehicle, his eyes on the sky. The other man spoke to him in Arabic, pointing. My friend nodded. I got out. Above Sabra and Shatila, the night was light as day. Dozens of incandescent pearls descended slowly over the camps, dancing through the air before going out. And then more, rising like arrows before falling in a blinding cloud.

'Flares,' Marwan murmured.

They got back in the car. I stood there alone, looking into the night that resisted the light of men.

'I'll take you to Shatila, but I won't go into the camp.'

I leaned into his window.

'What's going on?'

Marwan looked at me.

'Do you want to go to Shatila or not?'

I took my seat in the back. The night was warm, I was freezing. As Marwan started the car, I leaned my chin on the back of his seat. I sought his eyes in the rearview mirror.

'What's going on, Marwan?'

'The Israelis are lighting up the camp. They are looking for something,' the other Druze answered.

At the outer edge of Shatila, Marwan stopped his car and turned off the lights. In front of us, on the rampart that led to the first dwellings, Israeli tanks were napping. A soldier had climbed out and sat with his back to the turret, his feet on a jerrycan. The flares bathed him in white light.

'I'll wait here. I'm not going in,' Marwan repeated. The other man turned around. He nodded to me. I was about to open my door, get out. I stayed.

'Tell me what you think.'

My friend turned towards me. I didn't recognize the expression on his face.

'I know this silence too well,' Marwan answered me.

And he turned back.

'It's almost dawn. Go now.'

I took my bag. I left the car, the two men, what remained of my insouciance. I walked towards the tanks. I had decided to pass between two of them, where a soldier was smoking on the tank's armoured shell. I got as far as the tank treads. I was expecting a word, a shout, an order. The soldier and I looked at each other. He looked bleak. He turned away. I was nothing. I didn't exist. There was nothing around him any more.

I entered the camp. I entered the desert. Smells of burnt rubbish, rancid stench, sewage. I thought about Marwan's silence. The light of dawn was struggling to rise. Flares still lit Sabra, from the other side. I walked. Moved forwards, almost blindly. I had entered hell through an intestine, an alley so narrow I could touch both sides with my arms extended. I saw the first of the dead. A barefoot man in pyjamas. He lay on his stomach, crushed in the dust. I knelt down. I backed away, my hand over my mouth to escape the smell of rotting flesh. I looked around for help, knocked at the first door. It was half-open. Shoes were lined up beside the doorway. I thought about Goldilocks, the family of bears with my daughter in peace. The father's sandals, the mother's flip-flops, the children's small shoes. I stuck my head inside, called out quietly. I went in.

The father was collapsed on the table, his face in his own plate, lying in a pool of soup and blood. The sideboard was open, the linens put away. I was shaking. I didn't go into the bedrooms. I went outside. I ran in the narrow street. I called for help in French, in English. The daylight was so pale. A woman appeared in the red dust. A scarf on her head, one hand in the air, she cried, moaning words I didn't know. Another, behind me. Spectres, one by one, emerging from the depths of darkness. A shadow limped towards me, took my arm, dragged me. Dry-eyed, she screamed. Two old men blocked a covered entry, their throats slit. A man, his wife, her veil tightened around her neck like a noose. I recoiled. I was desecrating them. I was walking in human blood. I backed away from the door. The street was in tears. Piercing screams, wailing. The dead that one discovers, then the body one grieves. I moved forward. The doors were open, all of them. I didn't dare. At one corner, I stopped and sat on a concrete block. Nine men were piled up on the ground, open-mouthed, shirts and trousers soaked in blood. More, others, under a car. And more, fallen in a row along a wall, execution-style. A young man helped me get up.

'You have to keep your eyes open,' he said in English.

'One always has two eyes too many.'

I thought about the doctor from Shatila who was reluctant to restore my sight.

I walked. I saw a cane on the ground. An old man on his back, riddled with bullet holes, his arms spread. Another man, further down, the back of his head smashed in. A little girl called to me from her doorway. She pushed me inside. I lowered my head, looked at her finger, not the bed she was pointing at. The sheets were bloody. I followed her father's calvary across the floor. He had been dragged through the bedroom, the hallway, onto the threshold, then thrown into the brambles. In an alley, a body cut in two, the right leg discarded near the arm. A woman, fallen there, under a clothesline. Another, abandoned in a rubbish tip and covered in rubble. Near a cluster of cars, a funeral carriage. Three grey horses and five men, face-down on the ground. At another corner, an artificial leg torn from an old man prostrate against a metal shutter. A young man a few steps away, his stomach bloated, his face burnt, dried shit all over his legs. Everywhere, the dead. In the houses, in the streets, in the alleys, the terraces. Flesh chopped, crushed, gaping wounds, strings of brains in the bushes. The crazed eyes of a woman, popped out of their sockets like billiard balls. The sun sputtered. The obscene song of crickets. Hordes of flies, furious at being disturbed in their feast.

And then I saw the first infant. I feared it behind each door, I feared it after each scream. There he was. A baby, bare except for a torn nappy. Flayed. Flesh crushed live against a concrete wall.

I stopped. I was dry. My eyes. My heart. The air was thick. I breathed in spurts. To inhale was to ingest death. I wanted to take the child. Carry it. Brandish it in the camp, show it to Beirut, take it back to Paris, throw it at the whole world. I bent over him. A man shouted. He ran up to me. Pointed out the grenade with its pin removed, hidden under a beam next to the tiny corpse. And the string tied around the victim's foot, attached to a plank of wood. Move one, you move the other, and set off the explosion.

'They booby-trapped the bodies,' the man explained.

Now angels were guiding my steps. A little girl in a red shirt, her forehead split open, legs splayed. Another further down, in a corner, a plaid dress, her head against the wall and her back slashed open. A broken boy on his back, Mickey Mouse on his blue T-shirt. Four brothers piled up on the pavement and burnt. Flesh and clothing torn away, as if ground up, then melted back together. I abandoned resistance. I let myself be led. I passed from hand to hand, house to house in the shouts, the tears, all the flayed eyes searching mine. A woman led me to a bloody cradle. A wicker basket lined with grey, and white sheets. The baby's throat had been slit. He slept on his side, his head unglued, his hands behind him, one leg folded backwards, the knee broken. I wanted to offer him tears. I reached deep into myself. They didn't come. They filled my stomach, my heart, my soul. They refused my cheeks. I went back out like that, my face blank.

'Go straight ahead. After the tyre store, turn left. It's there,' Marwan had said to me.

I recognized the small field, the large painting that coloured the walls of the school, the office of Pierre the dentist. I stopped in the middle of the street. Imane's door was open. Women and men were crossing themselves as if they were lost. A press photographer was working. He raised his eyes to me. He was crying. I stood there, in the middle of everything, staring at the door. I waited. For someone to go in, come out, for a hand to appear through the bars of the window. And then I moved. I crossed the street step by step, my belly screaming with fear.

I had never gone inside Imane's house. The door opened into the kitchen, a tiny room overwhelmed by the table and chairs. They were knocked over. The table was set for dinner. This time, I didn't call out. I didn't shout. I looked at the door that led to the other room. The father was there, seated on the floor against the door frame, tilted to one side, his eyes open, his white keffiyeh stained dark. Imane had spoken to me of her younger sister, her brothers. The three of them were pressed together, stacked in the hallway. The morning light rushed through the window, searching each pool of blood the way a dog would sniff. I bumped into the table, the fallen chairs. Imane was in her room. She lay in silence, sideways, stretched across her bed. Her head hung over one side, her legs on the other. Her executioners had bound her hands behind her with wire. A part of her face had been torn off. Her cheek, her temple, a broth buzzing with flies. A gag had been stuffed into her mouth. Her throat was slit. The bodice of her dress was open, torn to the sleeves. Her breasts had been slashed. A green stain devoured her abdomen. Her black-and-white checked dress was pulled up. She was spreadeagled. Her stomach pierced. Her thighs were covered in blood, and her ankles. She had fought. She gripped a clump of hair in her fist.

I stopped breathing. My heart had stopped. I untied her. She was stiff, ice-cold, dead the day before. The wire was encrusted in her skin. I lay her straight on the bed, slid a pillow under her head. I lowered her skirt, buttoned the only button on her dress. On the table was her blue scarf. I unfolded it and placed it over her face, offering up only her red hair.

I almost prayed to my God. A few phrases from my childhood, then I gave up. Above her bed, Imane had framed a reproduction of an old Palestinian bank note. It was a clock. A small gilded purse hung beside it, attached to a rusted key as long as my hand. I recognized the purse. The Palestinian soil that Sam had given me. And the key from 1948. The one that closed the family home in Jaffa and was carried into exile by her grandparents.

'You will be the one to turn the key in the lock, my friend.'

I remembered Yassine, the Palestinian fighter. His promise to return. He had left with his defeated brothers. Left for Tunis in the wake of Arafat, with their weapons and their hopes, leaving their families defenceless.

I took down the key. It was heavy. A full shaft, an engraved ring. I opened the purse. I divided the soil into two equal parts, one for Imane, one for Yassine. I poured half into the palm of my hand. I sprinkled it over Imane's body. I wasn't crying. I wasn't shaking any more. I was Antigone leaning over Polynices. I scattered the sacred earth over her martyrdom. It was soft, this earth. Both dry and oily, flecked with sparks as shiny as diamonds. I dusted it over her scarf, her torso, her shattered legs, the palms of her hands, her feet. I sprinkled it, rubbing it between my fingers.

I bowed down before the tortured body. I took the key, the remains of Palestine in its gilded purse. I stepped over the brothers, walked around the father. I went out into the street. Outside, first responders from the Red Crescent were wrapping a little boy in a plastic bag. A zippered envelope. When I reached him, a nurse showed me the body. He held it out to me the way one asks a question. The schoolboy's eyes were white. The transparent shroud clung to his forehead, his nose, his chin. I thought I saw fog around his lips. I raised a hand. I wasn't a doctor, not a journalist. I put life on stage, but I could do nothing about that death. I took out Sam's notebook. I don't know why. To relearn a gesture. To put distance between myself and the blood. I wrote 'The End'. That's all. I surrounded the words with nervous circles, until the paper gave way.

And then I stopped looking. I walked in the middle of the street. Walked blindly towards the open air, followed by tears, screams, laundry drying pointlessly in the September sun.

Marwan was waiting for me, alone in the car. When he saw me in the distance, he got out and opened his arms to me.

'I know,' he said, simply.

We drove towards town. He made me sit in the back seat.

I held my head between my legs, my face in my hands. I asked him to open the windows. I stunk of death. We didn't speak. When we reached his house, he helped me out, helped me walk, with one hand under my armpit. I asked him for a shower, right now, immediately. To wash off the dust, the stench, the thousands of images. I ripped off my clothes. I scrubbed my face, leaning over the sink. I cleaned my nose until it hurt, tearing off pieces of soap to stuff up my nostrils. I opened the window of the bathroom, the taps, the wind came in bursts. It was warm, fetid. The water beat against me. It struck my skin like a wound. I washed my hair, my face again, my belly. Suddenly, the wind beat back the shower curtain against me. It clung to my torso, my legs. It redrew my face like a cadaver bag. Death had entered. It was in the room. Hovering. It smelled like vomit, wet dog, spoiled meat. It had followed me back from the camp to finish me off here. I screamed. I gripped the curtain with both hands. The rod gave way, the rings fell one after another. I slipped forward, fell to the base of the shower, dragging my drenched shroud. I hit my forehead. Blood. It was streaming from my wounded eyelid. It followed the furrows of the tiles, flushed by burning water. I shouted again. A mouthful of bile. And then I cried. I cried the tears that were left me, that had always threatened to come. The tears of the orphan picking a flower to say goodbye to his mother. The tears of the student not daring to touch the skin of a father too dead. I cried all the rage in me, the violence, the hatred. I cried for the children of Kiryat Shmona and Shatila. I cried to put an end to tears.

Marwan entered abruptly. He threw himself into the shower. Shut off the taps, swearing in Arabic. I was on the floor, in a ball. He lifted me gently, his head against mine. He took me in his arms, carried me away like a sleeping child. I was Antigone, head on one side, feet on the other, blood on my torso and thighs.

'It's over. You're going home. You're going back, George.'

'They killed Antigone.'

Just a breath of voice. To hear myself say it.

'It's Imane they killed,' Marwan replied.

He walked into the living room with his bleeding trophy. His wife cried out. She hid in the bedroom. The daughter buried her face in a cushion.

'They didn't kill Antigone,' my Druze repeated.

He put me on the bed, covering me with a sheet. He leaned over me.

'You are Antigone. And Sam. And Nakad and all the others. There are not enough of them to kill her.'

20

MIMI-CUCKOO

No one had ever really held me tightly in their arms. Before we reached the line, Marwan did, and I took shelter there. He crossed his hands behind my back, enfolding my shoulders and my chest. I pressed my face into his shoulder. He smelled of musk, and the leather of his vest. He held me like that, for a long moment, in the crowd of taxi drivers. Me, with my bag on the ground, my arms limp. And then he gently pushed me away, keeping his eyes on mine. His hands on my shoulders, he held me there, silently, at a distance. He turned around. He got back into his car. When he started it up, his large body was shaking. He was crying. Maybe. I'll never know. He didn't look back, didn't raise his hand through the open window. He went back to war without me.

I climbed into a minibus for the port of Jounieh. A cross swung below the rearview mirror, hanging from an olive wood rosary. Marwan's arms were still hugging me. I felt his warmth, his beating heart. He held me on the boat, he held me against him in Cyprus, when I boarded the plane, when I slept against the window, arriving at Roissy in a rainstorm. I didn't want to leave his arms for others. I wanted no refuge except his. I walked down the halls of the airport the way one walks to the scaffold. Fear gripped my stomach, my heart raced, trying to flee. When my bag arrived at the baggage claim, I went and sat down across from it, on the floor, against the wall. I stretched out my painful leg. I looked at all the live people. There were faces burnt by the sun, skin shining with salt, bare breasts under open silk, scents of Tahitian gardenia. There were words of vacation. There was the crowd, wild, inelegant life, pushing its way noisily towards the return. There was laughter that sickened my grief.

I stood up and walked.

When the sliding doors opened, I saw only them. My handful of life, in a cluster of welcomes. Aurora, Louise, two friends, a few buddies. I had so hoped they wouldn't be there.

I heard my name called in the hall, shouted like a bravo. I saw their arms in the air. The smiles spread across their faces. One fool was waving a Palestinian flag. I lowered my eyes. I was ashamed. I tried to manage a smile for them. I dredged the depths of myself. The brilliant smile of Imane, the warm smile of Marwan, the mocking smile of Charbel. I raised my head. I found something. I came back to them wearing Nakad's smile, when he forgave my unease at being too loved by him. A magnificent smile. The smile I could have offered back to him, I gave to these strangers.

Louise ran towards me. I put one knee on the ground, dropped my bag, my passport, everything in my hands. She ran into my arms, between Marwan and me. We were careful not to squeeze her too hard. She kept saying, 'Papa,' rubbing my cheek with the palm of her hand. I was bristly from the night. I expected the crowd, but they didn't approach. Not yet. Aurora kept her distance. Friends, too. Their respect told me I was hard to look at. I got up painfully, my hands full of tenderness. I put my arms around Aurora. I had imagined and feared this moment. Her perfume blasted me. It was flowery, like a honeyed sweet. She stroked my hair. I put my hands on her back. I didn't hug her. I congratulated her. She kissed my cheek, my lips, my lowered brow. She was eating me. Devouring what was left of me. She sought my eyes, ran her finger over the bad scars, cried over my fallen eyelids, my gaunt body. She told me that my face wasn't the same. She took a step back.

'It's you. It's really you!'

Louise was squeezed against my injured leg. That's when the others came towards me. There were more of them than before. Friends from Jussieu, class monitors from my school, teachers. They came for a taste of drama, to be part of it, to see up close someone who had seen. Aurora held my waist, my shoulders, my cheeks. My wife had ten arms. She only released one of my hands. I extended it to the others, who crushed it with the fervour of a liberated crowd. Now I was laughing. I was lost. Passed in a few hours from the arms of an armed Druze to airport hugs. People slapped me on the back, ran their hands through my hair, crowded me from all sides. One of them handed me a glass of champagne. He had brought a bottle all the way there. And one glass, just for me. Amid the hoopla, the bustle, he wanted me to celebrate my return. I took the glass. I drained it, throwing throwing back my head. And they applauded. I had just won a competition, a rally, beaten a record. A photographer friend flitted around me like a magazine reporter. Passers-by stopped to look, trying to recognize me. But of course, you know! An actor, I think. What's his name again? I let myself be led slowly towards the exit. I wanted to buy a newspaper at the arrival newsstand. Retrieve Beirut in the news. I didn't have the will to escape them. My daughter wore a plaid dress. I looked away. I saw it pulled up, her panties torn, and blood on her thighs. I let go of her hand. I pushed away Aurora's, that had moved from her tears to my skin. I asked for a little calm, just a little. And then they all understood. Calm. Of course, calm. How had they not thought of that? I was coming back from there. From what they pronounced in a whisper. After everything I'd seen, I must be exhausted, in shock. I needed air, silence, the time it took for us to regroup at the house.

'We'll meet up at the house?'

Aurora had organized a little party. Not much. Just a gathering to honour the day. With everyone who couldn't make it to the airport.

'Who else?'

Aurora laughed. What did I mean, who else? Her girlfriends, members of the Palestine committee, our friends!

We reached the car. She put my bag in the boot.

'You're not happy about it?'

Seeing all those people? Yes, of course. It was a good idea. I just needed a little time alone before they arrived. To catch my breath, gather my thoughts, to mask my rage and my disgust.

'There's something you're not telling me?'

I looked at Aurora. Her worried face. I shook my head. I had no words for her. I hid the dead that she would never know about.

When we reached the apartment, I asked to go out. The guests would arrive at eight. I just needed to see the neighbourhood. To walk alone. Please, Aurora. Please, Louise. Just long enough to wander a bit towards Saint-Lazare, in streets with no horns and no stares. Please, everyone. One hour to myself. To get these clothes off, this smell. I want to walk beside buildings with no bullet holes, see unarmed passers-by. I want to hear the sound of my footsteps on wet pavements. I want to see plane trees. I want the calm of street lights. I want window displays, shops closing, the rumble of the Metro underground in my belly. I want to walk into a bar. The whistle of a coffee percolator, cognac opened with a quick hit against the edge of a rubbish bin. I want to see the glasses at the edge of the counter. I want the theatre posters in the street. I want to pass young girls and boys. I want to be able to come home.

Aurora kissed me. She understood. It seemed hard for her to hear, but she understood. She thought about it. Then she suggested leaving Louise with a neighbour and accompanying my solitude. I refused, taking her hands in mine. She raised her eyebrows, opened her mouth. Okay. She understood. Later, then? My love, my wounded, my revenant. Until later, my husband forever. Until later, father of our frail child, who so, so very much wants a little brother.

Until later, future father whom I love. Until later, not long. Okay? Because the guests would be arriving soon. Yes. Of course, she would let me go. And, yes, in my place, she would have done the same thing. She would have gone into the streets to seek calm. But she would have taken me with her. That's right. She would have left the child with the neighbour and taken my arm. Because I was necessary to her, vital. And I, I would have been proud and happy that she trusted me. But no, of course she wasn't in my shoes. We weren't really alike, actually. It's surprising how many ways we were different. Not in the important things, though. But in lots of ways. The sooner I left, the sooner I'd be back? Of course. I was right.

'Yes, go.'

'Papa is leaving again!' Aurora cried to Louise as she entered the living room.

'Papa's coming back,' I answered.

And then I closed the door without waiting. I ran down the stairs. I feared the voice of one, the tears of the other. I arrived at the foyer, our letterbox, our names on it, my daughter's name in red pencil. Us, our life, our little box of news. The glass-paned door. The street. I turned left. I walked fast, fearing the first known faces. I walked up rue de Leningrad, I ran on rue de Rome. I entered the station at Saint-Lazare. A train was leaving for Dieppe. I hesitated. I decided against it. I walked slowly back up rue d'Amsterdam. I went back to my family the way a schoolboy returns to class on a Monday morning. My head hurt, and my stomach. My throat was dry. There was noise at the girls' house, through the open windows. I was the missing part that completed us. I climbed the stairs. Aurora had put on her record of Palestinian songs. I stopped on the floor below. I would like to be that neighbour. To go somewhere besides home. To have seen nothing. To know nothing. I climbed the final step. I put one hand on the door. I rang the bell. I surrendered.

* * *

A white spot fogged my right eye. A drop of water that bathed my surroundings. Wounds of 'foreign war' were not covered by my insurance. Or physical therapy or medical exams. Dr Cohen had recommended an ophthalmologist friend. He said I'd been lucky, but that nothing in my mind was intact. I worried him. He had found me three days after my return, sitting on the pavement across from the hospital. I hadn't wanted to go in. I hadn't been able to push the door open, take the lift up, walk down the corridor, pass the nurses' station, enter Sam's room, where he'd been asleep for a week. My brother had closed his eyes. He no longer responded, no longer moved. And I didn't want his silence.

'Do it for him,' the doctor had advised me.

Do what? Sit next to him? Adjust the sheets of his deathbed? Lie to him? Tell him about the triumph we dreamt of for *Antigone*? Charbel in majesty, Imane in beauty. His play applauded long into the night, from both sides of the Green Line. Make him dream once more with the words of a traitor?

'Then do it for you.'

For me? Share the blood with him? Splatter his sheets, his face, his hands? Let me tell you, Samuel Akounis. Here's what happened. Everything was going fine until the planes came. And you know what, Sam? They destroyed everything. Our actors? Scattered, running back to their trenches. Your theatre? Leveled by the last bombs. Antigone? Dead, Antigone. Her throat slit, her body torn, violated. You hear me? And you, how are you, my old friend?

The doctor reached out his hand to help me up, but I didn't touch it. He hoped I would go to Sam's bedside to tell him goodbye. I didn't move. He squatted beside me. He put his bag on the pavement the way a country doctor makes do with a kitchen table. He told me. Yes, he'd seen me the night before. And the day before that, here on the pavement. He had waited to avoid startling me. But this time, he decided to come. He examined my eyes, right there, in the street, asking me to follow the light in his hand. He listened to my heart. He took my blood pressure. Passers-by looked away. I was someone who'd had a sudden malaise while walking.

He said his hospital was open to me. Day or night, my time was his time. He would personally take me to Samuel Akounis. As soon as I had the courage. As soon as I wanted to. As soon as I needed to. He told me his days were running out fast. That I was fortunate he was still alive. He told me to think hard about it. He talked about words that come too late, through tears at a tombstone. He put his hand on my shoulder. He addressed me as a friend.

He said I should rest, sleep. That the damage wasn't just to my eyes. But everywhere else in my body, with no visible wound.

He gave me his card. I offered him my last smile.

* * *

Twice I came back and sat facing the hospital. Then I gave up. I couldn't endure another death.

Every morning, I took Louise to daycare. Aurora worked, I was on sick leave. After dropping off our child, I bought *Libération*, then, in the afternoon, *Le Monde*. I searched for Lebanon on their pages.

On 1 December 1982, the Israelis abruptly withdrew from Shouf, leaving the Druze and the Christians face to face.

'We will take back every inch of land with our teeth.'

I thought of Marwan's strength, Nakad's sweetness.

I knew Joseph-Boutros' men were ready for them.

I called often. Once I spoke to Haemon, twice to his mother. Marwan was in battle. He had replaced the pistol with a rifle. My winter began like that, watching for the names of mountain villages in the ink of newspapers. Late one afternoon, I forgot to pick up Louise at daycare. I went home without her, in the middle of the night. On Christmas Eve, I lit the burner under a pan of water and left the house. The radio announced that a Christian village had been martyred by Druze militia, that women and children had been massacred, that terrified civilians wandered the roads. Aurora got home in time. The handle of the pan had melted, the kitchen wall was black with soot. Neighbours had called the fire department. Everything tilted when I went in. My wife was crying about the sooty wall. I was screaming about the massacre of Christians. We were two adversaries, facing off, our eyes hard and our words harsh. My hands clenched. I wanted her to stop talking. To stop everything, now. Screaming, breathing, living. I wanted her to turn her back on me, renounce me, not say another word. Her hair covered her eyes. She was crazed with pain. I wanted to take her in my arms or strangle her, I don't know which. I reached out my hands, she screamed.

'Don't touch me! Don't touch me again, ever!'

She was afraid. I was afraid of myself. I heard her screaming the words of a wounded woman, a worried mother. Aurora didn't understand. Aurora didn't understand anything anymore. She said I walked the streets like a sleepwalker, indifferent to pavements, cars, stoplights. I didn't notice people around me. I wasn't the same. I woke up in the night. I didn't look her in the eye. I wasn't happy, never happy, ever, anymore. I hadn't smiled at her in months. Laughter had left our home. I didn't touch her. My body pulled away when she reached her hand towards my skin. I slept at the edge of the bed, one foot on the floor. I didn't see our friends. I never went out. At the park, on playgrounds, she was like a divorced woman. Louise was going to start nursery school in January. Did I know that? Where? What school?

'Answer me, George!'

I didn't know. I had lost interest in life. The night before, my daughter had handed me a drawing, her first man, with long legs and eyes as big as its head. I scribbled on the back of it as I listened to the war on the radio. We didn't eat together anymore. I ate only rice and bread. I didn't change my trousers or my shirt. I didn't speak. I banged my fist on the table, listening to the news. I cut out newspaper articles, underlined them entirely, line after line. I circled sentences. I added words endlessly, filled every margin, added question marks, exclamation marks, by the dozen. I tacked these crumpled papers to every wall of the living room, connected them with coloured strings. I talked to myself. I didn't respond to anyone. I was ill. I was crazy. I needed medical care. I had to see someone. To get help. She begged me. She loved me. She yelled that she couldn't take any more of this life. Louise was beside the door, sitting against the wall. I hadn't seen her when I came in. She was crying silently, her hands covering her ears. I spun around sharply, hit the kitchen door just above my daughter. I broke it the way one strikes an enemy, my fist caught in the wood. Louise sank to the floor, Aurora threw herself over her. Swept her up and ran to the bedroom without a word. I stood there, my hand a prisoner of the door. My head was spinning, I was shaking. I was breathing with my mouth open, a drum in my stomach. They were crying. Aurora whispered her love. I extracted my hand. I looked at it. It was bleeding. The wrist, the palm, the knuckles were torn. It wasn't my hand. Or my arm, or any part of me. A violence that was not my own. I wanted to go to the bedroom, reassure them, lick their tears, silence their weeping. I couldn't. I backed into the hallway. I opened the door. I left. I went and sat in front of the hospital. I left again. I walked. I rediscovered the war within me. I knew a person could die of rage. I knew I wasn't ready yet.

* * *

Louise turned three on 9 January 1983. I went back home in the early afternoon, unexpectedly, after a two-week absence. First, I had gone to a hotel. A ratty, miserable place in the Barbès quarter, with a flashing sign that intercepted my nights. Then I was taken in by a couple of friends who opened their sofa bed to me. Aurora knew. She had called me twice, but I couldn't answer. The sound of my fist in the door hung in her voice.

'Sunday is our daughter's birthday,' Aurora told me.

I took these words as an invitation.

I didn't use my key. I rang the bell. There was children's laughter inside. Coloured balloons decorated a wall, and a drawing of a fairy. Aurora opened the door. She wore the smile of someone greeting a child. She saved it for me.

'Papa!' Louise called out.

She flung herself against my legs. I squatted. I squeezed her. Aurora sat with us. We had recovered our circle of love.

'Come,' my wife murmured.

Six children were in the living room, seated in a circle around a clown. They were waiting for Aurora to come back.

'Oh, look at the handsome father who's late!' the clown laughed.

The children burst out laughing.

'Let's clap very, very, very loud for this father who's late!'

It was a woman's voice. The littles ones gave me an ovation. Four girls, two boys. Their faces were smeared with make-up and they wore paper hats.

'Now that everyone's here, do you want me to call Mimi-Cuckoo?'

The children yelled yes. The clown plunged an arm into a big red sequined bag. Pulled a sock puppet over her right hand, like an evening glove, up to her elbow. The puppet had very red hair tied back, red cheeks and a huge smile.

'Pippi Longstocking!' one little girl shouted.

'Ah, no! It's Mimi-Cuckoo!' the clown replied.

The puppet's head hung down, limp.

'But I think she's still sleeping. Shall we wake her up?'

Screams from the children.

'We'll have to call her very loudly! Let's go! Mimi-Cuckoo! Mimi-Cuckoo! Mimi-Cuckoo!'

I sat on the ground, in the corner. Louise chanted the doll's name, clapped her hands, happy to see her move. The clown was looking at me. It spoke to the children, then to me again. Insistent. I thought the clown wanted me to wake up Mimi-Cuckoo by clapping my hands, too. The clown watched Aurora attentively. They must be friends. I sought a face under the white cream and the plastic nose, searched the eyes circled in black. Mimi-Cuckoo awoke. She greeted the audience graciously. The clown was a ventriloquist. The puppeteer had a lovely, deep voice. The doll's voice was high-pitched. It asked the clown, 'So, I'm made of rags and you're a real person?'

And the clown said yes. She had a real house and real friends. The puppet only had her, and lived in a bag. That's how it was. If her hand stopped moving, the puppet couldn't move.

'Oh, really! Try it, let's see!'

The children laughed. I was entranced. Little by little, the clown lost its agility. Its movements became stiff, mechanical. Its eyes had left me, gone elsewhere. Its smile went out. Its speech had a brassy sound. Its voice was piercing. Mimi-Cuckoo was coming to life. She spoke with a lower voice, blinked her eyes, opened and closed her mouth, danced around, adopted the movements of her mistress. Life was shifting from one to the other. The clown gave up. It had been standing when it flopped to the floor and slid clumsily onto one side, overcome with fatigue. Only its arm moved, making circles that grew increasingly disturbing. No one was laughing any more. Even Aurora paled. I felt nauseous. Across from me, a boy. A blue T-shirt. Mickey, Shatila. I saw the boy lying in the dust, broken open from the back, his forehead blown off by a bullet.

Mimi-Cuckoo had killed the clown. It lay there, inert, one arm raised. The doll was snickering, looking at the children. It frowned, made faces, raised a fist, bared its teeth. Threatened them. Two of them jumped up, screaming, a third ran out into the hall. Louise started to cry. I crawled on all fours, like an angry cat. I pounced on this horridness, spitting and blowing hard. I ripped it off the clown's hand. I spun it in the air above my head, then smashed it violently against the wall.

'George!'

Aurora's voice. She screamed. I opened my eyes. The children were in a circle. None of them had ever moved. The clown was protecting its face with both arms, backing away towards the window. I held Mimi-Cuckoo by her undergarment, her smashed head hanging from my hand. The children scattered. Louise was crying. Aurora gathered them in the hall the way a teacher evacuates a classroom. There was fire, smoke, sirens by the thousands, bullets whizzing in all directions. The clown had shed its blue wig, its red nose.

'Don't hurt me!'

It was a woman. She was trying to escape. She crept slowly along the wall without looking away from me. I was leaning forward. I dropped the puppet. I looked at the empty room, the decorations on the ceiling, the paper plates on the table, the stars on the cups, the party napkins, the cartoon faces on the rubber balls. I looked at the mirror over the fireplace. My twisted mouth, my helmeted expression.

* * *

I slept. I slept for a long time, buried under the dead bodies. I had no more nights, only nightmares. I took pills even to breathe. The day I turned thirty-three, Louise made me a yoghurt cake that we ate in the clinic's park with Aurora and two friends. The spring went by that way, between the bed and the window. Then the summer. In June of 1983, I was allowed to go out, to venture into the streets. But I returned to sleep in its shelter. A soundproof room, newspapers, radio, television. I was safe there. The first few weeks, Aurora wanted me not to receive any news about Lebanon. I read papers of lace, the forbidden articles carefully cut away. And then they stopped doing it. Doctor Cohen had intervened, explained that hiding the problem would just postpone it. It wasn't his hospital. He only came to see me once, bringing *L'Orient-Le Jour*, which he had purchased at the Place de l'Opéra.

On 12 July, the eve of my official release, I got a letter from Marwan. It was short, dry, brutal. Nakad had been killed by Phalangists, along with three other young Druzes. None of them were fighters. Their car had wandered into enemy territory. By mistake. They were lined up against a wall and shot. I kept the letter in my hand for two days and two nights. I didn't eat or drink. I had to go see Sam. After Antigone, Haemon had just been murdered. I had to tell him. None of this could remain between me and myself. It was too heavy, too much, too painful for one man. I would go tomorrow. I would go into his room. He would have his eyes closed. I would have my hands covered in their blood. And we would share the silence.

I told myself all that. But I was unable to go through his door.

21

LÉOPOLDINE

I didn't know anyone. A few nameless faces, some sad looks, murmurs in the hall. I had seen this girl, that boy. Maybe at the theatre, maybe at Jussieu. I didn't know any more. Sam's casket had been closed without me, late in the morning. I went up afterwards, by the service stairs, postponing the moment of knocking at his door. Aurora had taken part in the vigil, with a group of actresses Sam had directed. They gathered for the night. I hadn't wanted to see him dying. I didn't want to see him dead. I stayed home with Louise. I took her to kindergarten. I stayed away from everything. I waited at the café for the stiff men to come and close the box. I watched through the window as they arrived, their suits too short, their shirtsleeves so long they almost covered their hands. I ordered a drink. A Calvados to strafe my heart. Another. Another.

I stood up when they came back out. I crossed the boulevard. As I neared the other side, I put Sam's kippah on my head. In the street, to feel its weight. The pallbearers would return early in the afternoon. I had two hours to be with Sam. I decided to go to the Bagneux cemetery after the ceremony. Once everyone had left. I didn't want to mingle my footsteps with theirs. I didn't want to follow them. I didn't want to line up, or shake hands, or greet anyone. I wouldn't go to the cemetery until the following day. I had failed. I had come back without Antigone, with nothing. I was abandoning my friend to the earth.

I tried to leave the funereal room. A young man held me back. He was Greek. He had heard a rumour about Antigone. He said that Sam had written out his last wishes on paper, over there. One page, cut out of a notebook, lay on top of the casket.

> *Each of my friends will recite, sing, and leave with two objects.*

That was it. A woman was leaving, a small box in her hands. Another took down the photo of the tank crushing the gate of the Polytechnic.

> 'Are you blind, or what? I'm right here! Here, don't you see?'

Sam was pointing to a black spot in the photo of the crowd.

> 'How do you know it's you?'

> 'I know, that's all. Look! I'm falling off the gate.'

I smiled. I made my way around the sofa, the table. There were about a dozen people, sipping drinks, not talking much. Duruflé was playing his requiem. I slid behind the armchair, leaning on it. I watched the people. And my reflection in the window. One autumn Monday, everything was said.

> *Demain, dès l'aube, à l'heure où blanchit la campagne, je partirai.*
> *Vois-tu, je sais que tu m'attends.*
> *J'irai par la forêt, j'irai par la montagne.*
> *Je ne puis demeurer loin de toi plus longtemps …*

I didn't raise my voice. I recited, looking out the window. Without seeing anything inside, without hearing a sound. I added no intonation, no colour. I let the words dress my voice. I was sad. Infinitely sad. But I had no more tears. The last of them had left with the blood, the water and the soap, in Marwan's shower.

No one applauded. Just as, earlier, a young woman recited a speech from *Electra*, by Giraudoux. People's eyes moved away. Their glasses went back to their lips. I had nothing more to do here.

I went into the study. I took the German cookbook. And Sam's bag, his Olympic Airlines shoulder bag in scratched imitation leather. I said my goodbyes. I exchanged looks with a few people, nodded to a few. Shook a few hands. And then I left my bottle of beer on the windowsill.

When I reached the street, I opened the book. I took out the portrait of Joseph Boczov, slipped between two pages, then I threw the German cookbook into the nearest rubbish bin. Before I went down the steps into the Metro, I looked at the man from the Red Poster. Sam had spoken to me about the executed man with words that were too broad. I hadn't understood anything about him. It took the silence of the aftermath of war for me to recognize him. I ran my finger across his hollow cheeks, the look in his eye, his thin lips.

> 'Look at him, George. He's about to die. There's nothing he can do about it. But he still dreams of ripping a soldier apart.'

A man was exiting the Metro. He looked at me, then looked away. I was sitting on the stone steps. Talking to a photograph. With the kippah on my head, I made a promise to this photo, to avenge it.

* * *

The only outdoor space we had was Parc Monceau. No family home or second home, a country locale where seasons change. On Sunday, 2 October 1983, for the first time since I left the hospital, Aurora had let me take Louise for the afternoon. I held her hand in mine. We walked along the paths in the park, examining the exhausted leaves. Slowly, at her speed, amazed at every step she took.

I pushed my daughter on a green metal swing. Next, she wanted to see the ducks, then the ponies. She asked me for a bicycle for Christmas, like the one the little boy was riding in front of us. I bought two tokens for the carousel. She sat in a chipped wooden car, then on a sinister-looking horse. I stood with the mothers, the fathers, the attentive, so full of love. Each time she passed in front of me, I raised a hand, chanting her name. I did what the others were doing. I mimed the papa. I saw myself, leaning towards the spinning ride with its sad music. So many of the living, it made my heart ache. One man was taking pictures of his son. A mother was wiping her child's knees. Louise wanted an ice cream. I said yes to everything. She rarely looked me in the eye. My gestures were exaggerated.

'Louise is afraid of you,' Aurora had told me.

At the sweet stand, two women were sizing each other up. One had gotten there first. The other disagreed. She accused her of jumping the queue.

'I couldn't care less!'

I had taken my place behind them. I was getting angry. I slowed my breathing. I had to calm down. Two women were at war with each other over a sweet, on a Sunday of peace? I lowered my eyes, my head. I listened to other things. Children's shouts, the whistle of the guard protecting the grass, the melancholy notes of the carousel. Louise asked for a scoop of chocolate ice cream. It was too big, wobbling on the waffle cone. After a few steps, it fell off. It landed at her feet. Louise was stunned. She looked at the crushed ice cream, her empty cone, back at the ice cream, and started to cry. In her blue parka, her face swallowed by the hood, I had never seen her so small. Her face was wet with tears, her feet turned in, one sock fallen down, her pink trousers too short. She was crying. And I wanted to silence her grief. I bent down. An ice cream? That's not so serious. What child cries over an ice cream? Really, a scoop of chocolate? Aren't you ashamed of yourself? I grabbed her by the shoulders. She wasn't listening. I jerked the empty cone from her hand, scraped the ground with it: the crushed scoop of ice cream, bits of dust and gravel. I handed her the brutal gift.

'Here! Eat it! Eat your ice cream!'

People were staring. I saw the harsh look of a mother. Louise backed away, stumbled. I didn't touch her, I swear. She caught her left foot behind her right ankle. She fell, face first, her hands behind her. Her forehead hit the ground, her cheek. I snatched her up. She was crying in pain, in astonishment. She called out for her mother. She was bleeding. Her forehead, her cheek. I pulled out the gravel stuck in her face, piece by piece. I repeated that she had fallen, I hadn't pushed her, it wasn't my fault, she had slipped, stumbled over her feet. She had tripped. It happens to everyone. And what a terrible idea, to put gravel in a children's play area!

I gathered Louise in my arms. I wiped her cuts with my sleeve. It was nothing, really. Just some scratches, some playground scrapes. I ran with her all the way home. Three times on the way there I stopped to catch my breath. I was angry. Picking up the scoop of ice cream from the ground. I had mismanaged a painful moment. I had yelled that elsewhere, in cradles, babies had had their throats slit. That children had been chopped to pieces, dismembered, crushed with stones. And my daughter was crying over a fucking ice cream? That, that was her misfortune? A scoop of chocolate fallen out of a waffle cone? The miseries of peacetime made me sick. A man approached me. He asked me to calm down. I stood up like a wild animal. He backed off without a word. I addressed him, the others. That was your problem? Scoops of ice cream? Skinned knees? Tangled hair after a bath? Those are your lives? This Sunday that stinks of Monday? These flocks of families? The smiles for a photo? This pathetic happiness? Louise was afraid of me. So I pulled her out of the sandpit, the park, the street, out of Sunday. I ran to the house to shelter her.

Aurora took our daughter in her arms. She said she had fallen. That's all. She had been on the swing, the carousel, she had seen the ducks, the ponies, and the leaves were red. She had three chestnuts in her pocket, for her teacher. She didn't mention the ice cream. Not a word. She had slipped. While her mother was running the bath, she asked me to wash her. I carried her to the tub. She threw her toys into the warm water. I watched her, sitting on the edge of the tub. Her eye was swollen. The scrape on her forehead was a wound. It was me. I had done that. I had hurt my child. I smiled at her. I patted her gently with a little water. And then I rubbed. Her hands, her feet, her body. I laid her down in the tub to wash her hair. Her strawberry shampoo. And the same question, as always.

'Does it sting your eyes?'

'No, it doesn't sting.'

I wrapped her in her towel, carried her to her room. I loved that moment, my wet child pressed against me, her hair against my cheek, her arms around my neck. We chose pyjamas.

'I can put them on by myself!'

I took her hand to walk to the kitchen. I had never done that. To step off the pavement, at the door of the school, right before the bell, but not in our hallway, crossing through the house. I caught Aurora's eye. She was smiling. She put her book down on the coffee table. Father and daughter, walking hand in hand through the watery strait of the hallway. She came to meet us in the kitchen. Louise wanted macaroni again. I added some bits of ham. She ate slowly, drinking noisily between each bite. I sat on the stool. Watching my daughter. Pressed against my back, Aurora wrapped her arms around my shoulders. She kissed me lightly on the neck. She had never done that.

'Are you in love?' our child asked.

I smiled. Aurora went into our bedroom.

'I'm going to bed. You coming?'

I sat next to Louise, on the edge of the bed, to tell her a bedtime story. I left the light on in the bathroom. I had trouble breathing. I looked at her damaged face, her hands, her hair, I stole the final images. Her eyes sank into sleep. She had her thumb in her mouth. She turned over. I read one more page. A white rabbit ran between the sky and the snow, unaware that colour existed. Louise was asleep. I closed the book. Went into the living room. I sat on the floor, in the dark, my back against the wall. I nodded off, I think.

At 4 am, I went back into my daughter's room. I leaned over her, as I had every night since I came home from Lebanon. I put my hand on her warm forehead, her chest. Every night I sought her heartbeat, fast as a small animal's, the blood beating at the base of her neck. Every night I listened to her breathing, inhaled her breath. Every night I feared my child might die before dawn.

Then I went into our bedroom. Aurora was sleeping, too, on her back, her mouth half-open. She had lit our candle.

The first time we made love, Aurora had turned out the light, then lit a candle. She thought she was overweight. She was afraid for me to see her nude. Hidden under the sheets, she played with the shadows. We had never made love except in this golden glow. Aurora put the candle in a glass. It was the vessel of our sacred fire. The old candelabra had come later. It was the first thing we purchased together, at an open-air market in Cancale. I had brought the bed, she arrived with her refrigerator, her stove, we transported our bookcases, our wardrobes. Her unmatched chairs, my table. We had my sheets, her pillows, our coloured utensils, her plates from Brittany, pans from Mayenne. But this copper candelabra was ours. She paid one half and I paid the other. She didn't see why only the man could give light.

I remember her eyes when she showed it to me, her hand raised above the cacaphony of the market. She was smiling, winking, flicking her tongue from side to side, frolicking like a child, tapping the air like an orchestra conductor with his baton. That same night, we bought candles and set up the candelabra for the first time. We took it with us on holidays, on trips, to friends' when we stayed overnight. By its light, we had made our Louise. Aurora counted the days in a notebook. This was it, tonight, now. The candle was almost dead. We lit the remains of the black wick. We made love until the wick gave out. Until the smell of the heavy smoke. Until the crackling. Until the darkness.

Aurora moved slightly. She put her hands under her cheek, turned onto her side. I turned, too. We were facing each other. I looked at her. Her night movements. Her expressive forehead. The tingling of her nostrils. I shifted onto my back, crossed my hands behind my neck. There was the park, then the bath, the meal, the bedtime story,

Louise's breath and Aurora's sighs. The candle went out. The smell of heavy smoke, crackling, darkness. The farewell ceremony was coming to an end.

I felt nothing. Not sadness or bitterness. I had no taste in my mouth, no emotion. I wasn't cold or hot, or hungry, or sleepy anymore. I no longer heard my own heart, or my thoughts, or the tumult that silence creates. I wasn't afraid. I turned my head. Looked one last time at the oval photo that I was leaving behind. The three of us. Aurora, laughing and beautiful. Louise, squinting in the sun. Me, smiling goodbye with my lips closed. We were destroyed. The war had made my wife a widow. It had made our daughter only half a child. And now it called me back. War claimed me as its own. It didn't fear my shouts, my blows, or even my expression. Only war truly hungered for me.

22

CREON

I left their life the next morning. Kissed Aurora, held Louise in my arms. Tonight, we'd all eat pizza on trays in front of the television. I was supposed to stop by the dry cleaner's, pick up our winter coats. When they left for school, I cleaned up our breakfast things. The bowls, the salted butter on the table, the glass of orange juice my daughter hadn't touched. I sponged off the table, swept the kitchen floor. Then I pulled the covers over our bed, fluffed the pillows before putting them back. I picked up a belt, my wife's blouse. I put away a book fallen from the table. I went into Louise's room. Her rumpled bed, the traces of her night. I picked up three stuffed animals, puzzle pieces. I put two pairs of trousers, two shirts and two pairs of underwear, socks and my toothbrush into a bag. I wrapped the key from Jaffa and the soil for Yassine in my grey scarf, with Sam's kippah. Also my copy of *Antigone*, annotated like a rough draft. The day before, I had transferred my money to my wife's account. And withdrawn enough cash to last a few weeks.

I had tried to write to Aurora and Louise. But none of my words made sense. They were too egotistical. I wasn't going to die tomorrow, like Joseph Boczov, yet I used the language of the executed. I wouldn't hang from a beam, yet I said goodbye like a broken old man. For Louise, I had drawn a winking sun. What was that? The sun mocking her? Leaving with a smile? Saying that it might come back? Then I drew stars on a white piece of paper, linking them together like a celestial dome. Papa in the sky. A funereal message.

So I wrote nothing, left nothing. Cleaning had erased every trace, and I had decided not to add anything. I put those attempts into my bag. I would throw them away in Beirut.

I turned out the lights in our apartment.

* * *

I figured out how to get back on my own. Cyprus, the boat, the port of Jounieh. The Beirut airport, now closed, had become the headquarters for the American forces. Going back to Lebanon forced me to take a circuitous route.

Marwan was there, leaning against his red car. He didn't have a smile for me. Didn't even welcome me. No more land, no more family to offer me. He spread his arms, I took refuge there. He hugged me the way he hugged Nakad. We passed through the Lebanese Forces' checkpoints. Marwan kept his eyes lowered. Their militia was fighting his people in the mountains. Three times, they searched us with our arms up. The boot of the car, the glovebox, underneath the seats, the shock absorbers. I was a theatre director and Marwan, my driver. Why a Druze? Because I lived at the Hotel Cavalier, in Hamra. A Druze hotel, so a Druze driver was more practical for me. Did we know what was happening in the mountains? Yes, of course we knew. The massacre of Christians? Yes, of course. The French press covers it in depth. What did I think of that? That it was atrocious, like all massacres.

We didn't speak on the way to Beirut. Once we crossed the Green Line, Marwan relaxed. He turned on the radio. At one corner, I was stunned. A bunker of sandbags with a sheet-metal roof surveilled the intersection. Inside, two French soldiers, their tricolour flag planted atop the fragile structure. I turned back to look. Two boys. They were young, helmeted, with a machine gun stuck out of the firing slot, and children playing around them.

'The Americans barricade themselves, the French repair our electric lines,' Marwan commented.

His first sentence. And the last of the day.

I thought I would stay at his house. He dropped me off at the Cavalier. I returned to the same room on the second floor. With war, the prices had gone up. Sammy, the porter, told me that there was credit on my account for the nights I'd been absent. I had three weeks ahead of me. He also asked me if we were going to perform *Antigone*. I shrugged my shoulders. Maybe. I didn't know any more. He offered me a welcome drink, a cream of Scotch and heather honey. In the dining room the aquarium was intact. The entrance hall was empty. I stepped outside. It was dark. Beirut was quiet. No gunshots, no glass breaking, no shredded steel, no howling sirens. A doctor had told me that truce brought worry. Men slept to the sound of a cannon. Tumultuous noise became the norm. When the racket stopped, no one slept.

'I've never prescribed as many antidepressants and sleeping pills as during a calm spell,' he said.

In the great silence, even little babies were in distress. Their mothers preferred the ruckus of a mortar shell to the threat of silence, and babies sensed it.

I walked around outside the hotel. I came back anxious. My return was unwelcome. Marwan hadn't understood why I was coming back. A key, a handful of soil, two symbols to return to a Palestinian fighter held no interest for him. First I had written to him to connect with his pain. His Nakad, my Haemon. He, orphaned by a son, me, mourning my dream. He didn't answer. So I called him. Ten times in three days, fire in my belly.

'I'm coming back, Marwan.'

I was leaving everything. I had nothing left to do in the arms of peace. In a world where children cried over a scoop of ice cream. He had been sharp, brutal. Leave what? My family? My country? And to do what here? What right had I to claim a place in this war? I answered that it wasn't that. I wasn't claiming anything. I just wanted to honour a promise, to give a man his land and his key, retrieved in Shatila. And after that? What would I do then? I didn't know. Not exactly. I would go home, of course. I would go back to my own country, to skies without warplanes, nights without fear, cellars that sheltered only wine. And he made me swear. To go home afterwards, to go back where I came from, to go back to my life, my love, my tenderness. To watch over my students, to drink an autumn beer on an outdoor terrace, to sit on the Sunday grass, to tremble watching a film, to close my eyes for a song, to laugh to his health, to his memory, to never come back for as long as his country was bleeding. And I promised. Over the phone. I swore, my hand raised. And he agreed to be my host one last time.

After being driven out of Beirut, the fighters loyal to Arafat had returned to Lebanon. They set up camp in Tripoli, in the north. Then they were pushed back, into the Beddawi and Nahr el-Bared refugee camps, by Syrian troops and Palestinian dissidents. Yassine was there, trapped with his comrades. Imane's brother resisted attacks with his back against the wall. A journalist from *Paris Match* had interviewed him. His portrait had appeared in the weekly magazine. Before he returned to combat, Yassine had given the reporter a letter addressed to me. In the letter, he told me that his sister had been murdered in Shatila. And his father, his entire family. That he was the only one left. He hoped I was in good health. He hoped my eyes were seeing beautiful things. He was saying goodbye.

I showed the letter to Marwan when I arrived in Jounieh. He shrugged his shoulders. Yassine was in Beddawi two months ago? So? Was he alive? Dead? How to find him? How to get to the front lines? And all that for what? Remind me? A key and some dust? I yelled yes, that's right. That if he didn't help me, I'd go alone. On foot, on all fours, on my knees like a penitent. He didn't want to? I understood. He could leave me there, at the port. Leave, with his red car. Go back to his mountain to massacre the last Cedars. He opened the car door for me without responding. We didn't speak again until Beirut.

The next morning at 6 o'clock, Marwan drove me to his home. He had picked me up at the hotel the way a cop summons his prey. His wife wasn't there, or his daughters. Nakad smiled at us from his black wooden frame. Marwan made me sit in his own armchair. An honour. He couldn't take me to Tripoli, but he agreed to drop me off at the Syrian outpost on the coastal road. Every day Western journalists tried to cross the front lines with the authorization of Palestinian dissidents. I could cross over among them. It was risky, but doable. Everything could shut down overnight, but today we could still get to Tripoli. If I wanted, he would be my driver. I would need consular authorizations, the recommendations collected for *Antigone*. Marwan's name was on an official Greek document, as an 'official translator'. I had to carry that pass with me. The press had a headquarters on the outskirts of Tripoli. He would drop me there and go back to Beirut. He wouldn't do more this time. He couldn't do anything else, for himself or for me.

I was in his armchair. He was standing, very straight, in the middle of the room. I would say yes to everything. Thank you for everything. He stopped me with a single sweep of his hand.

'You have contact information for your Christian actor.'

It wasn't a question.

'Charbel?'

'Whatever. You have it?'

'I have it, yes.'

Marwan sat. He opened a bottle of water without offering me any.

'His brother is one of the Kataeb leaders.'

'Joseph-Boutros?'

The Druze nodded. He repeated the first name of the man who recited Victor Hugo looking through the scope on his rifle.

'Whoever holds the mountains, holds Lebanon. Did you know that?'

Marwan wasn't looking at me. He stood at the bay window, his hands clasped behind his back. I didn't answer. I didn't know what to answer.

'We have liberated sixty of our villages, do you know that?'

I knew, yes. Almost 250,000 Christians on the roads of exodus.

'And thousands of Phalangist militiamen fell back to Deir el Qamar, you know that, too?'

French television had reported that, and French radio and newspapers. The Kataeb were defending 30,000 civilians in the city. Under siege by the Druze. Both sides feared an assault.

'Do you know that the American Navy has bombed our positions?'

The battleship *New Jersey*, yes. I knew.

'And that the Phalangists are desperately trying to get provisions to their trapped men?'

No, I didn't know.

'Your actor's brother is one of the men breaking our blockade.'

Marwan turned back to face me. His expression had changed. He wasn't Nakad's unhappy father, or my laughing Druze, or anything that I knew of him. He had become the man of Mount Lebanon. He had the look of a jailor. I was afraid. Not of him, of myself. I understood that I wasn't in this chair to listen to him and understand. I knew that something enormous was emerging between us. He stopped talking. Looked at me. He was waiting. I asked.

'What do you want?'

Marwan crossed his arms. He had time. I was his prisoner. He was going to toss me a bowl of food at nightfall and a bucket for my needs. I raised my eyebrows. I encouraged my future executioner.

'Your actor knows where his brother is. He must tell you.'

'Tell me? Why me?'

'Because his men killed Nakad. And your Imane, too.'

'His men?'

'Yes. His, not his. What does it matter? It was Kataeb troops that came to Sabra and Shatila. They were the ones who decimated our villages. Whether he was there or not, I don't care. He wears their uniform, their cross. He's one of them. He's made of all the others, as I am made of all the Druzes that people this earth.'

I thought hard for a long time. I looked at Marwan. My eyes told him yes.

* * *

Charbel was leaving. When I arrived, he had zipped up his bag. He opened the door for me. He took a step back, looked at me. We fell into each other's arms without a word. Since the bombings of 4 June 1982, we hadn't been in touch. He had crossed the street, his hand in the air, wishing Imane good luck. He had called her 'little sister' for all time. The young Christian let me in. His apartment was full of boxes. He and his family were leaving Lebanon for England. His village in Shouf had been destroyed. Two of his cousins murdered by Druzes. Only his older brother remained in the fight.

'How is he?'

'He's a killer like the others,' Charbel answered.

He apologised. He was packing books into boxes. Stopped looking at me. I sat on a mattress on the floor.

'Antigone died in Shatila.'

Creon started to raise his arm, stopped mid-motion, a dictionary in his hand.

'She was raped, suffocated, and her throat slit.'

Charbel turned his back to me. He sat on the floor, facing the wall.

'They killed her family, too.'

I stood up. I had to fill the room that he had just deserted.

'What do you want, George?'

'Your brother.'

Charbel turned slowly towards me.

'What do you mean, my brother?'

I was facing him. I felt like I was the jailer now.

'He was in Shatila.'

'And? That will bring her back?'

I made Imane scream, I showed her fighting off blows, shrieking in terror and rage, ripping hair from the scalp of her executioner. I told him about the blood dripping from her open throat, the pallor of her thighs smeared with excrement. Charbel stood up. Leaned against the wall.

'You know what's going on in the mountains? They're burning our churches, our houses. Our women are being killed, and our children! You understand?'

He reached into his bag, pulled out a statue of the Virgin, decapitated.

'That's all that's left of our convent. You understand that?'

'Imane had nothing to do with that.'

'But everyone has something to do with it in a war! If the Palestinians hadn't been there, nothing would have exploded!'

I showed him a poster, one I had designed and a friend of mine had printed. It was for *Antigone*. With our names on it: Charbel, Imane, Nakad, Nabil, Nimer, Hussein, Khadijah, Madeleine and Yevgenia. Sam's, mine, the logos of the consulates and the cultural associations. It was white, red, green and beautiful, with a cedar, like a genealogical tree, connecting enemies branch by branch to a trunk planted in a shared land.

'Show me who burnt your village, on this poster. Give me names. Who attacked your church? Imane? Nakad? He is dead. Nakad. Dragged out of a car and executed by your buddies.

'They aren't my friends!' Charbel yelled.

'Your brother's friends. Same thing!'

'No, it's not the same. I am not a killer. I have never killed anyone. I will never kill anyone. I am leaving, you understand? I am getting out of here. I don't want to stay in this country any longer.'

I put the poster on a box of dishes. I couldn't go any further. I held out my hand to Charbel, to Creon, to my friend, to the dream. He took it. I don't know which was more painful.

I was about to leave. I had turned away. I was giving up.

'My brother will be here tomorrow.'

I held my breath.

'He wants to wish me good luck.'

I didn't dare look at Charbel.

'Why are you telling me this?'

'I didn't tell you anything.'

I caught his eye. He was relieved.

'Can you live with that, Charbel?'

'And you, George?'

I didn't have an answer for him. I had nothing left at all. No legs, no head, no belly, no heart. I didn't extend my hand to him as I left. He didn't offer his. We had just condemned a man to die, he and I. Me for Imane. Marwan for Nakad. He, I never found out. I thought about Polynices and Eteocles. I was insane. In this brutal moment, I was dreaming of tragic beauty. Charbel had just handed me a knife and I was looking at myself in its blade.

I asked him not to be there the next day. He said he wouldn't be. He did not see me out.

'And you had come to make peace?'

I didn't answer him. I didn't dare tell him that a Druze killer would be with me. I had hidden Marwan. Tomorrow, I would let an enemy from the mountain into this Christian home. I didn't support him. I wasn't taking sides. I knew that villages on both sides were dying.

* * *

The militiaman stood on the doorstep. He rang twice, then slid the key into the lock. As he pushed the door open, I called to him.

'Joseph-Boutros?'

He turned. He understood. He got his hand into his vest just as Marwan and another man hurled him into the house. I followed them in. I closed the door. The Christian was on the floor, his revolver at the other end of the hall. The Druzes were kicking him. They broke his skull, his nose, his neck. I moved aside. I felt nothing. I was in Paris, in 1973, settling a score with a black rat. I knew these blows, this blood, the crack of bone giving way. Marwan crouched down, hitting the militiaman's face with both fists. He was howling in Arabic. I heard Nakad's name again and again as his fists fell like rain. He pulled him up by the hair, bashed the back of his head against the concrete floor. Again and again. Then he raised his foot to crush his face, a human soup stuck to his shoe. The other Druze pulled out a dagger. He knelt to slit his throat.

'Wait!' Marwan ordered.

He stood up. He went to fetch the Phalangist's Colt 45. He cocked the weapon with a quick motion, moved towards me and held it out.

I stood against the wall. I hadn't moved. I watched. Blood was flowing on the floor, a black sea mottled with grey bubbles. Marwan was facing me. He stood over his victim, his legs spread, dominating him. He handed me the weapon. After having refused me, the Druze abruptly proposed I take my portion of war. To close the door behind me forever. I looked at his peasant hands, his damaged fingers, his nails broken one after another by life. I looked at the well-shined pistol, the grip emblazoned with a cedar tree. I had seen this symbol all along the road to Shatila. Scouts had marked the killers' route. The cedar tree, logo of the Lebanese Forces. So they wouldn't get lost. Let's go, brothers-in-arms. The camps are disarmed. The men sailed off, holding up Vs for victory. Their women are here for the taking. Their children, who will be our enemies tomorrow. Their elders. Let's go! Leave them alive, they'll add to their ranks. Think of the martyrs of Damour. Blood for blood.

I took the weapon held out to me. Marwan let me take his place standing over the Christian. My legs spread, I squeezed his body between my feet. He had no face left. Something was flowing across his cheek that looked like an eye. He was kicking his feet, his arms, convulsing like a wounded animal. I took the revolver in both hands. I held my breath. My legs were shaking. I was going to kill a man. I looked at Marwan. His look was sombre. Not anger or hate. I understood that I could still renounce. Step away from this living wound and go home. He wouldn't have held it against me. I looked at the Druze again. He had deserted me. I was alone. My body, this heavy weapon in my hands, the hammer cocked, my finger on the trigger. I had shot a pistol in the woods. With both hands. A jerk to the shoulder, a rumbling sound, exploding bark.

I aimed for the head. I pressed slowly. The impact was violent. It surprised me. I thought my finger would go further. I was wrong. I shot the forehead, between the two open wounds that were his eyes. Stupefied by the flesh dripping down my trouser leg, I stood there like that, buzzing, weapon in my hand, looking at the wisp of smoke. I stood there. I had just killed a murderer. I was a murderer. I had joined the war. Delicately, Marwan took the weapon from my hands. He threw it on the body of my tortured victim.

We went out to the street. They led the way. I followed behind, reeling. We had just executed a Phalangist leader in his fiefdom of Achrafieh. It was terrifying. Marwan left in a car stolen the night before on the coastal road. The other Druze took me on his motorbike. I held him the way a woman shelters herself against her man. I was shaking. I was cold. He was going too fast for what I'd just been through. I needed to walk, sit, think. I had just killed, which meant I had died. I could no longer look a child in the eye. They know, children do. They sense evil. They see the devil in the eyes of an adult. Louise would never see a father again, only an ogre. Aurora would never see a husband again, but a threat. My dreams would all become nightmares. My days would be soot. I had killed. I could kill again. I felt nothing. My heart pounded, like after a wild race. I needed water, a bath, a beer. Ready to do it again? Why not. So easy. Anyway, that one was almost dead. I had spared him from agony. Not killed him, freed him. I was sorry Charbel hadn't been at the door. I imagined myself facing him, draped in a white toga, forbidding him to bury his brother. I envisioned myself magnificent, powerful, refusing this bastard a tomb, depriving him of funeral rites. I liked myself as king of this world, offering his cursed corpse to the crows. I was crushed against the Druze. I held him with both arms. I had my mouth open, but no tears. I wanted to offer some to Joseph-Boutros, to Nakad, Imane, Sam, Aurora, Louise, to myself. I was afraid to die without crying.

23

TRIPOLI, NORTHERN LEBANON

Thursday, 27 October 1983

'I didn't see it! Shit! I didn't see it!'

Marwan braked suddenly in the dark. He put the car in reverse. The day before, this Syrian roadblock wasn't here. Every night the soldiers from Damascus moved their checkpoints around the city. This one was hidden behind a tree. When we drove past without spotting it, a soldier fired in the air.

'Don't talk. Let me handle this,' the Druze muttered.

Three soldiers from Damascus walked slowly towards us. Two aimed their weapons at us, the third was eating a tomato. Marwan lowered his window, the car's registration in his hand. The officer kicked the door, stepped back, ordered him to get out. Marwan got out, his hands up. A harsh command. He knelt down. The other soldier approached. He spoke quietly, pointing to the sentry-box, the sandbags, the Syrian flag, the face of President Hafez al-Assad. The driver hadn't seen it? Is that right? Didn't see the flag? Or the president?

I was about to get out. A Syrian signalled me to stay in the car. He examined my passport upside down. Another was searching the boot of the car. Suddenly, Marwan was back.

'He wants water,' he whispered.

I gave him our bottle. The taxi driver walked back towards the soldier, holding out the water. And got back on his knees. The soldier started to drink, spat it out. Too warm. He yelled, poured the rest of the water on my Druze's head. And then ordered him to stand up. Took him into the bunker. Showed him the tomato. Asked him a question. Marwan answered. The other man forced him to kiss the flag, the photo of the president, then hit him violently and kicked him in his side. Marwan fell, got up. Brushed himself off as he came back to the car. His hand was shaking. He started the car. Saluting the soldiers who were looking at something else. Further down the road, he spat out the open window. My friend had been humiliated. I had been wounded for him. I was upset with myself for having witnessed this deadly ritual.

'He gave you back your passport?'

I nodded.

'What was he doing with the tomato? I asked.

'He wanted to know whether I was Palestinian.'

The Syrians were chasing down Arafat's fighters. When they arrested a man, they showed him a tomato and asked him what it was called. With their accent, the Lebanese would reply '*banadora*' and the Palestinian '*ban'dora*'. Hundreds had been arrested that way.

'Why don't they just answer like the Lebanese?'

Marwan gave me a look.

'Because they are proud.'

* * *

Forty minutes later, on the coastal road, our taxi faced a Syrian tank. I had fallen asleep.

'George, get out!' Marwan yelled, opening his door.

24

GEORGE

'You have seen death, but you haven't killed,' the old man murmured.

He lit a cigarette, sat on his heels. Then he stopped talking, watching the shy light of dawn rising.

I looked at my leg. Blood was spurting out. I felt pain in my head, nausea, cold, desire to sleep, I didn't know any more. Outside, shouts, more shouts. Two men ran into the garage, throwing themselves beside us in the hole. One was wounded in the arm. He spoke in Arabic, fast and loud.

'The Syrians have us surrounded, they're shooting anything that moves,' the old Palestinian translated for me.

I thought I was alone with him in the shelter. But at the back of the ruin, other shadows. And then more, behind a half-destroyed wall, in the former reception area, under the burnt-out cars, in the repair pit. There were about thirty of us, besieged. The old man readied his rifle.

'If we stay here, we're dead. Let's all go out together!'

He gave a sharp order. The same clack of rifles being armed everywhere in the darkness. And then he began to pray, on his knees, his hands raised. Two Palestinians attempted a sortie, alone. The first fell at the door, covering Marwan's body. The second ran back in to take cover.

I pulled the soil from Jaffa from my bag.

'Where are you from?' I asked the old fighter.

'From Jordan in July 1971.'

'But before that?'

'My home, you mean?'

I nodded. He smiled. He lit another cigarette.

'Bethlehem.'

I opened Imane's small gilded purse.

'Open your hand.'

The old man hesitated for a moment, then offered his palm to me, his eyes on mine. I poured the dust into the crevices of his black wrinkles. He raised his head, looked at me.

'What is it?'

'Soil from Palestine.'

He looked astonished. Looked at me again. He closed his fist around it. I was in pain. Feverish. My whole body screaming. A man went out. He fell. Another. And another. Machine-gun fire. The tank had stayed in position. It was sweeping our hideout. The door, the wall, the roof, flew to pieces.

The Palestinian crouched down, turned towards me.

'What's your name?'

'George.'

He nodded.

'*Ahlan wa sahlan*. My name is Mahdi.'

I smiled.

'We're going to die, George, you know that?'

I looked at him.

He spread the soil over his hands, then rubbed his face with it, his forehead, his nose, behind his ears, slowly, as if he were doing ablutions before prayer.

I took out Sam's kippah. The Palestinian startled.

MAHDI

Are you Jewish?

GEORGE

No.

MAHDI

What do you mean, no?

GEORGE

(*He stands with difficulty*)

I am nothing any more.

MAHDI

Where are you going?

GEORGE

I am going home.

MAHDI

Outside you will die.

GEORGE

No one leaves this world alive.

CHORUS

The old man looked at George. He motioned to hold him back. The Frenchman had Sam's kippah on his head, the key from Jaffa in his hand. He left his bag on the ground. He hobbled towards the

> exit, his belt a tourniquet around his thigh. From the shadows of the garage, the ghosts watched him leave without a word, with his dead leg. Anouilh murmured to him that tragedy was calm, straightforward. In drama, with its innocents, its traitors and avengers, dying was becoming complicated. We struggle against it because we hope to evade it. It was utilitarian, ignoble. Whereas in tragedy, it was gratuitous. Without hope. Vile hope that ruined everything. Tragedy was for kings. Twice, George fell. He got back up. He bumped into a fallen beam. Then he reached the door of the garage. He crossed the fourth wall, the one that protects the living.

Death took him like that. A kippah on his head and a key in his hand.

EPILOGUE

'And there we are. Without little Antigone, it's true, everyone would have been at peace. But now it's over. They are at peace. Everyone who had to die is dead. Everyone who believed one thing, and those who believed the opposite – even those who believed in nothing and were caught up in the story without understanding it. Dead just the same, everyone, stiff, useless, rotting. And those still living will begin to forget them and mix up their names. It's over.'

– Jean Anouilh,
Antigone (1942)

TRANSLATOR'S AFTERWORD

Oscar Wilde wrote: 'Life imitates art far more than art imitates life.'[1]

Francis Charles McGrath elaborates, 'Far from art imitating life, Wilde holds that art sets the aesthetic principles by which people perceive life. What is found in life and nature is not what is really there, but is that which artists have taught people to find there, through art.'[2]

Frank Jones, in 'Tragedy with a Purpose: Bertold Brecht's Antigone'[3] explores the question of tragedy:

> In Brecht's view, the tragic effect is more than emotional or even moral: it is intellectual; it should arrive, not from personal sympathy with any of the characters, but from understanding of the total situation in which they are involved.

---

1 'Life imitates art far more than art imitates life [...] results not merely from life's imitative instinct, but from the fact that the self-conscious aim of life is to find expression, and that art offers it certain beautiful forms through which it may realize that energy.' Oscar Wilde, 'The Decay of Lying – An Observation.' *Intentions* 1891.

2 McGrath, Francis Charles. 'Brian Friel's (post) colonial drama: language, allusion and politics.' *Irish Studies,* Syracuse University Press, 1999. First Edition.

3 Jones, Frank. 'Tragedy With a Purpose: Bertold Brecht's *Antigone.*' Pages 39–40, *Tulane Drama Review 1957.* MIT Press, Boston.

> In Sophocles' handling of the story, the tragic issue is more individual than social. [Brecht's] presentation of the story ... encourages the audience to think about the story as one thinks about necessity and free will in history. Whereas Sophocles seems to be saying, 'Character is fate,' or 'People are like that,' Brecht seems to be saying: 'Nothing is inevitable, except that violence begets violence.'

This book incorporates all of those ideas. Without assuming to prejudge the characters, Sorj Chalandon offers his reader a range of interpretative choices. Each equally logical. Just as the public and critics approached each production of *Antigone* with various, even contradictory assessments of the characters' intentions and motives. *Antigone*, the nexus of this book: Sophocles' original tragedy, Brecht's reinterpretation, Anouilh's production, and, finally, the individual understanding of the play offered by different characters in the book. Their unifying feature: tragedy, the alignment of the book with the play, the merger of life and art, the rupture of the Fourth Wall.

Cheney Crow

October 2025

ENDNOTES

1. PROLOGUE

Translations of Anouilh's text are the translator's. p. vii

2. SAMUEL AKOUNIS

CRS (Compagnie Républicaine de Securité): French national police force. p. 7

Commune: refers to both the 1871 violent uprising and the socialist-inspired government that ruled Paris from 18 March - 28 May 1871. p. 10

'students': the plural is masculine unless all are female. p. 10

'dictatorship': a feminine noun. p. 10

Regime of the Colonels: a right-wing military junta that engineered a coup and ruled Greece from 1967–74. p. 10

Mikis Theodorakis: Greek composer, dissident, future Minister of State. p. 12

17 November: declared a Greek national holiday to honor this uprising. p. 13

Rebetiko Theatre: a style that originated in Greece, combining actors with puppetry, music, (often folk tales), and more recently video projection. p. 15

Asphalia: the Greek National Security Service. p. 16

3. ALOIS BRUNNER

Red flag: emblem of the French Communist Party. p. 20

The People's Cause: newspaper of the Proletarian Left, founded in 1968. p. 20

Epic (political) theatre: In France, '"Le Théâtre Empêché" is described by Henry Bauchau as the embodiment of the imagined scenario; it only achieves the status of art, of creation, when the plot extends beyond the internal allegories of the play, when its language becomes actualized.' (Myriam Watthee-Delmotte, FNRS-Université catholique de Louvain, '*Le Théâtre Empêché d'Henry Bauchau,' DOSSIER THEMATIQUE, p. 123, Revue international Henry Bauchau, 'L'écriture à l'écoute — numéro 7, 2015*.)

Epic Theatre in England: 'The Brechtian legacy ... has provided models of dramaturgy, and it also provides a theory of political theatre, a framework of ideas through which critics and audience members can look at contemporary works in order to understand how they function (politically) in relation to other contemporary works and to those of their predecessors ... Epic theatre [accommodates] ... political opposition in theatrical representation. Brecht's work has proved useful for playwrights with leftist social commitments ... Many useful applications of epic theatre strategies and techniques mark the work of [British] Leftist writers.' Reinelt, Janelle. Introduction, *After Brecht, British Epic Theatre*, University of Michigan Press, Ann Arbor, 1994. p. 25

Translator's note: Bauchau references Brecht, as do works on Bauchau, naming theatre as a source of political activism. The Watthee-Delmotte citation is paraphrased in translation.

4. NATALIA STEPANOVA

Roger Planchon: director of film, theatre and other organizations (including the Théâtre National de Paris), also an author, a proponent of decentralized, popular theatre, he labeled Brecht a 'complete man of theatre'. p. 33

Patrice Chéreau: director of opera, stage and film, he infused his work with intimacy and broad social critique. p. 33

5. LOUISE

Louise Michel: 'the teacher who chose black over red, mourning the illusions of our soldiers': a reference to Stendhal's *The Red and the Black*, a novel in which red represents the clergy and black the military, two paths out of poverty. Another noteworthy contrast of black and red is the black anarchist flag and red communist flag.

'Louise Michel, an educator and anarchist, inscribed in the history of Paris. She fought on the barricades with the revolutionaries of the Commune in 1871, was deported to New Caledonia, spent 8 years in prison, went straight back to lecturing, fighting for equal rights. In 1886, she moved to England after publishing a memoir that included these words, "Revolution, beloved mother who devours us/Giving equality/Take our broken destinies/And make of them a dawning."' Excerpt from Higgins, Lynn A., 'Review of *The Red Virgin, Memoirs of Louise Michel*', Tulsa Studies in Women's Literature 1, no. 2 (Autumn 1982) pp. 212–16. p. 37

'Penn Sardin': (Breton for sardine-head), was a nickname given to workers in sardine canneries in Douarnenez known for their activism. p. 37

(Women in France did not get the right to vote until 1944, under Charles de Gaulle. Prior to the Renaissance, women could hold office, own and inherit separate property, and run businesses.)

'our flags came back out of the closets': 8 May 1945, end of World War II and the Nazi occupation of France. p. 42

Armbands worn during civil unrest in France (beginning May 1968): leftists, socialists and communists wore red, anarchists wore black. p. 44

May 1968: violent protests, strikes and civil unrest in France. p. 44

6. JOSEPH BOCZOV

Harki: Algerian Muslims who fought with the French army against Algeria during the War of Independence (1954–62). p. 47

Michel Sardou's song 'Le France': a song used as a rallying cry for the right. ('Le' is intentional, a ship's name). p. 49

Red and brown: Communist/Maoist (red) and Fascists (referred to as 'the brown plague'). p. 54

Brown refers to 'Brownshirts', a nickname for the original paramilitary wing of the Nazi party notorious for violent street fights with political rivals (Communists, Social Democrats) and for intimidating Jews.

Valéry Giscard d'Estaing: president (1974–81). p. 57

Maréchal Pétain: World War I hero who surrendered France to Hitler in World War II. During the Nazi occupation, he led the Vichy government that collaborated fully with the Nazis. He was convicted and imprisoned for treason after the war. p. 57

Mont-Valérian: a fort (named for a nearby mountain) used by the Nazis in World War II for executions of Resistance members and prisoners. In 1960 Charles de Gaulle established the Memorial to Resistance Martyrs there. p. 58

The Red Poster: a Nazi propaganda poster with mugshots of ten Jewish resistance fighters, members of the Manouchian Group (FTP-MOI). The poster's text - "Liberators? Liberated by The Army of Crime" (what they called the Manouchians). All were executed on 21 February 1944. p. 58

FTP: Franc-Tireurs et Partisans Français, an armed resistance organization created by leaders of the French Communist Party in 1939. The name 'Franc-Tireurs' derives from irregular military formations used during the Franco-Prussian War (1870–71). p. 58

7. AURORA

Polisario Front: (abbreviation for Popular Front for the Liberation of Saguia el-Hamra and Río de Oro, formed in May 1973): a politico-military organization striving to end Moroccan control of the former Spanish territory of Western Sahara, populated largely by Sahrawis, indigenous nomads. p. 60

10 May 1981: Election of François Mittérand, France's first Socialist president. p. 63

La Bastille: site of the turning point of the French Revolution. p. 63

8. JEAN ANOUILH

Boulevard Theatre: popular theatre that began in the 18th century on the Boulevard du Temple, mostly light-hearted, fast-paced comedy, melodrama and farce, created for the general public. p. 67

Druze: an ethno-religious, esoteric, monotheistic group considered one of the five Muslim communities in Lebanon (with Sunni, Shiite, Alawi and Ismaili), though they do not practise the Five Pillars of Wisdom and are no longer considered Muslims. In Lebanon, Druze and Christians lived in harmony, with few exceptions, for almost three centuries. p. 69

Syriac Christians: Eastern Catholics, recognized by the Pope, among the earliest Eastern Christians, they follow the doctrine of the Council of Chalcedon (451 AD). p. 69

Maronite Christians joined with the Druze to found modern Lebanon in the eighteenth century, with a social and political system known as 'Maronite-Druze dualism'. p. 69

Shiites: like Sunni Muslims, they believe Allah is the one true God; the split into two factions arose over who would be the successor of the Prophet Mohammed after his death in 632. p. 69

Shatila: a Palestinian refugee camp established in 1949. p. 69

"Les Pétroleuses": a name given by their accusers to a group of 5 women activists (Communards) who were tried, convicted, and sentenced without proof during the 1871 revolt (The Commune) in which Louise Michel was an organizer. p. 73

Chaldeans: Eastern Catholics united with the Roman Catholic Church since 1830. p. 74

10. MARWAN

Jumblatt: a Druze political dynasty since the 18th century. Walid Jumblatt, leader of Lebanons' Druze community, succeeded his father Kamal after his assassination. p. 93

Sabra: a predominantly Palestinian neighbourhood adjacent to the Shatila refugee camp established in 1949. p. 110

11. IMANE

Amal Movement: (Hope Movement) a political party founded in 1975 by a Shiite cleric. This militia became one of the most important Shiite militias during the Lebanese Civil War. p. 106

12. JOSEPH-BOUTROS

Kataeb: member of the Kataeb militia, also known as Phalanges, from the word's Greek origin. Formed in 1936 as a Maronite (Syriac Christian) paramilitary youth organization, it evolved into the Kataeb Party, a Lebanese Social Democratic Party. (Kataeb means 'Batallion'.) p. 117

Nasserien: Arab nationalist, follower or supporter of the political and social ideology of Nasser, an Egyptian prime minister. p. 119

bas, khalas, Arabic: that's enough, stop. p. 122

Green Line: 1975–90, a demarcation line established to separate the Christian (East Beirut) and Muslim (West Beirut) factions during the Lebanese Civil War. p. 123

'*Demain dès l'aube*' (Tomorrow, at dawn): Tomorrow, At Dawn, a famous poem by Victor Hugo about a father going to put flowers on his daughter's grave. p. 134

green holly and heather in bloom: images in the final lines of Hugo's '*Demain dès l'Aube*'. p. 134

13. NABIL, NIMER, HUSSEIN AND KHADIJAH

kameez: long tunic-like shirt. p. 138

sura: section of the Quran. p. 139

14. HAEMON

Lebanese white coffee: infusion of orange blossoms with sugar or honey. p. 144

tarboosh: flat, round hat. p. 145

15. SIMONE

RPG: rocket-propelled grenade. p. 149

peristyle: a row of columns in the interior of a building. p. 150

'Address each other informally': 'shift from formal (vous) to informal (tu) pronouns in French, indicating closeness. p. 159

bekanntmachung, German: public notice, announcement. p. 168

Montoire: the village where Maréchal Pétain surrendered France to Hitler. p. 168

Wahhabism: an Islamic reform movement founded by Muhammad ibn 'Abd al-Wahhab in the 18th century in central Arabia and adopted by the Saudi family. Wahhabism is prevalent in Saudi Arabia and Qatar. p. 170

chokrane, Arabic: thank you. p. 171

16. ESHKOL COHEN

komboloi: Greek worry beads. p. 176

Betar: movement founded in 1923 in Riga, Latvia, by Ze'ev Jabotinsky; it became the official youth movement of Zionist revisionists in 1925. p. 180

Tsahal: Israeli Defence Force. p. 180

17. THE CHORUS

follow spot: a spotlight that follows a performer. p. 187

Blue Helmets: a UN peacekeeping force (UNIFL: United Nations Interim Forces in Lebanon). p. 208

18. NAKAD

Anta majnoon, Arabic: you're crazy. p. 221

19. ANTIGONE

Red Crescent: the name and emblem adopted in Islamic countries; Red Crescent and Red Cross are partner humanitarian organizations. p. 232

20. MIMI-CUCKOO

Mimi-Cuckoo: Mimi is a nod to Mimi-Pinson (pinson means 'lark', a bird), an activist who formed a group offering evening classes in the arts to seamstresses who became known as the "Mimi Pinsons" by the end of the 19th century. Many joined the war effort when WWI broke out. The second part of the puppet's French name is Linotte (French for 'linnet', a bird). A common expression, 'tête de linotte' (linnet-head), often a tease, refers to someone whose mind is elsewhere, not in the reality around them. Hence cuckoo, used relative to a state of mind, also a tease. p. 236

'He addressed me as a friend': Shifting from formal 'you' (vous) to informal 'you' (tu). p. 243

Libération and *Le Monde*: newspapers with different political perspectives. p. 244

21. LÉOPOLDINE

Léopoldine: Victor Hugo's young daughter. The poem Demain, dès l'aube, describes a plan to visit her grave. p. 252

'*Demain, dès l'aube*': Victor Hugo's poem, 'Tomorrow, At Dawn'. p. 254

22. CREON

Cedars: Guardians of the Cedars, a Lebanese nationalist party and militia, predominantly Christian. p. 266